THE FALLS OF DEATH

THE FALLS OF DEATH

Christopher Nicole

Severn House Large Print
London & New York

This first large print edition published in Great Britain 2006 by
SEVERN HOUSE LARGE PRINT BOOKS LTD of
9-15 High Street, Sutton, Surrey, SM1 1DF.
First world regular print edition published 2004 by
Severn House Publishers, London and New York.
This first large print edition published in the USA 2006 by
SEVERN HOUSE PUBLISHERS INC., of
595 Madison Avenue, New York, NY 10022.

British Library Cataloguing in Publication Data

Nicole, Christopher
    The falls of death. - Large print ed.
    1.   Missing persons - Investigation - Guyana - Fiction
    2.   Guyana - Fiction
    3.   Suspense fiction
    4.   Large type books
    I.   Title
    823.9'14 [F]

    ISBN-10:   0-7278-7506 X

Printed and bound in Great Britain by
MPG Books Ltd, Bodmin, Cornwall.

This is a novel. The characters and events are invented and are not intended to portray real characters or events. But Kaieteur is there, the Eighth Wonder of the World, once seen, never forgotten.

What dreadful noise of water in mine ears!
What sights of ugly death within mine eyes!

William Shakespeare.

Prologue

'Damn, but that is hot.' Woo-woo staggered down the steps from the officers' mess, blinked in the sunshine and then did an involuntary pirouette. Then she stamped, as even through her lace-up leather shoes the heat rose from the tarmacadam of the roadway to scorch her feet. The American air force base at Atkinson Field in the British colony of Guiana, which fronted the Caribbean Sea to the north of Brazil, was situated only a few degrees north of the equator; the temperature this afternoon was well over a hundred degrees Fahrenheit – in the shade.

Woo-woo was a WAAC, and she was in white tropical uniform, although this was distinctly untidy at the moment, the tie knot slipped down, the tunic askew, the skirt crushed, one of her stockings laddered – and she had lost her sidecap. She was a plain woman facially, but she had a head of brilliant yellow hair, which curled extravagantly, and a body to match. Harry caught her arm before she fell into a flower-bed. 'One glass of port too many,' he suggested at large. Harry was a lieutenant in the navy, tall and thin; his khaki uniform clung to him like a second skin, but that was partly sweat.

'Some stopover,' Lynette commented. Small and dark and generally petite, with attractively tight features, she also was a WAAC, but relatively sober, despite the long and alcoholic lunch they had just finished. 'Say, you guys, do you know that till yesterday I didn't know where this place was? I thought British Guiana was in Africa.'

'But as you've just come from there,' Don pointed out, 'it can't be.' Don was a lieutenant jg; like Harry he flew one of the blimps that operated out of Atkinson Field in the continual search for U-boats prowling the Caribbean Sea in this summer of 1942. Nineteen years old, he was a recent arrival from the States and was still imbued with the romance of being in uniform. He also had recently learnt that moral attitudes change in war time, and he knew that these two young women had only arrived at the base last night, and were leaving again tomorrow morning. He thought Lynette might prove a fun companion for this night. And interesting. What were two WAACs doing in Africa, anyway, with Rommel beating the hell out of the Limeys and the general situation fairly grim? Woo-woo had said something about Cairo, and then clammed up at a glance from Lynette.

'What do you reckon the temperature is, Major?' Woo-woo asked.

'Hundred and forty, maybe.' Clark Smailes was plumply laid back. He wore a moustache, which he felt went well with his rank; like the other officers, he was in uniform.

'Jesus,' Woo-woo commented. 'I'm for the pool.'

From whence they could hear the sounds of laughter and splashing. Otherwise the new base, twenty miles up the Demerara River from the capital city of Georgetown and carved out of the thick bush, was fast becoming somnolent in the afternoon sunshine. 'Siesta time,' Don suggested, casting Lynette a meaningful glance.

'Flying,' Harry said. 'Let's go for a spin. You sober, Major?'

'I am always sober,' Clark reminded him. Which was true enough, Don thought; he had never actually seen Clark Smailes drunk, no matter how much he might have consumed.

'Fly where?' Lynette enquired. 'I flew all day yesterday, clear across the ocean, and I'm told we're flying all day tomorrow. What's out there, anyway?' She waved her hand to the south. 'Just a lot of bush.'

'There's some pretty fantastic country in there,' Don said, seriously. 'A few hundred miles of jungle, sure, then a great prairie the locals call the Rupununi.'

'And then there's Kaieteur,' Clark said. 'Now that is the wonder of the world.'

'Kaiewhat?' Woo-woo asked.

'You ever been to Niagara?'

'Once.' Woo-woo giggled. 'It was a week-end thing.'

'Compared with Kaieteur, Niagara is a boy pissing in a stream. I'll show you. We'll go up there and have a look.'

'Like, now?'

'Why not? There's gotta be something fuelled up. Shit, it's only a hundred and fifty miles.'

Lynette looked at Don, who she regarded, with reason, as the most sensible of the men. But Don merely grinned and shrugged. 'It'll be a jolly.'

'Say, Major,' said the control tower. 'You sure you're fit to fly?'

'Clear me, goddamit,' Clark said into the mike.

'I gotta have a destination and an eta.'

'Kaieteur, man. The Falls. We're going to have a gander at the Falls.'

'Give me a return time.'

Clark looked at his watch; it was two fifteen. 'Make it three hours, to be safe. Five fifteen.'

'Okay, Major. You're cleared for take-off. Have a nice time.'

The twin-engined Dakota roared down the

shimmering runway, lifting into the sky as Clark pulled the yoke back. Harry, acting as co-pilot, checked the instruments. 'All systems go,' he remarked.

'Ooooh,' Woo-woo was exclaiming in the cabin behind them, nose pressed to the window. 'There's gotta be more trees down there than in Africa.'

'More rivers, you mean,' Lynette said, from the other side of the aircraft.

'This country has more big rivers, for its size, than any other in the world,' Don told them. 'That's where it got its name. Guiana, or, more correctly, Guyana, to use the old spelling, means land of many waters.'

'Say, we're learning things all the time,' Woo-woo said. 'Just how big is it, anyway?'

'About the same size as England,' Don said.

They were out of sight of the airfield, and below them was nothing but jungle. Clark was only flying at four thousand feet, and Lynette stared down at the trees, close-packed, green, almost inviting. 'So who lives down there?' she asked.

'Nobody.'

'You're putting me on.'

'God's truth. That forest is empty. Of human beings, anyway.'

She shivered. 'What would happen to us if we came down in it?'

'Well, presuming Clark got off a mayday

11

before we went in, they'd know where we were, and they'd get us out. But it could take a little time. Say, that'd be something, eh? The five of us, shacked up in that jungle for a week or two?'

'Sounds grim,' Lynette commented. She had accepted the possibility that Don was going to make a play some time this evening, and hadn't yet decided how she was going to handle it, especially considering what she was carrying in the body belt under her skirt. But Don was rather sweet, even if he was still wet behind the ears.

Another huge river unfolded beneath them. 'That's the Essequibo,' Clark shouted back at them. 'It's the biggest of the Guianese rivers.'

'How big?' Woo-woo wanted to know.

'Well, the Nile and the Amazon are both over four thousand miles, the Mississippi just under. The Essequibo is about six hundred and fifty.'

'And these falls are on this river?' she asked.

'No, no. Kaieteur is on the Potaro, that's a tributary of the Essequibo. We're just about there.'

'What's that?' Lynette pointed through the window. 'A forest fire?'

'That's mist and spray,' Don told her. 'Those are the Falls.'

Both women gaped as the aircraft swung

over the trees and into the immense gorge. In front of them was a solid wall of water, beginning where the river rolled slowly up to the lip, and ending in the huge cloud of spray, rising hundreds of feet into the air.

'Jesus!' Woo-woo whispered.

'That river is three hundred and fifty feet wide,' Don said. 'And the fall is over eight hundred feet, seven hundred and forty-one sheer drop.'

'Jesus!' Woo-woo said again.

'We'll take a closer look,' Clark shouted over his shoulder, and drove the Dakota straight at the water wall, some two hundred feet below the lip. 'That's a sight you won't even see repeated. Wheee!'

One

Partners

The woman entered the hotel foyer through the revolving glass doors, which immediately shut out the noise of the London traffic behind her. She stood just inside the door, looking left and right as she got her bearings. While the clerk behind the reception desk looked at her. She was worth looking at. Although not as young as would really have suited him, about thirty, he reckoned, and with somewhat blunt features, her figure was very solid, her legs excellent and her hair yellow and straight, below her shoulders. As she carried both a laptop and a briefcase he guessed she was here on business. Now she approached him. 'Good morning. I'm meeting a Mr O'Ryan.' She was definitely an American.

'Miss Richards? Mr O'Ryan is in the bar, Miss Richards.'

'Thank you.'

The clerk thought she looked even better walking away than towards him. She stood in the doorway of the bar for a moment, again appearing to size up the situation before making her decision. Then she went up to the man on the stool at the very end of the counter – he was one of only five men present. 'Mr O'Ryan?'

He turned his head, slowly. 'That's me.'

'Shirley Richards. We spoke on the phone.'

She felt a sense of acute disappointment. She knew Tom O'Ryan was about forty, but she had expected better than this. The man was tall, and had powerful shoulders and regular features. But the effect was dissipated with too much alcohol, from the over-red complexion to the distinct paunch. Had she made a wasted journey?

'So we did,' O'Ryan agreed. 'Drink?' Shirley Richards looked at her watch, and O'Ryan grinned. 'I thought only Englishmen drank by the clock.'

Presumably he was one Englishman who did not. She assumed he was English from his accent. If he no doubt had Irish forebears, it had to have been a generation or two back. 'I'll have a half of lager,' she said. The barman filled a glass.

'Let's sit down, shall we?' Shirley invited, and led O'Ryan across the room to a table in the corner, where they would hopefully be out of earshot of the other drinkers; she laid her two cases on the table, sat down.

O'Ryan followed with the glasses. 'So you

want to pick my brains about Guyana.' He sat beside her.

'You answered my ad,' she reminded him.

'Was I the only one?'

'Heavens, no. There were dozens.'

'And you've been buzzing around the world interviewing all of these people?'

'No. Only those I considered interesting or genuine. And as it happened, most of them were in England. I suppose that follows: sixty years ago Guyana was a British colony, where...' she opened her laptop, booted it up and pressed a few keys '...your father worked as a forestry officer.'

'That's right.' Tom O'Ryan sipped his drink while he studied her. Unlike her, he was very happy with what he was contemplating. She looked cool, she had a well-filled shirt and good legs. She was a lot of woman. Presumably, if she could read his mind she'd slap his face. She looked like that sort of woman, too.

'Thus he would have spent some time in the interior,' Shirley Richards said.

'Most of his time.'

'Right. Did he ever talk to you about it?'

'Often. He was a keen photographer. He has stacks of albums taken when he was up there. He was a bachelor then, you see.'

Shirley nodded. 'Did he ever visit Kaieteur?'

'Several times. He said it's the wonder of

the world.'

'A lot of people agree with him. Those that have seen it, anyway. Your father was in Guyana, or British Guiana as it then was, in 1942, wasn't he?'

Tom nodded. 'He wanted to quit and join up, but his was considered an essential occupation. He did manage to get out a year later, and saw some service.'

'But he was there in forty-two. Did he ever tell you about an aircraft that disappeared?'

'Quite a few have done that. The Guyanese jungle is no place to come down.'

'I'm talking about a US army Dakota that went missing on July 7th 1942. Did your father ever mention that?'

'He may have done. I'm afraid I don't remember.'

'This was the one that some people say went into the Falls.'

Tom O'Ryan contemplated his empty glass, and signalled the waiter to bring over two more drinks. 'He did tell me about *that*. Caused quite a sensation at the time.'

'So?' Shirley sipped her second lager.

'It's pure supposition. These five Yanks ... I beg your pardon, I meant Americans, three men and two women, took off in the middle of the afternoon, and gave their destination as the Falls. They were never heard of again, and their plane was never found. But like I said, this has happened more than once in the Guyanese interior.'

'The business was hushed up, wasn't it?'

'Well ... with respect, Miss Richards, from what my dad told me I'd say they were all drunk. They had no business being up in an aircraft at all. Naturally, the officers at Atkinson Field played the whole thing down. Well, let's face it: if they crashed into the Falls they'd have to have been drunk.'

'Do you remember the names of the people on board the aircraft?'

'Haven't a clue.'

'One of them was Lieutenant jg Donald Wishart, USN.'

Tom frowned; she had not been looking into the computer. 'Someone you knew?'

'My grandfather.'

'Your ... wait a moment. A junior grade lieutenant is usually about twenty. You're saying this character was married and a father?'

Shirley's mouth twisted. 'No. He'd only been out in BG for a few months. Just before he left home he and my grandma got together, and bingo. They did mean to marry, when next he had a furlough, but then he went and disappeared. So Grandma had to have her baby all by herself.'

'I'm sorry.'

'I'm not. If she'd done something silly like aborting I wouldn't be here, right? So after a while, her daughter, my mother, got married to this guy Richards, and here I am. Don't tell me you don't have black sheep in your family.'

'Most people are of the opinion I'm it,' Tom confessed. 'But this grandfather of yours really seems to have been a wahoo.'

'I don't believe he was,' Shirley said, choosing not to take offence. 'I told you, he did want to marry Grandma when he got home. She never doubted that.'

'Meanwhile he takes a couple of young women up on a drunken flight over the BG jungle.'

'Okay, so they were a bit wild around then. There was a war on, remember? But no one knows exactly what happened.'

'And you'd like to clean away some of the mud. Won't the US army, or navy, help?'

'Not a chance. Even more than sixty years later they're not admitting that three of their officers went flyabout while drunk.'

'Then what about the Guyanese government?'

'They have nothing to offer, officially. In 1942 Guyana was a British colony, and the people presently holding office, or their ancestors, had to keep a very low profile. But in any event, Atkinson Field was US territory, leased to Washington by Churchill for ninety-nine years in exchange for fifty old destroyers. They handed it back after the war, but what went on up there *during* the

20

war was strictly US business.'

'Then I'd say you've had it. In any case, don't you think it'd be better to let sleeping dogs lie? I hate to be disrespectful, Miss Richards, but is there anyone in the world today, outside of your immediate family, who even remembers Lieutenant Wishart, jg, much less how he died?'

'I accept that. And I was prepared to let it go, as you suggest. Then I came across this in a three-month-old Guyanese newspaper.'

She closed her laptop, and opened her briefcase instead. From it she took a newspaper cutting. Tom read it, a faint frown gathering between his eyes. *STRANGE HAPPENINGS AT TAKDAI. INHABITANTS TERRORISED BY GORILLA-LIKE CREATURE. VILLLAGER FOUND DEAD IN BIZARRE CIRCUMSTANCES.*

Tom looked up, his frown deepening. 'Takdai is downstream of the Falls. Five miles or so.'

'That's right.'

'And this happened three months ago? So what exactly are you trying to say?'

'I wrote to the Guyanese government, asking for more information on what happened. They weren't very helpful. They suggested that it was an oversize monkey who went berserk. Apparently the local police did investigate the incident, but their report has never been made public. Don't you find that suspicious?'

'Or merely incompetent.'

'I find it suspicious. I've done some research. I suppose the biggest Guyanese monkey is what they call the howler, because it inflates its lungs and makes a huge noise, like a lion roaring, when it's scared. But the biggest howler ever known doesn't stand four feet, and there is no record of it ever attacking a human being. Nor was any roaring heard around Takdai on the night of the killing.'

'More probably a jaguar. Were there claw marks on the body?'

'Nobody knows, save for the local authorities, and they aren't saying. But if it had been a jaguar, why the hush-hush? That is a perfectly straightforward explanation. But there's something else. I did get to talk on the phone to a Guyanese journalist, who to begin with was quite helpful. He knew about this attack, of course, and said he presumed the police were still investigating it and would release their findings in due course. Although, he went on, they never did release their findings on those disappearances ... there I'm afraid I jumped the gun, and interrupted him. What disappearances? I shouted. Then he clammed up. Sorry, he said, slip of the tongue. Forget it, and he hung up.'

'You have his name?'

'Surely. Claude Diamond.'

'Did you follow him up?'

'I tried, but he was always busy.'

'What about other newspaper references?'

'Just the couple that I've been able to find. The dead man had his throat torn out. He had been hunting with a companion, but they had become separated. The companion heard his friend scream and caught a glimpse of this ape-like creature before finding the body. The creature ran off into the jungle. Then I found the report of a teenage girl having gone missing from another village near the Falls, about six months ago. It was supposed she'd gotten too close to the river at the wrong time and been nobbled by an alligator or something. It really was a small item.'

'Which could be true. You suggesting that the death of the man and the disappearance of the girl are related?'

'Diamond used the plural – disappearances. Tom, I think something very odd is going on in that jungle.'

'Connected with your grandpa? You are saying that that aircraft did fly into the Falls, and that someone, or more than some *one*, survived the impact, and that having done that...' He stared at her. 'That was more than sixty years ago.'

'I know what I'm saying. It would have to have been more than some *one*. Don't you see? Sixty years! My grandad would be just about eighty, if he were still alive. That's a bit old for rushing around the jungle terrorizing the natives. But if *two* survived, a man and a woman...'

'And had children? You're still talking about fifty-year-olds.'

'Not if the children had children.'

'Incest on a grand scale.'

'Isn't that how we all began?'

Tom rubbed his chin, looked as if he intended to order some more drinks, then changed his mind. 'Okay. So let's suppose there were survivors. Why didn't they just walk into Takdai and get help? Why, for sixty years, didn't their children do that? Like I said, the village is only five miles from the Falls.'

'I don't know. But there must have been a reason.'

'Because you feel sure some of them survived. Okay. They didn't, or couldn't, contact civilization, just stayed shacked up together. Tell me, how has this incestuous family survived, all of these years? According to your info these attacks on the surrounding villages are all pretty recent.'

'We don't know that. They've only been getting publicity these last few years. We don't know when they started. As for the survival itself...' she gave a little shudder. 'Have you ever heard of Sawney Bean?'

'You have got to be kidding.'

'He really happened, didn't he?'

Tom nodded, slowly. 'Sawney Bean lived on the west coast of Scotland, some time in the fifteenth century. He was an outlaw, and when the law got too close he disappeared, with his wife and family. The authorities thought they were dead, and forget about them. Then stories started, about people disappearing. It got so notorious that the king himself, one of the Jameses, I think it was, decided to do something about it. He led an army, personally, and they found Sawney Bean and his family. And a situation it takes a strong stomach even to think about.'

'Sawney Bean,' Shirley took up the tale, 'and his wife and children, had been living in a large cave on the west coast of Scotland. They had been entirely incestuous, and had spawned a huge family. They had lived by waylaying lonely travellers, kidnapping them to their cave, robbing them and then cannibalizing them. When they were captured dozens of half-eaten bodies were found.'

'And you think this is what may have happened to your grandad? Or whoever survived the crash?'

'I think it is important that I find out.'

Tom leant across the table to hold her hand. 'Sawney Bean, and every member of his family, was executed. Just as horribly as

25

they knew how, in the fifteenth century. And that was a time they knew a lot about making people suffer while they died.'

'I know,' Shirley said. 'We don't do that sort of thing nowadays. But isn't that an even more important reason to find out just what happened – is happening?'

Tom gazed at her for several seconds. Then he said, 'I would say so.'

'So, will you help me? From what I've already experienced, I'd say I'm going to encounter nothing but brick walls from the Guyanese government. Half of my letters haven't even been answered, and, as I say, the one journalistic contact I have just clammed up on me. If you have any contacts out there that could be of help when I go...'

'I have one or two,' Tom said. 'But I don't think you're going to get very far. On your own.'

'Just what do you mean by that?'

'I'm coming with you.'

'You?' Her gaze drifted up and down his body.

He grinned. 'So I'm not quite the man I once was. I can still do a safari, even in the Guyanese jungle.'

She flushed. 'I didn't mean that. It's just that I'm on a very strict budget. A small one.'

'I'm cheap.'

Once again she appraised him. 'Why?'

He shrugged. 'Maybe I've always wanted to go back. And this is one hell of a story, if it's true. I write. Not too successfully. This could put me on the map.'

'Hold on just one minute,' Shirley said. 'You said go back. I didn't know you'd been there.'

'You never asked. After the war Dad went back to his old job. Then he got married. Then he begat, me and my two sisters. Then, when things turned really nasty, he brought us home. That was in the seventies. I was just a kid, ten years old, but I can remember certain things.'

'How nasty did they get?'

'You could call it a civil war. Actually, it was an ethnic war, which had been going on for years. The Brits wanted out, but it was a question of who was going to run the country: the blacks, descendants of the slaves imported to work the sugar plantations in the eighteenth century, or the Indians – they call them East Indians out there to differentiate them from the real Amerindians, the indigenous population. The East Indians are the descendants of the indentured labourers hired in places like Calcutta to work the sugar plantations after the blacks had been freed and quit in the nineteenth century. The two races didn't get on. So a lot of blood was spilt before things settled down.'

'And they are settled down?'

'You could say that. But the process, plus the fact that Guyana became pink going on red, ruined the economy. We're talking about Third World and then some.'

'I thought pink going on red was dead and buried since Gorbachev?'

'Not in the Caribbean. Certainly as long as Castro is about.'

'You make it sound pretty grim.'

'Which is another reason for you to have a man about. The reason that these attacks and disappearance that have you excited have not been very well reported is that such things are not exactly unusual in Guyana. While, if you do turn up something like Sawney Bean, I reckon you may need someone to hold your hand.'

Another long consideration. 'You could be right,' she said at last. 'How do you think we should handle this?'

'The one thing we do not want to do is blow a bugle and announce that here is the investigative journalist plus interested party arriving to discover what is stinking up the Mazeruni. That is the sure way to find ourselves staring at brick walls, even supposing we're not immediately deported. We have to be a pair of tourists, nothing more.'

'Do they have tourists in Guyana?'

'Sure they do. It's one of the few unspoilt places left on earth. Simply because almost every tourist who goes there gets mugged and robbed, if not raped.'

'Cheer me up.'

'That's why you're having me along.'

'But two people, man and woman, travelling together...'

'Oh, we have to be lovers,' Tom assured her. 'Or, as they say nowadays, partners.'

'Well, you can forget that for a start.'

He raised his eyebrows. 'Don't tell me you're not into men?'

'Are you trying to make me say something rude?'

'Ah,' he said sadly. 'You mean you're into men, some men, but you're not into me.'

'I've only just met you, Mr O'Ryan.'

'Just now you were calling me Tom. Okay, we're cardboard lovers. But we have to put on a good show for the natives. What I mean is, we need to share the same room, etcetera, etcetera.'

'As cardboard lovers. I hope you remember that.'

'I don't see how I'm going to be allowed to forget.'

'So ... what do we do first?'

'We need shots and passages and visas, and various other things. But first ... how about dinner?'

Not for the first time, Shirley Richards found herself asking herself what she was doing. As a small child there had been something enormously exciting about her grandfather disappearing into the South American jungle; she had read everything she had been able to lay hands on about the explorer Fawcett. Of course, Fawcett had disappeared into a much more famous jungle, the Matto Grosso of Brazil, but it was still South America, and, in fact, as the Brazilians were ruthlessly exploring and destroying their jungle, while the Guyanese were not, the interior of Guyana was now a much less known place than the Matto Grosso. And the thought that Grandpa might actually have flown into the world's greatest waterfall was breathtaking.

Nor had she been put off by the obvious fact that Grandpa had been a bit of a rotter. As she had told O'Ryan, if he hadn't been at the least an impatient lover – by the standards of 1942 – she would not have been here, or, at least, what she was. She was entirely satisfied with what she was, would not have had her looks or her personality, or her character, changed one iota. So what was wrong with being narcissistic? Or self-possessed, in the most literal possible sense of the word? She sat in front of the dressing-table in her hotel room and gave herself a slow, secretive smile. She knew she would never be beautiful, or perhaps even pretty, but she had good features, and an even better body.

Grandpa was responsible for that, too. She had first heard the story of his disappearance when she was about six, she supposed. It had stuck in her mind. Grandpa's pre-disappearance misdemeanours had by then been sufficiently history to be forgiven, and Ma had been quite prepared to trot out fading photograph albums to show her daughter what Grandma had looked like, and what her lover had looked like, too, before dashing off to disappear into the wilds of the then British Guiana. He had been a handsome man. But then Ma had been a handsome woman, as she had had a handsome daughter. Ma had never doubted that her father, or whoever had been piloting the aircraft, had flown into the Falls. By the time *she* had been old enough to do anything about it, British Guiana, on its way to becoming Guyana, had sunk into the ongoing civil war that Tom O'Ryan had talked about.

Odd to think that had Ma had the guts or the money or the time to go to Guyana then she might have met the boy O'Ryan, or his parents. Ma had had none of those things. Principally she had been preoccupied with getting married. And then getting pregnant, and then nursing her baby girl. By the time all that had been sorted out Ma had been past thirty and losing the desire to adventure.

Nor had she had anything to go on. If Don

Wishart and his friends *had* flown into the Falls, that was that. No one had any idea of what lay behind that enormous and almost solid sheet of falling water, or if anything did. Everyone was agreed that no one was ever going to find out. Yet Ma had continued to be fascinated, had collected every photograph of Kaieteur and the surrounding country, now known as Kaieteur National Park, and every news item that she could. There had not been much in the way of news items. But she had passed on all of that excited enquiry to her only child.

Shirley had made capital out of that at school. She had always kept a photograph of the Falls in her satchel, would take it out and show it to new acquaintances, and proudly announce that her grandfather had flown into that, and disappeared. She had undoubtedly been obsessed with that single most important fact in her family history. Heaven knew what a psychiatrist would have made of it. But she had never been to a psychiatrist. Perhaps she should have. She was well aware that such an obsession was a bad thing for anyone. It had turned her in on herself. Quite a few of her schoolmates had grandfathers who had died in the Hitler war; that was a fact of life. A great many more had fathers or uncles or brothers who had fought in Vietnam, and some of them had got killed as well. That was an even grimmer fact of life. No doubt all of American youth had been traumatized by those two epic periods of history, so at odds with the guarantees that tomorrow would be a better and happier and more prosperous time that were part of their heritage – certainly until 9/11.

But she was the only one out of them all whose grandfather had flown into the world's greatest waterfall. That simple fact dominated her life, coloured all her relationships. It had actually prevented any true relationships from forming. She had had affairs, some of them quite serious, at least from the other person's point of view. For her they had always been experimental, a desire to feel, a real wish to share ... but that was impossible. Soon the affairs had become irrelevancies. She had not slept with either man or woman for four years.

Because, slowly growing larger and larger in her life, had been the certainty that somehow Grandpa had survived that crash, at least for a while, and that a cousin of hers might actually be alive out there. She had never been able to explain the certainty to herself, much less attempt to do so to anyone else ... until she had found herself confiding in that dissipated bear of a man, who was obviously going to be a handful – but who was so strangely reassuring, if only because of his size. As for what might have actually happened after that plane crash, and might have been happening ever since, that was just too horrible to contemplate. But she had to find out.

Two

Threats

'So what have we accomplished, so far?' Shirley asked, as they sat at dinner in a booth in a small and inexpensive bistro. They had eaten here the previous two nights as well.

'No trouble with visas,' Tom said, handing back her passport. 'And the passages are booked. But they will need paying for.' He waited, watching her sip her diet Coke. She was a most attractive woman. More handsome than pretty, but with a lot of body. And a lot of personality, too. To get her into the sack would be a dream. He didn't doubt he could do it, no matter what pre-nuptial agreement they might come to. But he wished he knew more about her, what was going on behind those dark-green eyes. She was obsessed, that was certain. Well, perhaps he might also be obsessed if he had a grand-father who had disappeared in most unusual circumstances. But she was obsessed with the idea of what her grandfather, or his descendants, might have become. Her possibilities did not bear thinking about. Probably, a psychiatrist would say she needed analysis. But then, he thought, don't we all?

The fact was, he was no less obsessed. Not with men who might have turned into monsters, but with Guyana. He could remember very little of it, as he was only ten when his family had finally left. Heat, rain and dark faces were a confused blur. But he had been shown enough photographs of it, and his father had been equally obsessed by the beauty and majesty of Kaieteur Falls. It was a place he had always intended to visit, without quite knowing how he was going to accomplish it. He supposed life had somewhat passed him by, with a certain amount of assistance from himself. With a gift for observation and description, and a wayward sense of humour that he could inject into the written word, he had slipped into journalism almost without thinking, on the paper of the town where his parents had settled. He had done well, and moved to a provincial paper. Then a national. But the deadlines and abrupt uprootings had got to him. That and his marriage.

Cynthia had been a lovely girl, and a loving one, but she had found the pressures even more exacting. He thanked God they had never had children, which had made the separation the easier to bear. He wondered what she was doing now ... The divorce had accentuated the drinking problem. He refused to consider himself an alcoholic, while realizing that there were few alcoholics who did. But though the drink had never interfered with his work, it had interfered with his relations with various bosses, and from national he had slipped back down to provincial. All this at the age of thirty-five. From there, the only way had been down.

Unless he could put his name back up on the front page. This could be his big chance. Supposing he kept sober. But he intended to do that, at least in public. As Shirley Richards had noticed: no wine with dinner. That he intended to have a few quick vodkas when he got back to his flat was something she need not know about.

'I've also been through a lot of newspaper files,' he said. 'There is nothing, but nothing, about any US plane disappearing into the Guyanese jungle in 1942. On the other hand, there was so much going on elsewhere in the world an item like that wouldn't have seemed important to any UK editor.'

'I understand that,' she said, contemplating her glass of Coke.

Who knows? he thought. I might convert her to my way of thinking; she obviously feels like a drink.

'So I turned my attention to more recent happenings,' he said. 'But, there again, I drew a blank. Reasonably. The odd disappearance in the interior of a Third World country like Guyana is hardly going to make the news in Britain, where a young girl or woman disappears almost every day. Not all monsters have fuzzy chins or look like gorillas.'

She nodded. 'I didn't expect anything different. So when do we go?'

'Wednesday. I have seats booked. Economy. I thought that's what you'd prefer.'

'Thank you. What about shots and things?'

'I've made an appointment for Monday. We can be jabbed in tandem.'

'How exciting,' she remarked. 'And then it's into the unknown.'

'It's not unknown,' he protested. 'At least to me. I have a list of names of several people who knew my father. One or two even owed him a favour. There are also people I was at school with. One in particular.'

'How long ago were you at school with these friends?'

'Well, thirty years.'

'And you've never been in touch since?' She blew a raspberry.

'I also know the country.'

'Which you left when you were ten.' She raised one eyebrow, a disconcerting gesture; clearly she was wondering if she might not have made a mistake in accepting him as her partner. 'Just what is in this for you, Mr O'Ryan?'

He held up his finger. 'Tom. Don't forget that we are lovers.'

'The modern word is partners, remember? You haven't answered my question.'

'What's in it for me? A chance to tell a headline-making story. To get my career back on track.'

'That makes some sense.'

'Now can I ask you one?'

'You can ask.'

'What do *you* do for a living?'

'I work in PR.'

'Pays well, does it? With long holidays.'

'If you must know, my mother recently died and left me some money. So you could say I'm taking a holiday, yes.' She stood up. 'Thanks for the meal. Oh, I forgot. I assume I'm paying, as usual.'

'I'm sorry about your mother. And I would happily pay if I had any money.'

'Don't worry about it. I reserve the right to fire you, whenever you get too obnoxious. You may call us a cab.'

They drove back to her hotel. 'Shall I get rid of this fellow?' Tom asked.

'That's up to you. I have no idea how close you live.'

'I thought we might still have things to

discuss.'

'There is one question. When do we leave?'

'I told you. The tickets are for next Wednesday. Returning in a fortnight.'

'That doesn't give us a lot of time.'

'So we can miss the return flight. But we have to have a reasonable return date or they won't let us in. And, as you seem to have forgotten, they also have to be paid for.'

'They will be, tomorrow morning. Well, then...' the taxi was slowing. 'I'll say goodnight, Tom. I'm looking forward to our expedition. I really am.'

'So am I. When do I call? I mean, Monday.'

'You don't call Monday,' she told him. 'I'll find my own way to the doctor. You present yourself at Heathrow, at the appropriate terminal, in time for our flight. If, in the meantime, you manage to come up with any additional information, it can keep until we're on the plane.'

'There's one small matter: my fee.'

The taxi driver was waiting patiently, as she was half out of the car. 'Your fee? There isn't one, Tom. You volunteered. I'm picking up the tab for an all-expenses visit to Guyana, out of which you will get a story, which, as you say, should put your name back up in headlines. I think, at the end of the day, you will owe me.'

Tom lay on his back and stared at the ceiling

above his bed. He was just realizing that this was the first time in a very long while that he had gone to bed absolutely sober. He wondered if he was going to sleep, decided that he wasn't, got up and padded out of the bedroom into his small lounge to find his bottle of vodka, and was checked by a knock on the door. He looked at his watch: a quarter to eleven. He went back into the bedroom to pull on a pair of trousers, and the knock came again, more urgently.

He opened the door and gazed at a rather pleasant-looking young man. 'Mr O'Ryan? I've a message for you. May I come in?'

Tom hesitated. But he was bigger than his visitor, and he was sober. Nor did the fellow look the least aggressive. He took the chain off the hook and stepped back, with instant regret. The pleasant-looking young man entered the room with some force, and was immediately followed by a large black man, who didn't look half so pleasant.

'Just what the hell do you think you're doing?' Tom demanded.

The black man closed and locked the door.

'No trouble,' said the young man. 'Why don't you sit down?'

'I'll stand,' Tom said.

The young man shrugged, and sat down himself. The black man remained standing by the door. 'You and your lady friend have been asking questions,' the young man said, as pleasantly as ever. 'About a US air force plane that went missing in the interior of Guyana. In 1942.'

Tom did sit down, on the far side of the room. 'So?'

'Tell us why. That plane disappeared more than sixty years ago.'

Tom considered. There was nothing illegal in what Shirley Richards was doing. Nothing even of interest to any other party, unless ... It occurred to him that these two goons, out to discover what he was after, might give him more information than anything he could give them. 'My lady friend is the grand-daughter of one of the pilots,' he said.

'So why is she so interested in what happened to her grandfather?'

Tom shrugged. 'She's compiling her family tree.'

The black man twitched, and the white man gave a sour smile. 'You want to remember that this is a serious business, O'Ryan.'

'There are degrees of seriousness,' Tom pointed out. 'Look, this woman has a crazy notion that her grandad may have survived the crash. She wants to find out about that. She's employing me to help her. Who am I to argue? It's money, beer and a return to the place I was born. And maybe a story at the end of it.'

The white man studied him for several seconds. Then he asked, 'What about the other people in the aircraft? She interested in any of them? There was a Major Clark Smailes. There was Lieutenant jg Donald Wishart. There was Captain Harry Craig ... Which one was the grandfather?'

'Don Wishart.'

'Right. There were also two dames, Josephine Hopkins, known as Woo-woo, and Lynette Marshall. These were both WAACs, on their way back to the States from Africa. That was the route then, Dakar, Georgetown, Miami. Out of the way of enemy activity. Any of those ring a bell?'

'I'm afraid not.'

'Your girlfriend never mentioned any of those names?'

Tom shook his head.

'Well, I'll tell you what you do, O'Ryan. You ask her about them. Find out how much she knows about them. We'll contact you, and you can tell us.'

'Are you going to give me a reason why I should do that?'

The white man grinned. 'If you don't, we might just ask her ourselves. And when we've done that, she might just wind up not worth going on holiday with.' He stood up. 'I know you're a sensible fellow, O'Ryan. So I know you're not going to call the police when we leave. They won't catch us, but we'll know they were trying, and that'll give us another reason for calling on the lady.

42

Right?'

Tom remained seated. 'I'd be even more cooperative,' he said, 'if I knew why the men Shirley's grandad were with are so important.'

'Not the men,' the white man said. 'Lynette. She had something with her. Something we want. Something we'll get, if it's at all possible, like if she survived that crash. We'll be in touch.'

They closed the door behind them, and Tom remained sitting still for several seconds. So what was Shirley Richards really after, if not her grandfather? That was something he had to find out. Now. He picked up the phone, punched the number of the hotel.

'Do you realize the time, sir?' asked the reception clerk.

Tom looked at his watch. 'A quarter past eleven.'

'Do you suppose Miss Richards will wish to speak with you at this hour?'

'Yes,' Tom said. 'Or I wouldn't have rung.'

There were clicks and bumps, and a buzzing sound. 'What?' Shirley asked. 'Hello? What?'

'I'm afraid I have a call for you, madam,' the clerk said. 'I do apologize, but it seems to be urgent.'

'Wake up,' Tom said. 'It's me. Get up. Put something on. Or not, as it takes you. I'm on my way. We have a problem.'

Getting across London by tube well after the shows were out was a relatively easy matter, and Tom was at the hotel in under an hour, which included changing trains unnecessarily to make sure he wasn't being followed – although he didn't suppose they'd bother; they knew where to find him, and they knew where to find Shirley. At the moment they were holding all the high cards. 'Miss Richards is expecting me,' he told the clerk.

'Oh. Yes.' He was not enthusiastic. 'Number three hundred and seven. I should warn you, Mr...'

'Smith,' Tom said.

'Smith, that this hotel takes a dim view of disturbances, at any hour, but especially after midnight.'

'I'll be quiet as a mouse,' Tom promised him, and rode up.

Shirley wore a brocade dressing gown; material that heavy concealed everything, but he couldn't see the collar of a nightgown or pyjamas.

'This had better be important,' she remarked.

'It could be, if you'd let me in.'

She stepped back, closed the door behind him. 'You look as if you've seen a ghost.'

'Maybe I have. Two of them. Even more interested in your grandad's misadventure than you are. Maybe.'

Shirley sat down on the bed. 'That's not possible. Who are they?'

'Well, they're both younger than me. That's not difficult, in the thug world. But I would say they could both be younger than you, as well.' He sat beside her. 'And they weren't really interested in grandad. They wanted to know about one of his passengers. A WAAC lieutenant named Lynette Marshall.'

Shirley was frowning. 'She was one of the party, yes. What's important about her? Was she their grandparent, too?'

'That's unlikely, unless she was of African descent.'

'You mean...'

'One of them. No, it appears that this WAAC lieutenant, who made the mistake of going gallivanting around the Guyanese bush with your grandfather, was carrying something.'

'What?'

'I'm hoping you are going to tell me.'

'I have no idea what you're talking about.'

'You'd better have. These characters had it in mind to beat what they wanted out of me. I talked them out of that, but then they began having sadistic thoughts about you.'

Shirley clasped both hands to her throat. 'Did you call the police?'

'I came here. I like to know what I'm into.'

'You say this woman was carrying something...'

'It would seem so. And that's logical. If it was something sufficiently important, or valuable, to be removed secretly from Africa for delivery in Washington then it was something she was not going to let out of her sight or off her person. So it seems logical that, when the plane went in, she had it on her. Do you suppose your grandad knew about it?'

'I shouldn't think so. As far as I have been able to gather he only met the two WAACs on the day of the flight. They were on passage, just overnighting in Guyana.'

'Which lends credence to the theory that she was some kind of delivery girl.'

'Maybe. But, anyway, if it was some World War II secret she'd hardly confide in Grandpa.'

'Darling, there is no World War II secret left short of information that Franklin D. Roosevelt was actually a German spy that would have anyone today running around threatening to kill someone to get it.'

Shirley's hands had unclasped. Now they tightened again. 'Did you say kill?'

'I have an idea that's what my friends were talking about, yes.'

'What are we going to do? The police...'

'I don't think involving them is going to be any help. I can't even prove the men were at my place tonight.'

Once again her fingers relaxed. 'That's

true. You can't.'

He grinned at her. 'But they were. And I saved my skin by promising to get the information they're looking for out of you. So if you don't have it we're up shit creek without a paddle.'

'And you still don't think going to the police will be any help.'

'None in the least. When they hear you're going looking for a long lost grandfather they'll likely lock you up for being mentally unstable.'

'Thank you very much. In that case...'

'There is absolutely no use in losing your temper. You simply have to look at things from the other chap's point of view, sometimes. Let's be logical. One. WAAC Marshall leaves Africa carrying something of considerable value. I'd say enormous value. Maybe WAAC Woo-woo was in on it too, but that's not relevant now. What is relevant is her original departure point. Any chance of finding that out?'

'Maybe,' Shirley said cautiously. 'But if it was a Pentagon secret they'll clam right up.'

'You'll have to try. Two. As was usual in those days when most aircraft had a strictly limited range, she crossed the Atlantic on what was virtually a shuttle service between Dakar, which was Free French, and British Guiana, which was British. This was the safest possible route as it is the narrowest part of the ocean, and outside any usual enemy activity. Three. She had to overnight at the American base at Atkinson Field before catching her onward flight up to the States. Four. While in Atkinson she agrees to go for a jolly with a bunch of drunken airmen and is never heard of again. Those are facts. With five we enter the realms of supposition. What was the reaction of the Pentagon, or the State Department, or whoever started her on her mission, to this catastrophe? Nobody knows. One would presume they uttered a few hearty curse words and then wrote the whole thing off. One thing was certain: if the aircraft did crash through the Falls there was no way anyone else was ever going to get hold of whatever it is she was carrying in her knickers or wherever. But, of course, governments never forget, certainly where it is an important item that has gone astray. Or do they? Somebody didn't forget. Sixty years is a long time. So maybe the file is locked away some place and the odd happening in the interior of Guyana didn't excite anybody. But when somebody else – you – suddenly ups and starts asking questions about that plane's disappearance under the guise of researching the fate of her long dead grandad...'

'It is not a guise,' Shirley snapped.

'They apparently think it is a guise. So may many other people.'

'Meaning you.'

He shrugged. 'I'm in your pay, ma'am. You want my help to find out what happened; I'm going to give you my help on the terms we agreed. But I'm entitled to my own opinion.'

'As I'm entitled to fire you.'

'You are. But it wouldn't make much sense. You won't find anyone quite as well qualified as me, and you'll be left all alone to cope with my two friends.'

'Supposing they exist.'

'Like me, you're entitled to your own opinion.' He grinned again. 'Before you make a decision, I'll just finish my analysis. The key to this whatever went missing with your grandad is: who was WAAC Marshall's despatcher, and who are his or her descendants? Even if he was a shavetail lieutenant in 1942, he's going to be in his dotage now. But even if he is, or if he is dead, he passed on some information to somebody who has suddenly been activated by your appearance.'

'Those two were probably secret service people.'

'Whose secret service?'

'Well, I suppose, logically, it would have to be the CIA, or something.'

'My dear girl, I don't know a lot about the CIA, apart from the fact that it wasn't in existence in 1942, but what I have read leads me to suppose that if the CIA felt you were muscling in on their territory or their secrets they would deal with you. Not your aimless drunken sidekick.'

'Okay. So what's your theory? You seem to be full of them.'

'As you have nothing to offer, I don't have a theory. Not about 1942. But I do have one about 2004. Those characters said they'd be in touch. I believe them. Therefore, I, and you, need to be some place where they can't reach us, if you're still with me, when next they get the urge.'

'Didn't you say we're booked out on Wednesday? I was going to get the tickets tomorrow.'

'We need to be out of here tomorrow.' He looked at his watch. 'Today.'

'Tomorrow ... today is Sunday.'

'Planes fly on Sundays.'

'You mean you want me to change our flights to tomorrow? Today. That's very short notice.'

'Changing our flights to today won't help a damn,' he pointed out. 'They'll trace us easily enough. We have to get out of here by some other means, and reach Guyana by some other means. I would say we fly to the States and get a flight out of there.'

'Won't they be able to trace that?'

'Given time. We need the time to get to Guyana before they decide to stop us.'

'They'll know where we've gone.'

'Absolutely. But once we're there, they'll have to show their hand, if they mean to stop us.'

'The way things are, you'll need another visa.'

'Not if you make the booking here, so that I'm strictly in transit.'

'What about our appointment for those shots?'

'Forget them. I would say the odds on our getting some dread disease are better than taking on those two.'

She hugged herself. 'You're sure this whole thing isn't some nightmare you've dreamed up?'

'Nothing I could dream up about you could ever be a nightmare,' he assured her. 'Did I ever tell you that you are the sexiest possible woman in a nightdress?'

'I am not in a nightdress,' she snapped, and checked, flushing. 'I'm in a dressing gown.'

'You are turning my imagination loose. It is my considered opinion that it would be highly risky for you to sleep alone. Or, for that matter, for me to sleep alone. So we're stuck with each other.'

'Forget it,' she said.

He sighed and stood up. 'Never fall for the boss, they say. You do realize you may never see me again?'

'It's a risk. However, if I do see you again,

it should be at the BA desk at nine tomorrow morning. This morning. I'll be taking your advice and catching the eleven o'clock for Kennedy.'

'I'll be there. One thing more. You taking that laptop with you?'

'Where I go, my laptop goes.'

'And you have an Internet connection?'

'If I can get my modem within reach of a phone line.'

'Or even your mobile, right? I'm sure you have one. Then give me your email address.'

'Why?'

'Let's say that I'm not entirely lacking in friends.'

Shirley sighed, and wrote down the address.

It was all very well for her, he thought, as he walked back to the tube station ... It was him the two goons regarded as their go-between. If they knew he had been to see her ... He was very tempted to go to an hotel himself for the night. But he needed his gear. And more than that, if the people around him were preparing to play rough.

He took a train south of the river, walked a couple of blocks to a rundown block of flats, rang the bell, waited patiently.

'Yes?' asked the brogue.

'Tom O'Ryan.'

'Jesus! Ye know what time it is?'

'I thought you guys never slept.'

'Is this a tip or something?'

'It's a favour. For not tipping someone else.'

There were various clicks. 'Come up,' said a woman's voice. Tom pushed the street door in, went up the stairs three flights, found another door open. The woman had red hair and wore a dressing gown, otherwise she was unremarkable.

'We don't owe you nothin',' she pointed out.

'I've an Irish grandfather. And I know enough about you lot to shop you.'

She stood aside, and he entered the small bedsit. The man sat on the bed. He wore pyjama bottoms and looked tousled. The woman closed the door.

'That's a good reason to put a bullet in your brain.'

'You'll not do that, Maureen,' Tom said, easily. 'Firstly, there's the matter of my diaries, with names and addresses, which the police will find because I've left instructions where they're to be found.'

'Bluff,' Maureen commented.

'Then there's the fact that if you do me this favour I'll be leaving the country.'

'For good?' asked the man.

'I hope not, Brian. But you never know.'

'Ye'll not be going home?' Maureen asked.

'Ireland is not my home,' Tom pointed out.

'Nor will it be as long as it is inhabited by murdering thugs like you.'

'Will ye listen to t'e man?' Maureen demanded. 'And him coming calling in t'e middle of t'e night, lookin' for a favour.'

'What favour?' Brian asked.

'A shooter. Something small, handy and man-stopping.'

'You ever shot somebody?'

'As a matter of fact, no. But there's a first time for everything.'

'Ye know ye'll be breakin' t'e law, just by havin' one?'

'Like I said, I'm leaving the country. Name your price.'

'Jesus,' Brian said. 'T'e man's serious, Mo.'

'Mother-in-law trouble?' Maureen asked, grinning.

'Wait till you read the papers. Will you help me, or not?'

Brian waved his hand and Maureen opened one of the drawers in the bureau. Tom stood at her shoulder and gaped. 'Holy shit! You planning to start a war?'

'We're fightin' a war,' she pointed out. 'Now, t'is little one here is what ye're after.' From the assorted hardware she took out a snub-nosed revolver. 'Point t'irty-two calibre, doesn't make too much noise, does t'e trick. Ye don't want to be too far away from t'e target, mind.'

Tom took the revolver, balanced it in his

hand. 'Feels good.'

'T'ey always do. How many cartridges would ye be needin'?'

'How many can I have?'

She produced a box. 'Twenty-four in there. T'e gun takes five, so ye've a few spares. T'at'll be t'ree hundred pound.'

'You'll take a cheque, I hope. I don't travel with that kind of money.'

Maureen looked at Brian, who shrugged. 'We know where to find him.'

'He's goin' abroad.'

'We'll find him if we have to. Won't we, Tommy boy?'

Tom sat at the table to write the cheque, to Mr and Mrs O'Reilly, which happened to be the name they were currently using.

'Ye say ye're leavin' t'e country,' Brian remarked. 'How?'

'Is it important?'

'Supposing ye're flyin', just how do you intend to get t'e gun t'rough?'

'Hold baggage.'

'Ye might just be t'e unlucky one for an X-ray. Ye have to split it up.'

'Eh?'

'God save us from amateurs,' Maureen remarked. 'Like t'is.' She took the gun back, fiddled with it, and a moment later it was in four parts on the table. 'Can ye put t'at back toget'er?'

'I doubt it.'

'Well, practise,' she recommended. 'Ye want four bags, see. Clothes and shoes and wash items, hardware like soap and brushes, some in each bag. T''en ye put one piece of t'e gun in each bag, too. Ye'll see t'e butt comes apart, so even an X-ray machine isn't goin' to identify it too easy. T'e bullets ye wrap up in your undies, all separate. Got it?'

'What about a camera case. And a camcorder?'

'Useful.'

'You don't reckon that, using so many bags, I'm increasing the risk of getting caught?'

'We use t'at met'od all t'e time,' Brian pointed out. 'And we don't get caught. Well, not too often. It's an acceptable risk.'

'Yeah, well...' Tongue between his teeth, Tom carefully reassembled the revolver. Then he put it and his box of bullets in his jacket pocket.

'Don't hurry back,' Maureen suggested.

Tom wondered why he dealt with such people? But they were useful. And the odds were they'd blow themselves up before they actually got around to blowing up anyone else. And there could be no doubt that with the gun in his pocket, even at the moment unloaded, he felt a whole lot safer. Meanwhile, he had things to do. Shirley might genuinely not have a clue as to what Lynette

Marshall had been carrying, but he had a few secrets of his own. He returned to his flat, punched out a telephone number. It rang several times before it was answered.

'Gifford.'

'And the top of the morning to you, old son.'

'You are drunk. Do you know the time?'

'I am not drunk, and it is a quarter to two.'

'Don't you ever sleep?'

'I can't afford it. Lionel, old son, I need a favour.'

'Why?'

'Because we are old chums and you were best man at my wedding.'

'Which was a mistake for all of us.'

'Be serious. You still on the Africa desk?'

'It's a living.'

'I'm trying to trace a WAAC named Lynette Marshall who left Africa with something of great importance and went missing. I need to know what this something was. Or if that is impossible, who was likely to have been her boss.'

Gifford, who like all top feature writers reacted to the possibility of a story like a retriever spotting a falling bird, was clearly making notes. 'When?'

'July 1942.'

There was a brief silence. Then Gifford asked. 'What did you say?'

'If it was easy, Lionel, I'd do it myself.'

'Sixty-two years? Are you out of your shitting mind?'

'If anyone can do it, Lionel, you can. My faith in you is infinite. Now listen, I'm leaving the country in a couple of hours.'

'Don't tell me you're on the lam.'

'Only in a manner of speaking. So you won't be able to reach me for a few hours. How long will it take you to find out what I want?'

'About two years.'

'This is a serious business, old son.'

'Well, maybe a week. If I drop everything else.'

'Do that and I'll cut you in on the story when I get it. I don't know where I'll be in a week, but I'll be available. Write this down.' He read Shirley's email address.

'Shirley dot Richards? Who the hell is she?'

'My alter ego. Get working, old son.'

He slept soundly, almost too soundly, and arrived at Heathrow only ten minutes before check-in expired. At least he had not noticed anyone following him.

Shirley was chic in a pink trouser suit. 'Thought you'd dropped out,' she remarked.

'I had things to do. Do we have seats?'

'Just. But one of us will be upgraded. I have miles.'

'Which one of us goes up?'

'Me,' she said.

Well, he supposed he was only the hired help. He watched his various bags disappear with a sinking feeling. 'You travel heavy,' Shirley remarked. She only had the one carry-all.

'We may be gone a long time,' he pointed out. 'And I don't suppose you're going to wash my shirts and knickers for me.'

She snorted and led him through security. Once again his heart seemed to do hand-springs, as both camera and camcorder case slipped behind the curtain. 'Has it ever occurred to you,' he remarked, when he had regained possession, 'that security at most airports is very lax, despite the terror threat?'

'They figure that the mere fact that there is security will put most people off, while the real bad guys know how to smuggle their guns and bombs through anyway.'

'Good point,' Tom said thoughtfully. 'Well ... see you at Kennedy.'

They were reunited at luggage reclaim. 'Which movie did you watch?' he asked conversationally.

'The latest Emma Thompson.'

'Ah. They weren't showing that in economy. Have you booked us into an hotel for the night?'

'No. You said we had to hurry. Our onward flight is in half an hour.'

'And don't tell me: you're flying business

again, while I...'

'You are flying economy. Don't worry about it: we're staying at the same hotel. There aren't all that many in Georgetown.'

He slept most of the way south, and when he awoke it was dark, the cabin lights dimmed. He peered out of the window, looking down at nothing but darkness. The passengers by whom he was surrounded were all either black or ethnic Indian; Guyana, as he had told Shirley, had a population of just about half Indians from India, induced to travel across the ocean some hundred and fifty years ago in order to replace the freed slaves as labourers in the cane fields, the freed slaves having shown no desire to work for wages for their erstwhile masters. Now, as in Trinidad and Jamaica, they formed a very important ethnic group. Everyone was very friendly, but he was by now conditioned to be suspicious, and kept to himself, wondering how Shirley was getting on up front.

Stepping off the plane at Timehri Airport, as Atkinson Field had been renamed since independence, even at nine o'clock at night, was like entering an oven ready for baking. It was very still, and there was low cloud; from the pools of water lying around the tarmac he guessed there had been recent rain. The jungle, which began just beyond the airport, seemed to seethe, as did the insects closer at hand. How it all came back from even his childhood memory.

'God, the heat,' Shirley remarked, joining him in the arrivals hall. 'Does it ever cool off?'

'Not really,' he said, with malicious pleasure. But he was very uptight. This was the real crunch.

'May I ask the purpose of your visit?' asked the pleasant, young, uniformed black man. 'Miss...' he opened her passport. 'Richards?'

'Vacation,' Shirley said.

This seemed to surprise him. 'You have come to Guyana on vacation?'

'Is there a law against that?'

'By no means. We are pleased to see you. It is merely that we seldom have individual tourists, especially female. Most of our visitors come in groups.'

'I'm not alone,' Shirley told him. 'This is my partner.'

The immigration officer looked Tom up and down, his expression quizzical but clear enough: what is a good-looking chick like you doing with a beat-up old wreck like this? He took Tom's passport, flicked it open to the date of birth, raised his eyebrows again and then frowned. 'You were born in Guyana, Mr O'Ryan?'

'I was born in British Guiana, old son,' Tom said.

The immigration officer stared at him for

several seconds, but at last decided it had been an attempt at humour. 'May I ask when you left Guyana, Mr O'Ryan?'

'1973.'

'Ah.' The immigration officer checked the date again. 'Your parents were British. Returning home, as they used to say.'

'That's right.'

The immigration officer handed back both passports. 'Have a nice visit.'

'If you intend to spend the entire trip rubbing the natives up the wrong way,' Shirley remarked as they went towards customs, 'we are going to travel very slowly.'

'Couldn't resist it,' Tom said, trying to stop his heart leaping around his stomach, or vice versa. Their bags waited on the counter, and a grim-looking uniformed black man was standing above them.

'You together?' he enquired.

'Yes,' Shirley said.

'Do you have anything to declare? Drugs, alcohol...' He grinned. 'Firearms, seditious material?'

'No,' Shirley said.

The customs officer looked at Tom. 'I'm with her,' Tom said, amazed that his voice sounded as calm as usual.

The customs officer scribbled on the bags with chalk. 'Have a nice visit.'

'Why is your hand trembling?' Shirley

asked, as Tom picked up the various items and draped them round himself.

'Customs officers always make me nervous,' he confessed.

'Georgetown?' asked one of the very few waiting taxi drivers. 'I got to tell you this, boss, it is twenty-five miles. So there is a flat rate, right?'

'Right,' Shirley said.

The taxi driver looked from Tom to her and back again, then shrugged, and started loading the bags into the boot. 'Where you all staying at?'

'The Olympus.'

'Is that a fact. You all sit comfortable now, eh?' He got behind the wheel. 'My name is Harrison, see?'

'Is that a first name, or a last name?' Shirley asked.

'Whatever turns you on, ma'am.' He started the engine at the fifth turn of the key.

'When I was a lad,' Tom remarked, settling his thigh against Shirley's, 'this drive used to take about three hours, over about the worst apology for a road you ever did see.'

'I'm not sure how much of your humour I can take,' Shirley said, and added, 'My God!' as the taxi moved from a standing position to fifty miles an hour in ten seconds, behind a blaring horn. 'Belts. I don't see any belts. Don't you have belts, driver?'

'Well, ma'am, is a fact, I don't have belts,' Harrison confessed. 'I did have belts one time, but some guy tore them out. He was drunk,' he explained.

'Then aren't you breaking the law?' Shirley broke with all her principles and grabbed Tom's arm as they rounded a corner on two wheels.

'I don't think they going bother with me,' Harrison said. 'They knowing who I am.'

'Jesus,' she muttered.

The horn blared as the taxi followed its headlights into the night, scattering puddles left and right and then swerving to avoid a stray cow, also firmly situated in the centre of the road.

'I did hit one of them one time,' Harrison said. 'Man, you know what? It bust up my radiator.'

'What about the cow?' Tom asked, putting an arm round Shirley, who now seemed firmly anchored to his chest.

'I ain't knowing about that,' Harrison said. 'She done wander off.'

'Do you think he was sent to kill us?' Shirley whispered.

Tom hugged her closer. 'Not unless it's a suicide mission.'

They drove through a village, not that the taxi slowed much. People stood on the roadside and bellowed curses as water splashed away from the tyres. Then it was out on the open road again, and more blaring horn to scatter various animals. Tom wasn't sure how long the journey took, but it was a fraction of the time it did in the old days, even if the danger level was magnified enormously. At last there were big houses, and metalled roads, and streetlights. And even more people.

The taxi slowed. 'They got speed restrictions in town,' Harrison explained, regretfully.

'Don't they have them out of town, too?' Shirley asked.

'Well, yes, ma'am. But out of town nobody mind too much.'

'Do they need to in town?' Tom asked, peering out of the window at the various potholes, some, he estimated, more than a foot deep.

'Oh, yes, man,' Harrison said. 'Some of these people does drive too bad.' He swung into a driveway and came to a halt with a screeching of brakes, his front bumper just touching the back bumper of a car parked outside the large building. He pushed his head out of the window. 'Man,' he bawled, 'you can't take up space so.'

'Man,' remarked the other driver, getting out, 'if you dent my bumper I going bust your ass.'

'You and who else?' demanded Harrison, also getting out.

'Look,' Tom said, 'why don't you guys settle your difference after the lady and I have been dropped off.'

'This the hotel,' Harrison said. 'Hey!' he shouted. 'You working?' A young man wearing a mauve jacket and a mauve peaked cap ambled out of the hotel doorway. 'These here are your guests,' Harrison explained.

'You got bags?' the porter asked.

Tom got out and assisted Shirley. 'Yes, we have bags. Mind the cameras.'

Harrison opened the boot and the porter began taking out the bags. 'Man, but what you got in there?' he enquired. 'A gun?'

'Chance would be a fine thing,' Tom riposted, hoping that no one could hear the pounding of his heart.

Shirley was paying Harrison; he apparently accepted US dollars. 'I hope you're insured,' she remarked, as she followed Tom and the porter into the hotel lobby.

Here all was bright lights, with music issuing from a disco to the right. But there was only one weary looking female clerk behind reception, and their porter was equally the only one about. 'You all got a reservation?' asked the receptionist.

'Name of ... ah...' Tom looked at Shirley.

'O'Ryan,' Shirley said, and waggled her eyebrows.

'O'Ryan,' he said enthusiastically.

The woman ran her finger down a list on

her desk. 'Oh, yeah,' she said. 'I got it.' She sounded surprised. 'You got a passport?'

Tom gave her his, and she opened it and peered at the writing. 'Yeah,' she said, again apparently surprised. 'You take these people up, Leo,' she told the porter. 'Here is your key, Mr O'Ryan.'

'Thank you. The passport?'

'I keeping this till tomorrow,' she said.

There seemed no point in arguing. Tom ushered Shirley into the lift behind Leo and the bags; it was a tight squeeze. 'I ain't knowing if she going carry all this,' Leo said. But he pressed the ascent button anyway. There was some hesitation, then the car began to climb.

'What happens if it stops?' Shirley asked.

Leo giggled. 'It ain't going to stop, ma'am. If we don't go up, we come down. Kind of fast.'

'How did I let you talk me into this?' Shirley muttered.

'You have that wrong,' Tom pointed out. 'You talked me.'

Before she could think of an adequate reply, the lift did stop, fortunately on the fifth floor. And held its position while Leo hastily pushed their bags out of the door and into the hallway. 'Is that door there,' he gasped.

Shirley nearly tripped over him in her haste to be away from the lift. Tom followed, unlocked the door and switched on the light. 'Looks comfortable,' he remarked.

'That is a double bed.' Shirley pointed. 'I specifically requested twin beds, and was told I would have them.'

'Well,' Leo said, panting as he carried the bags into the room, 'they always saying that, and that is a fact. But there ain't no twin beds in the hotel.'

'Oh my God!' Shirley remarked.

'An understandable mistake,' Tom said, and tipped Leo. 'You've done a splendid job, old son.'

'Yes, sir,' Leo agreed. 'The room does have everything. You seeing this fridge here? Well, now, it is open. It shouldn't be that.'

'Is there anything in it?'

'Oh, yes, sir. Well ... there ain't no ice; that done melt. But it got everything else. You close the door, and you will soon have ice.'

'Thank you,' Tom said. 'How do we eat?'

'Well, the dining room done close, and that is a fact. You have to call room service.'

'And they'll reply?'

'Oh, yes, sir. They have to reply.' He didn't promise anything more than that. 'Well ... have a good night.'

Tom closed the door behind him, and turned to look at Shirley, who was gazing pensively out of the double-glazed window at the lights of Georgetown.

'At least it's air-conditioned,' he said. 'I

think we need a drink.'

'Don't we have dinner?'

'Drink first, room service after. Hey, there's a billet-doux from the management.'

She returned to stand above the coffee table, on which there was a sealed white envelope. 'Probably the bill, in advance.'

'I can see travelling doesn't agree with you,' he remarked, and slit the envelope. Then sat down, slowly, in the nearest chair.

'It *is* the bill,' Shirley suggested.

He handed her the sheet of paper, on which were typed the words: *Leave Guyana and live. Stay, and you die.*

Three

Policemen

'Oh my God!' Shirley exclaimed. 'What are we to do?'

'Have that drink,' Tom said. For once she didn't argue, just sat on the settee, knees pressed together, trying not to tremble. By now her pink trouser suit was decidedly crushed. The champagne was lukewarm, but he thought that might be a good thing; it should get to them more quickly. He gave her a glass. 'Here's to us.' The glass clattered against her teeth as she drank. 'You didn't really suppose those goons were going to let us get away from them, did you?' he asked.

'I didn't really believe there were any goons. But ... they can't have got here yet. That means...'

'That they have contacts here on the ground in Guyana. That figures.'

'Tom! I'm frightened. We're in a country where nobody really cares what happens to us. And where we're probably actively disliked by the government, and now we know there are people looking out for us...'

'They aren't looking, darling. They knew where we are. But, as I said, I have a few contacts of my own. We'll start on them tomorrow. Meanwhile, I suggest we eat.'

'I couldn't eat a thing at this moment.'

'You'll feel better when you've finished your drink.' He began to empty his suitcase, laying his clothes on the bed.

'You mean you're not scared?' she asked.

'Less than you'd think.' He began to take out the various parts of the gun.

Shirley was watching him, but for a moment what he was doing didn't register. Then she put down her glass. 'What is that?'

'It is a small revolver, which will stop a man and perhaps even kill him.'

'Where did you get it?'

Tom was assembling the gun, tongue between his teeth. 'From a friend.'

'Do you know what would have happened if you'd been caught smuggling it in?'

'I'd have been locked up.' He grinned at her. 'You'd have been locked up, too. Interesting places, South American gaols, so I've heard. *Voilà!*' He fitted the chamber, gave it a twirl and unpacked the various bullets to load the weapon. The other bullets he put in his pockets. 'Now I feel a whole lot safer.'

'Well I don't. Do you intend to walk around with that thing?'

'I do indeed. And if those goons show up, I may just use it.'

'But that's not legal.'

'Neither is an attempt on my life, or yours. I remember a film once where the hero, accused of illegally carrying a gun, said, "I learnt a long time ago that it is far better to have a gun and not need it than to need a gun and not have it." Safer, too. Now, let's see. Room service. Chosen yet?' He waved the menu at her.

'I have the shakes.'

'I'll order for you.' He did so. 'When do you think that will be ready?' he enquired.

'Now, how am I going to know that, man?' the woman asked. 'When it ready, it coming up.'

'Patience is clearly the name of the game.' He hung up. 'I suspect we could be thinking in terms of half an hour. Look, why don't you have a shower? You must feel like one. I know I do.'

'While you do what?'

'I know what I'd like to do.' He opened the bathroom door. 'That shower stall is big enough for two.'

'Well forget it.'

'Right. Then I'll wait for room service.'

She looked into the bathroom herself; it had a door but no bolt. 'Promise me you're not going to try anything.'

'Listen,' he said. 'We can't spend the next fortnight or whatever in a state of suspended antagonism. I have indicated that I am not going to lay a finger on you until and unless you invite me to. What more do you want?'

'But you do expect, in your male egotism, that I will invite you to before very long.'

'I'm the eternal optimist.' He grinned.

She gathered up her suitcase and disappeared; he heard the sound of a chair being placed against the door. He stood at the window and looked out at the night; the city glowed with light, although the double-glazing kept the noise at a distance. For all his apparent confidence for Shirley's benefit, he was beginning to wonder if they were biting off more than they could chew. If she was really only trying to trace her long-lost grandfather, without any knowledge that there might be something else involved, they

72

were plunging into a morass without knowing if there was a bottom. His instincts were telling him to cut and run. But, Shirley apart, the idea that he could be on the brink of uncovering something really big ... supposing he lived long enough to write the story.

'Tom!' The voice beyond the door had a note of urgency. 'I can't turn the shower off.'

'Open up, and I'll do it for you.' There was a moment's hesitation, then he heard the chair being moved, and the door was opened. Shirley was wrapped in a towel that was tucked under her armpits, but the towel was as wet as the rest of her, while water sprayed everywhere; it might be quite a large shower stall but it was rather a small bathroom.

'Shit,' he muttered, and stepped into the stall to wrestle with the circular tap. She took the opportunity to get past him, taking her suitcase with her, and by the time he had succeeded in turning the tap off she was wearing a dressing gown.

'What are you doing?' she demanded, as he stripped.

'I'm taking off my wet clothes,' he said. 'And it really wouldn't be a lot of good doing it in there.'

'Well, really.' She turned her back on him, looking out of the window as he had been doing earlier, but turning back at the knock on the door.

'Dinner,' Tom announced, wrapping himself in a sheet.

The food was surprisingly good. The wine wasn't, but after the champagne and their very long day they weren't inclined to take it seriously.

'I'm sorry you got all wet,' Shirley said.

'Goes with the job, I reckon.'

'So, where are you going to sleep?'

'In that bed. I'm so tired I wouldn't be able to do anything anyway. Why don't you just relax. In any event, don't you want me about, just in case things get rough?'

'Well, turn your back while I put on my pyjamas. And you put on yours.'

'I don't have any,' he told her.

He had to have been as tired as he claimed, because despite the nearness of the woman he slept heavily, and awoke with a start to find himself alone in bed, which had been divided into two by a row of pillows. Shirley was in her favourite position by the window, wearing a yellow sundress and sandals, peering out.

'It's raining.'

'It usually is. This is one of the wettest places on earth. You ordered breakfast?'

'I don't breakfast.'

'I do.' He rang room service, then wrapped himself in the sheet, riffled through the phone book and tried another number.

'Isn't it a little early to be waking people up?' Shirley asked.

'It's a quarter to eight. That's late, in Guyana. Hi,' he said into the phone. 'I'm trying to get hold of Cal Simpson ... Mrs Simpson? Well, hi again. I didn't know he was married. I'll congratulate him ... Right. We were kids together. Queen's College, yes ... Is that a fact? When do you reckon he'll be at his office? Fifteen minutes. Great. What's that number again?' He wrote it down. 'Thanks a million, Mrs S. Hopefully I'll get to meet you some time.'

He grinned at Shirley. 'He's already left for the office.'

Breakfast arrived, and Shirley accepted fruit juice and coffee, while Tom, having dressed, tucked into a meal. When he was finished, he used Shirley's laptop

'What are you doing?' she enquired.

'Just letting my back-up know where I am in case he needs me.'

She snorted, but Tom finished the message, giving Gifford the name of the hotel. Then he called the number Mrs Simpson had given him, and gulped. 'Would you repeat that...? Right. Then may I speak with Superintendent Simpson? Tell him it's an old school friend.'

'I should think that'll put him off,' Shirley remarked. 'I always run a mile when I hear an old school friend is getting too close. But did you say superintendent?'

'I did. We could have fallen on our feet.'

'Or be on the next plane out of Guyana.'

'He's a friend. He *was* a friend ... Cal? Tom O'Ryan ... O'Ryan. Tommy the Trundler.' Shirley raised her eyes to heaven. 'You got it,' Tom said. 'I never knew you were a policeman ... Yeah. Right here in Guyana ... At the Olympus ... Well, it's part business and part holiday. Listen, I'd enjoy it if we could meet up ... How about lunch? Can your wife make it? ... Great. Lunch.'

He hung up. 'We're on our way.'

'How well do you know this character?'

'We were in the same form at school, played cricket together, chased the same girls together...'

'You said you left Guyana when you were ten. But you were already chasing girls?'

'I was a boy genius.'

Shirley sighed. 'So, how much are you going to tell him?'

'With your permission, of course, I think we should lay our cards on the table and check out his reaction. I don't think we should mention the other guys as yet. We are innocently looking for some news of how your grandfather died.'

'That's what we *are* doing. Me at any rate.'

He finished his breakfast, and they went downstairs, where they were accosted by the manager, who returned Tom's passport. 'Good morning, Mr O'Ryan. Mrs O'Ryan.'

'Actually—' Shirley began.

'We're just good friends,' Tom explained. 'Is that a problem for you?'

'It's a free country, Mr O'Ryan. What I was wondering was how long you wish to stay with us. The room is only booked for two days. But you have not come all this way for two days, surely.'

'No, no,' Tom said. 'What we would like to do is make a safari into the interior.'

'Where exactly? It's a big country.'

'Well,' Tom said, 'we'd like to see the Rupununi, of course. And the goldfields. Oh, and there's that big waterfall ... What's it called?'

'Kaieteur.'

'That's it. How do we get there?'

'You can go up by boat and road, if you wish, but it is a long way. Most people use an aircraft. There are in fact regular charter flights to the Falls. It would be cheaper for you if you joined a scheduled party.'

'Sounds great. Can you arrange it?'

'Yes. That is a day trip, you understand.'

'Oh, but...' Shirley bit her lip.

'Miss Richards is rather keen on spending a couple of days up there,' Tom said. 'Is there nowhere to stay?'

'Not at the Falls themselves. But ... there is an hotel in Takdai...' the manager sounded doubtful.

'We don't mind roughing it.'

'It is a quite comfortable hotel, I believe. But ... well...' he changed his mind about what he would have said. 'Shall I radio through and book you a room?'

'We need twin beds,' Shirley said. The manager raised his eyebrows. 'My partner is a very restless sleeper,' she explained.

'Ah. Right. I will see what I can do. Shall I see about the Rupununi flight as well? You'd have to come back to town to change planes, for Lethem. That's right on the Brazilian border. There is a very good hotel at Lethem. I could book you in there for a few days.' He smiled. 'With twin beds, if possible.'

'That sounds great,' Tom said. 'But we'd like to do Kaieteur first.'

'No problem. When would you like to go?'

'How about tomorrow?' Again the manager raised his eyebrows. 'Then, when we're finished, we could come back here and spend a few more days with you. What's your name, by the way?'

'Whitling,' the manager said.

'Mr Whitling. Now, we're expecting friends to lunch. Do we need to book a table?'

'Might be a good idea. I'll do it for you.'

'Great. We'll probably be in the bar when they arrive. Our guests are Superintendent and Mrs Simpson.'

'Superintendent Simpson is a friend of yours?'

'Has been for years.'

'Well, hell, man, why you didn't say so right off? I'll look after all of these bookings right away.' He hurried off.

'Magic words,' Shirley muttered.

'I'm hoping it permeates. Has it occurred to you that the only way that note could have got into our bedroom last night was for someone in the hotel to put it there? It didn't have a stamp.'

'Jesus! That *hadn't* occurred to me.'

'So letting the whole world know that Cal and I are buddies might prove useful protection.'

'Sometimes you do sound like a genius. It's ten o'clock. What do we do until one?'

'Not one,' he told her. 'Everything in Guyana is moved forward an hour or so, because it gets too darned hot to do a lot around one. So lunch will be at eleven thirty.'

'That still leaves us an hour. The rain has stopped. Let's take a walk.'

'After we've checked your laptop. I'm expecting a message from my back-up.'

'You really have a back-up?'

'Doesn't everyone?'

'I don't have one.'

'You have me, darling.'

There was nothing from Gifford, but Tom knew he had been absurdly optimistic. So

79

Shirley put on her hat, a large straw that matched her light dress and sandals, and they went down the stairs. 'Mind how you go,' said Leo, their porter from last night.

'Which way is Main Street?' Tom asked.

'Just turn left at the gate, man. It's at the corner.'

'Well, hi.' It was Harrison the taxi driver. 'You folks want to go riding? I'll take you up to the Botanical Gardens. Now that is one beautiful place. It got manatee and all.'

'Maybe later,' Tom said. 'We just want to take a stroll.'

'Yeah, man. Now is the best time to take a stroll.'

'What did he mean by that?' Shirley asked, as they walked out of the gate.

'I imagine, two things. At half past ten in the morning we are less likely to be mugged than at most other times.'

'Oh, cheer me up. What was the other reason?'

'Simply that while the sun is shining at this moment, it will probably start raining again around midday.'

Shirley squinted at the sky through her dark glasses. 'There's not a cloud in sight.'

'They lurk,' he told her. 'And spring out when you least expect them.'

'This has got to be the flattest city I have ever been in,' Shirley commented. 'I thought you said this country was full of mountains.'

'It is, in the interior. The coastal strip is just the leftover of centuries of mud brought down by the rivers, and is, as you say, about the flattest place on earth. It's even beneath sea level. There's a sea wall to keep the water out. In my day, it was the place to meet your girlfriend after school. Probably still is.'

They reached the corner and gazed at a wide, tree-lined avenue with a pedestrian walkway up the centre. 'That looks rather good,' Shirley remarked.

'Apart from the potholes.'

'Why don't they do something about those?'

'Money. Or lack of it.' There were not a great number of vehicles, apart from some very decrepit-looking buses, but a large number of cyclists, and getting across to the pedestrian walkway was hazardous. Once there, however, they could sit on one of the benches, in the shade, enjoying the morning, which was steadily heating up as the sun began to reach its apogee. Immediately they were the centre of attention both from passers-by, quite a few of whom greeted them with 'Morning, man' and small boys and girls, who clustered at a safe distance and giggled. Also from a group of black youths, who stood some yards away to survey them.

'I suppose these are your would-be

muggers,' Shirley suggested. 'Are we safe?'

'I don't really know. As our friend suggested, one would have supposed so, in the middle of the morning.'

'Do you have your little gun?'

'I do. But I don't think it would be a good idea to flash it in public. I'd rather put my trust in our friend over there.'

A large black policeman, resplendent in dark-blue trousers, light-blue summer shirt, black beret and heavy black boots, was slowly parading towards them, swinging a lengthy and clearly heavy baton from his right hand. 'You all troubling these white folk?' he enquired at large.

'Man, we just talking,' one of the youths said.

'Well get off and do your talking somewhere else,' the policeman recommended. 'I coming back this way just now, and I don't want to see your faces.' He drew level with Tom and Shirley, touched his beret with his baton. 'Morning, sir. Morning, madam. Having a nice day?'

'Brilliant,' Tom told him.

'Well, you all go on doing that,' the policeman suggested, and continued on his way. The youth gang was already wandering off.

'Well,' Shirley said, 'it makes me feel a whole lot better to know that man mountains like him are on our side.'

'Ah, but try thinking what it would be like

if he changed sides, and you found yourself in a police cell with said man mountain, with him asking the questions.'

'You sure can cheer a girl up. We haven't broken any laws.'

'Yet. You look as if you could use a drink, and the clouds are coming. Let's go back.'

The sky clouded over with remarkable rapidity, and they actually had to run the last hundred yards as it began to drizzle. By the time they were seated in the hotel bar drinking rum punches the rain was drumming on the roof. 'Is there a dry season?' Shirley asked.

'September,' the barman told her. 'It don't rain all that much in September.'

Shirley raised her eyebrows, and then raised them some more as the doorway was filled with another large man, wearing, in contrast to the constable, a peaked cap and, even more unlike the constable, dressed below that in a khaki bush jacket and shorts, with khaki stockings and brown Sam Browne belt. Calthorpe Simpson was a good-looking man; his ebony skin seemed to gleam. His wife, a petite figure barely half his size, was no less attractive.

'Cal!' Tom was on his feet. 'I'd have recognized you anywhere.'

Cal shook hands. 'You've changed a bit. This is Patricia.'

More hand shaking. 'And this is Shirley,'

Tom explained. She shook hands in turn, feeling distinctly overawed. Rum punches were served. 'Must be thirty years, just about,' Tom said.

'That is a fact. Good to see you, man. Good to see you.'

'And you, a copper. Who'd ever have thought it?'

Cal grinned. 'Set a thief, eh? But what brings you back to Guyana?' His gaze flickered to Shirley. 'You ain't working?'

'As a matter of fact, I am. Partly.'

'I understood you were on vacation,' Cal said, revealing that he had had them checked out with immigration. 'You know you can't work here without a permit.'

'It's not that kind of work. I'm trying to trace someone.'

'You a detective, nowadays?'

'Just an enthusiastic amateur. I don't suppose you remember the story of a US air force plane crashing into Kaieteur in 1942?'

'Man, that was before either you or I was born,' Cal pointed out.

'My dad was working up there then, and he told me about it.'

'Yeah,' Cal said, thoughtfully.

Shirley realized that he did know about the plane – perhaps all there was to know. 'My grandfather was on board that plane,' she said.

'Oh, you poor dear,' Patricia Simpson said.

'Now that is one hell of a thing,' Cal agreed. 'So?'

'The thing is, there's no proof the plane actually went into the Falls,' Shirley said. 'It could have crashed anywhere out there in the bush.'

'As I remember from what I've read about it,' Cal said, 'the Americans carried out a pretty extensive search of the whole area, and found nothing.'

'You mean you did know of it,' Tom said, grinning.

'It's my business to know everything,' Cal said, also grinning. 'So tell me, just what are you folks aiming to do?'

'Go up to Kaieteur and have a look around.'

Cal shook his head, slowly. 'Waste of time. More than sixty years? Even if that plane did come down in the bush, there'd be not a trace of it now.'

'Steel doesn't rot. Nor does aluminium.'

'It sure can rust, and get too overgrown to see. No, sir, Tommy, and you, Miss Richards, my advice to you would be to enjoy your stay here in Guyana. By all means go up to the Falls. They are the ultimate wonder of the world. But enjoy them. And then go home again.'

'You wouldn't by any chance be warning us off, Cal?' Tom asked, pleasantly.

'Why should I wish to do that?'

The luncheon gong went.

The two men reminisced over the meal, while the two women exchanged small talk. Cal deftly steered the subject away from the Falls, but it was his own wife who reintroduced it. 'I think it's real romantic,' she said. 'You coming all this way, Miss Richards, to find out where your grandfather you never even saw died.'

'I can't help feeling that maybe he escaped the crash.'

'That simply isn't practical, Miss Richards,' Cal said. 'If they went into the Falls, kaput. If they came down in the jungle, and weren't found in a hurry, as they weren't, again kaput. But even if anyone managed to survive the crash, and exist in the jungle, man, they'd be more than eighty now.'

'That's not too old, nowadays,' Shirley said quietly.

'That's true. Well...' he ate for some seconds. 'So you mean to go looking.'

'Have you any objections?' Tom asked.

'Not at all. It's a free country. I'm thinking of you. These forest communities are kind of tight-knit. You want to be careful about treading on anyone's corns, right?'

'I thought Kaieteur is now a national park?' Shirley asked.

'Sure it is. That don't mean they have

super-highways and high-rise hotels. It's just as empty, most of the time, as it ever was. Sure we'd like to see a big tourist trade; we could do with the hard currency. But it ain't happened yet.'

'What possible corns can we tread on if we're just looking for a vanished aircraft?'

Cal shrugged. 'You're only looking because you reckon your grandad survived. If he survived and nobody knows about it, it could be that he reached what he thought might be help and didn't survive *that*. We're talking about these people's grandads, too, right?'

Shirley looked at Tom, trying to share an estimate of how much they should tell this pleasant but vaguely hostile policeman.

'Wouldn't that be a criminal matter?' Tom asked.

'After more than sixty years?'

'There's no statute of limitations on murder, is there?'

'No there isn't. But there sure is a statute of limitations on proof. Sixty years is just too long, man.'

'Is there a lot of crime up there?' Tom asked. 'According to my dad, there was very little when he was stationed at Takdai. Everyone knew each other too well.'

'Things change, in sixty years. People certainly do.'

'You mean there is crime.'

Cal's eyelids flickered. Obviously he would

know all about the recent murder and the spurt of strange disappearances. But he wasn't about to share his knowledge. 'Crime gets everywhere nowadays, Tom. But there's nothing up there we can't handle. On the other hand, we don't have the manpower to offer you any personal protection. I just want you to know that.'

'We accept that.'

They drank coffee. 'The guy you want to talk to,' Cal recommended, 'is named Fuller. He's an anthropologist. American, like you, Miss Richards, but he's lived here for years, prowling around the bush. If anyone knows anything about what might be behind the Falls, he's your man. When were you thinking of going up?'

'Tomorrow morning.'

'That's a bit short notice for getting hold of Fuller. By the Grumman?'

'That's the idea. We want to do the tourist bit first. You know, landing on the river, taking off over the Falls...'

'Yeah. It's great.'

'Have you done it, Mrs Simpson?' Shirley asked.

'Oh, yes. I went up with Cal, earlier this year, when...' she bit her lip.

'When he was investigating something, I'll bet,' Tom said with a grin.

'That's right,' Cal said pleasantly. 'Honey, we should be going. I have to get back to the office.' He stood up. 'That was a splendid lunch, and it's been great meeting you again, Tommy. And you, Miss Richards. Have a good trip. Maybe we'll get together again when you return to Georgetown.'

'I'd like that,' Shirley said, and was a little surprised to realize that she meant it.

'Do you reckon we're any further ahead?' she asked, when she and Tom had retired to their room for the obligatory siesta.

'Well, I reckon we've confirmed that there are some odd goings-on up there.'

'But no one is likely to tell us what they are, so I don't see that we've advanced. If no one at this place Takdai is willing to talk to us either ... We going to follow up on this man Fuller?'

'I think not. We don't want the whole world to know what we're at. We're not entirely out of ammo. What about your reporter friend?'

'I told you, he wouldn't talk to me.'

'That was on a long-distance phone. It's too easy to hang those things up. I think he might change his mind, face to face.'

'How do we do that?'

'You have the name of his newspaper, don't you?'

'The *Daily Story*.'

'We'll trot along there this afternoon and have a word.'

'Shouldn't we telephone first, and make an

appointment?'

'And have him duck out, or at least prepare his defences? We need to take him by surprise.'

To Shirley's surprise, she actually slept. She put it down to a combination of the air-conditioning after the heat of downstairs, the alcohol she had had with lunch and the exhaustion produced by nervous tension. Together with the oddly reassuring presence of Tom. And his gun?

He was, as she had come to expect, hopeful. 'Lying down in your clothes is a detestable habit,' he remarked.

Shirley kicked off her shoes. 'It's one you are going to have to take up, while we are resting.'

'I am making plans to re-educate you,' he said. But she fell asleep before he could commence. When she awoke he was standing by the window, drinking cold beer from the can and looking down at the street. 'Thought you were never going to surface,' he remarked.

'God, my mouth tastes like the inside of a sewer,' she muttered, and went to the bathroom.

'All ready?' he enquired when she returned, having washed her face and looking slightly more alert. He had finished his beer.

'As I ever will be.'

* * *

They had a new taxi driver, who was less communicative than their friend of the previous night. He also drove more slowly, and his rear seats still had their belts. It was only a five-minute trip to the newspaper office, which was situated down a side street just off Water Street, the riverside business area.

'We'll need someone to take us back,' Tom said as they got out.

'You want me wait?'

'I think that would be a good idea.'

The driver adjusted his meter, tipped his straw hat over his eyes and appeared to go to sleep.

'Won't that be very expensive?' Shirley asked as they went inside.

'We're not planning on spending the afternoon. Mr Diamond in?' he asked the receptionist.

'Who's calling?'

'Tom O'Ryan. He doesn't know me.'

'You got an appointment?'

'No. But I have a news item that I know will be of great interest to him.'

The woman considered for a few seconds, then tapped a switch. 'Guy down here says he has an important news item.' She listened, then looked up. 'Give it in at the desk.'

'No way,' Tom said. 'This goes direct to Diamond, or I'll go to another paper.'

She spoke into her mouthpiece. 'Guy says

it's you or another paper. Yeah. Okay.' She closed the key. 'Says you can go up. Two flights, first on the left.'

'No lift?'

'You got legs,' she pointed out.

'You should've told her you're a friend of Superintendent Simpson,' Shirley said. 'Look at the effect it had on the hotel manager.'

'I'm saving that trump.' He began to puff as they reached the second floor.

'That's it,' Shirley said.

The door had printed on it, in gold letters, CLAUDE DIAMOND, ASSISTANT EDITOR. Tom knocked, and the door was opened by a woman.

'Mr O'Ryan?'

'The very one.' She looked at Shirley. 'My bodyguard,' Tom explained.

She stepped back to allow them into an outer office where they could see several people sitting before computers, some actually typing. She led them across this and tapped on the inner door, then opened it. Claude Diamond didn't get up. He was a somewhat small man, fair skinned, with a little moustache. Once upon a time he would have been good looking, Shirley reckoned, but he was running to stomach and his cheeks to jowls. He looked vaguely surprised to discover that his visitors were white.

'You all ain't local,' he suggested.

'Spot on,' Tom said. 'In a manner of speaking. I was actually born here. Tom O'Ryan.' He held out his hand, which was taken, limply, after a brief hesitation. But like everyone else they met, Diamond was looking at Shirley. 'And this is Miss Shirley Richards,' Tom explained.

Diamond frowned at the name. 'You and me met?'

'We spoke on the phone, a few weeks ago,' Shirley said.

Diamond considered her for several seconds, while the penny was apparently dropping. 'Jesus,' he commented at last.

'Mind if we sit down?' Tom asked, and gestured Shirley to the chair in front of the desk. There was a straight chair against the far wall, and he placed this beside hers, to sit himself.

'Listen,' Diamond said. 'I told you on the phone...'

'You didn't tell her anything, Mr Diamond,' Tom said, pleasantly. 'You hung up. Now, is that any way to treat a lady?' Diamond glared at him. 'So,' Tom said, 'we would like the information you were reluctant to give over the phone. About this murder up by the Falls. And the disappearance of that young woman.'

Diamond clearly needed time to think. 'You know the girl?' he asked.

'Sadly, no. But we want to know what

happened to her.'

'She disappeared,' Diamond said. 'You ever been up there?'

'Sure I have,' Tom lied.

'Then you must know these things happen. That is wild country. Miles and miles of empty bush. Jaguars. Alligators. Comoodi. Any one of those could have got her. Or she could just have fallen into a river and drowned. Or got eaten by pirai.'

'What's a comoodi?' Shirley asked.

'It's the local name for the anaconda, the water boa,' Tom explained. 'Some of them can grow twelve feet long.'

'Twenty feet, man,' Diamond said.

'Have you ever seen one that big?'

'I ain't, personally. But they grow, man. What about this python they got in Indonesia? Four hundred feet, man.'

'That's Indonesia.'

'And what's a pirai?' Shirley asked, disinclined to become involved in a zoological dispute.

'Local name for piranha,' Tom explained. 'However, to the best of my knowledge piranha only eat human beings in Hollywood, and there is no record of a comoodi attacking a fully grown adult. I assume this young lady who went missing was full grown? Now, what about the man who was attacked and killed by some kind of critter? His throat was torn out.'

'Could have been jaguar,' Diamond suggested.

'There is no record of any jaguar ever resembling an oversize monkey. Am I right, Mr Diamond?'

'Listen, man,' Diamond said, 'you trying to cause trouble, or what?'

'That's certainly possible, Mr Diamond,' Tom agreed. 'If we don't get some answers. It may interest you to know that we had lunch today with Superintendent Simpson. And he suggested we chase you up.'

'Me? Why he couldn't tell you himself?'

'Tell us what?'

'Whatever it is you want to know.'

'I think he preferred that it should come from you.'

'Man, that don't make sense. What's your interest, anyway?'

'Tell him,' Tom suggested.

Shirley went through her routine, while Diamond stared at her in growing consternation.

'Now,' Tom said when she had finished, 'don't say it. More than sixty years is a long time, blah, blah, blah. Tell us, first, why you hung up on Miss Richards when she called you.'

'Well ... okay, as you've spoken with Simpson. There has been more than one happening up there in the Falls National Park. Six people have disappeared over the past three years. Well, you know, these things happen. But there ain't that many people up there, so after the first two or so people began to ask questions. The police tried all the usual things, sex crimes, blood feuds, but there were no leads. These people simply disappeared.'

'All women?'

Diamond shook his head. 'Two were men. Well, at that time there was no reason to hush it up. But now, this murder, well ... we got the message. If there is some kind of yeti or bigfoot roaming around the park, keep it quiet. We don't get that many tourists as it is.'

'And this last time was the first time this creature was actually seen?' Tom asked.

'Save maybe by the people it killed or abducted. There's been tracks before, mind. But with all the rain they get up there they haven't been too distinct.'

'But there *were* tracks,' Shirley said. 'Surely they've been analysed, and they know whether they were human or not.'

'I guess maybe they have. But the government put a clamp on it.'

'And you let them get away with that?' Tom was incredulous.

'Listen, man, when the government seals something, this government, it stays sealed. '

'That's why everyone keeps reiterating that it's a free country. But it may interest you to know that we intend to get to the bottom of what is happening, and when we do, and I write up the story, I am going to say how unhelpful you have been.'

'Man, you can't frighten me.'

'I should mention,' Shirley put in, 'that for anyone who *is* prepared to be helpful, there could be a handsome reward.' Tom gave her a quick glance. But maybe she was thinking about whatever the WAAC named Lynette had been carrying.

'Yes, well ... Look, I have nothing to offer, man. Like I said, this man was attacked by some outsize critter. It sounded like news so I went up there myself and learnt about the disappearance of that girl. Then it turned out she'd been the third in the last year, and there'd been others before that. That sounded even more like news. Then I found out that over the past twenty years or so there have been sixteen disappearances. Not all from Takdai, of course. From the goldfields, from other Mazeruni villages ... It covers a fairly wide area. So maybe there is something up there. Each case didn't get the publicity it deserved. So it sounded big. So I came back down to town to do a story, and before I can boot my computer along come the police.'

'Simpson?' Tom asked.

'No, this was Lemonde, CID. Said the story was *sub judice*. All of it, no matter how far I wanted to go back. Lemonde isn't the kind of guy one argues with.' He looked from face to face. 'And that's the truth, man.'

'You'll never believe this,' Tom said, 'but I believe you. There's still something you can do for us, though. When this Lemonde character told you to bury the story, he didn't say anything about your files, right?'

'Well ... no.'

'Well, then, we would be most appreciative if you would dig up all the files, say for the past sixty-odd years, relative to Kaieteur, and let us have a look at them.'

'Man, you're talking about a lot of work. There wasn't nothing like computers around then.'

'*Most* appreciative,' Tom said. 'I'm sure you can spare the rest of this afternoon. Tell you what, why don't you have dinner with us tonight. Is there a Mrs Diamond?' Diamond shook his head, slowly. 'Then we'll expect just you. We're at the Olympus. Eight o'clock?'

'Do you suppose he'll turn anything up?' Shirley asked, as they drove back to the hotel.

'Maybe, maybe not. But we need to cover every inch of the ground. What may have appeared totally insignificant to someone not sufficiently clued up, could provide us with a vital lead.' She looked sceptical. 'Now,' he said, when they regained their room, 'you can tell me where this extra money you have suddenly discovered came from. Or is coming from.'

She looked sulky. 'I have a little put by for emergencies.'

'Like bribing newspaper reporters. But I'm a newspaper reporter. As well as your guide and bodyguard. How come you've never thought about bribing me? And I'm not even asking for cash.'

'I didn't think you were the sort of man who takes bribes,' she replied pertly.

'You know what—' He checked as there was a knock on the door.

They looked at each other. 'Have you still got your gun?' Shirley whispered.

Tom tapped his pocket and moved towards the door. 'Who is it?' he asked.

'Whitling here, Mr O'Ryan. The manager.'

'Oh. Right.' He unlocked the door.

'Just to let you know I have all your bookings for you. I'm afraid it's an early start tomorrow, to get you up to Timehri for the Grumman.'

Tom nodded. 'Just give us a call. By the way, we're expecting a guest for dinner.'

Whitling nodded. 'I shall arrange it.' He bustled off.

'An early start won't give us much time to look at those files,' Shirley remarked.

'We can study them all night and sleep on the plane,' Tom suggested.

They showered, with careful segregation, and then went downstairs to have a cocktail before Diamond arrived. There were quite a few other people in the bar, but none seemed interested in the Caucasian couple. And there was no sign of Diamond.

'Suppose he doesn't show?' Shirley asked.

'He'll show,' Tom promised. But when eight came and went Diamond still had not arrived. Whitling hovered, anxiously and inquisitively.

'Our guest is Mr Diamond, from the *Story*,' Tom explained. 'He must have got delayed.'

Whitling returned to stand by their chairs at half past. By then they were on their fourth cocktail, and feeling that the evening was getting away from them.

'May we have a telephone book?' Tom asked. One was produced, and the home number of Diamond's flat found. Tom called, but there was no reply after several rings. 'I think we'd better eat,' he told Whitling. 'He's gone some place. And it isn't here.'

'Damn,' Shirley said as they had their meal. 'You had me feeling that we might really be on to something.'

'We still could be,' Tom said.

'You're an incurable optimist,' she pointed out. 'Have you forgotten we're leaving here at dawn tomorrow? Your friend has gotten cold feet all over again.'

'He'll turn up. I'll sort something out with Whitling if he doesn't show until tomorrow. Let's at least have coffee and brandy in a civilized manner.'

They sat themselves in a corner of the bar and watched Calthorpe Simpson come in. He was in plain clothes, but had the air of a policeman on duty. He came directly to their table, and Shirley was aware of some very uneasy sensations. 'You guys pay a call on Claude Diamond this afternoon?' Cal asked.

'That's right,' Tom said. 'Anything illegal in that?'

'I wouldn't say so. When did you see him after that?'

'He was to join us here for dinner, but he never turned up.'

'I can tell you why he didn't,' Cal said. 'He's dead.'

Four

Running Water

Tom sat down with a bump. Cal sat down also. 'Dead?' Shirley asked. 'How can he be dead?'

'He was shot, Miss Richards. At short range with a point two-two automatic pistol, as far as we have been able to judge.' Tom glanced at Shirley. 'Listen, man,' Cal said. 'This is a serious business. Claude was a much-liked man. I know you went to see him at his office this afternoon. What happened after that?'

'What do you mean?' Shirley demanded. 'Nothing happened after that. Concerning us. We told you, he was coming here to dinner, but he never turned up.'

'You went to see him to ask about this fairy-tale idea of yours,' Cal suggested.

'We don't happen to think it is a fairy tale.'

'So what did he tell you?'

'He didn't actually tell us anything, save that your police had put a clamp on the story.'

'What story?' They gazed at each other, then Cal shrugged. 'So, what was he going to tell you this evening?'

'This evening?'

'Listen, Miss Richards, Tommy, we may be several thousand miles away from Scotland Yard, but we're not exactly hicks down here. Someone from this hotel telephoned Claude at eight forty-five this evening. We got the records from Telecomms first thing. I reckon that had to be you. Why did you do that?'

It was Tom's turn to shrug. 'Like we said, he was coming to have dinner with us. So he said. When he didn't show, I called him to find out why he'd changed his mind.'

'And what did he say?'

'He didn't say anything. There was no reply.'

'Because he was already dead. As near as we can figure. Claude Diamond was shot just after seven, as he was about to get into his car. His body was found half in and half out of the front seat.'

'And you think we did it? That doesn't make sense.'

Cal sighed. 'Of course I don't think you did it. You were returned here by taxi just after four this afternoon, and you didn't leave the hotel again. We've checked that out. And, as you say, it doesn't make sense, if you were looking forward to meeting up with him again and hearing whatever it was he had to say. What was it you were hoping he was going to say?' Again Shirley and Tom exchanged glances. 'If he was finding out something to tell you,' Cal pointed out, 'we might have a motive for his murder.'

'You don't think it could all be coincidence?' Tom asked. 'Robbery, for instance?'

'No, I don't think it was a coincidence, or a robbery,' Cal said. 'Claude's clothes were untouched. If it had been a robbery, his pockets would have been turned out. As it happened, his wallet was still in his inside breast pocket and his card case was in his side pocket, untouched. Nor do I think it could have been a personal motive. Like I said, Claude was a well-liked man in the community, and he had very few vices. He did not womanize, and he did not pick up small boys. He has, had, a long-standing girlfriend, who is currently under sedation. I know most things about what goes on in this city, and I can tell you that he did not have an enemy in the world. So you see, all I have is the fact that within three hours of meeting with you two he's dead. You have got to tell me why, otherwise I am going to arrest you and charge you with being accessories.'

'That's not legal,' Shirley protested.

'It is in my book, Miss Richards. And you know what? I don't think you'd enjoy even one night in our cells. The facilities are poor, and the company mainly unpleasant.'

'Was there anything in his car, or lying by his body?' Tom asked.

'No. What should there have been?'

'Just files. Diamond promised to look up his newspaper files back to 1942 for anything that may have happened in the Falls National Park, and bring them along this evening.'

'So whoever killed him took the files,' Cal mused. 'Why?'

'We haven't seen them, remember?'

'Listen,' Cal said. 'I damn well know you're not giving me the whole thing. Nothing is making sense so far. A plane goes missing more than sixty years ago. It happened to have your grandfather on board, Miss Richards. So you want to find out exactly what happened. After such a long time that doesn't make much sense, but it has a weird sort of logic. You also happen to believe that the disappearance of that plane and a few crimes that we've been having in the interior are linked. That makes even less sense, after sixty years, but nothing is impossible. What does not make any sense at all is what has happened since. No one knew you were going to visit Claude this afternoon; there was no appointment. Therefore, you were followed there, by the murderer or by an agent of his. Now tell me, why should he do that? What's so important about you and your weird theories?' He looked from face to face, and, getting no response, continued. 'Because something is. The killer knew that Claude was coming here tonight, and he also knew, or he figured, that he'd be bringing something of interest. Something so interesting that he was prepared to kill to get it for himself. Well, he killed, and now he has it. You have to have some idea what it was. Is.'

Shirley opened her mouth, and Tom squeezed her hand to shut her up. 'We came here looking for anything that might shed some light on what happened in 1942, Cal, and what has happened since. Okay, so it's a hell of a long shot that anyone survived that crash, and that he or his descendants might have survived for sixty years without anybody knowing about it. But while there is the slightest chance of that having happened Miss Richards is entitled to want to find out if it did. There's nothing criminal about that. You've been talking about things not making sense. The thing that is making least sense is the slightest possibility that Claude Diamond's murder could have had anything to do with us. So you say the clothing wasn't disturbed. But whatever Claude was carrying was taken. It was armed robbery, and the fellow lost his head, grabbed what he could and ran off. Those are the facts. Policemen work on facts, don't they?'

Cal regarded him for several seconds, then

he nodded. 'Sure they do. What they don't go for are coincidences. Claude Diamond could have been mugged any night in the last ten thousand. But he was mugged on the night he had just seen you, and was coming to see you again.'

Another pause, but Tom merely smiled. 'And I can only repeat, he was bringing what information he could get from his files regarding any odd happenings around Kaieteur over the past sixty years. And, Cal, the only people in the whole world, certainly in Guyana, who knew what we were after, apart from Claude himself, were you and your policemen. Right?'

Cal's head jerked. Then he grinned. 'Nobody ever told you it pays to be on good terms with the fuzz, man?' He got up. 'You still aiming to go up to the Falls tomorrow?'

'It's all arranged. As part of a general sightseeing trip. Or are you meaning to put us under hotel arrest?'

'I wouldn't dream of it, old man. You go ahead with your sightseeing tour. The only thing you have to remember is that there is a guy wandering around prepared to kill for the information Claude was bringing to you. Whether he's got it or not, he's likely to keep looking.'

'But you're going to pick him up, aren't you, Cal?' Tom asked, innocently.

★ ★ ★

'God, I'm scared,' Shirley confessed, as they went up to their room. 'Why didn't you tell your friend about those people in London? Get us some police protection.'

'Because if I had, our little expedition would have ended right here. Cal would have taken over. He's a policeman.'

'Mm.' She went into the bathroom, while he stood at the window, looking through the drapes at the hotel yard and the street beyond. Never had he felt so lonely. Once he had called this place home. Now he was a stranger, and an unwanted stranger. A stranger whose very presence had caused the death of a well-liked and well-known man. But how...?

Shirley's thoughts had apparently been running on parallel lines. She returned from the bathroom, wearing her black and white striped pyjamas and brushing her hair. 'God! Tom ... let's go home.'

'And forget about your grandad?'

'I don't think he's worth dying for.'

'Unfortunately, we are already in that slot. If we just catch the next plane out of here, don't you reckon that our friends will deduce that we got what we came for ... and come after us?'

She sat on the bed, both hands clasped to her neck. 'What a shitting awful mess.'

He blew her a kiss. 'Which you created, my dearest girl.'

'Oh, get lost.' She slid beneath the covers and pulled them to her neck. Then apparently had a thought, because she sat up again. 'Do you think there could have been something important in those files?'

'Somehow I doubt it. My idea was to get him here, on our turf, if you like, ply him with strong drink, and maybe get some real information out of him.'

'But the murderer must have thought there was something worth having or he wouldn't have taken them.'

'The murderer, my pet, wouldn't have had the time to look at them. He just shot his man, grabbed his briefcase or whatever, and fled. They're being examined now, I would say.'

'Shit,' she muttered. 'You shoot all my best theories down in flames.'

'Was that a theory?'

She lay down again, and this time switched off the light. He supposed it was a measure of his own concern that he did not even feel like making a pass, tonight.

Their alarm call was for five, which, so close to the equator, meant it was still dark. It was also raining, quite heavily.

'I don't believe this climate.' Shirley stood at the window and looked at the steady downpour; she was wearing a khaki tunic and skirt and heavy boots, carried a khaki slouch hat and looked ready for the worst. 'Can they fly in this?'

'I think they've practised.' Tom had also dressed as he considered practical, in jeans, a loose shirt and boots. 'Anyway, there's no saying it's raining in the Mazaruni. Come,' he called to the knock.

Breakfast was wheeled in, the waitress being followed by Whitling, in a highly agitated state. 'That guest you were expecting to dinner last night, Mr Diamond—'

'Has been murdered,' Tom guessed. Whitling stared at him with his mouth open. 'Why do you think Superintendent Simpson dropped by last night?' Tom asked. 'According to the superintendent, it was a mugging that went wrong.'

'That's what the papers say, yes. But your name is mentioned.'

'Come again?'

'You are mentioned as having been amongst the last people to have seen Mr Diamond alive.'

'Oh, cheer us up,' Shirley said. 'Now we're marked.'

'Then the sooner we're out of here the better. Is our car waiting?'

'It will be here in half an hour. That is plenty time.' Whitling hesitated. 'I must let Mr Simpson know that you have gone.'

'Do that. He already knows we're going.'

* * *

The taxi-driver was their friend Harrison. 'Oh, no,' Shirley said. 'Can you drive in all this rain?'

'No problem, ma'am.' He grinned. 'Less people on the road.'

'But you don't have a wiper.'

'Now that is a fact,' Harrison agreed. 'It come off some time last week and I ain't had the time to get it fix. Maybe tomorrow.'

'But we're driving today.'

'No problem. I can see through this rain. And the other one is working.'

'But the wheel is on this side.'

'No problem, ma'am.'

Shirley looked at Tom. 'Would you care to look closely at my hair, and start counting the grey?'

'In the car,' he promised.

Whitling waved them off, standing securely in his hotel porch while Leo loaded their knapsacks – they were leaving the main part of their luggage until they returned. They were wearing kagools but by the time they were in the back of the car they were both wet through.

'Is the rain going to stop?' Tom asked, as they hurtled out of town behind a blaring horn; as Harrison had promised, there weren't many people about, both because of the hour and the rain, but those that were were clearly living dangerously.

'Oh, yes, boss,' Harrison said. 'It must

stop. It always does stop.'

'When, do you suppose?'

'Well, they saying tomorrow. But it could stop today,' he added brightly.

'Jesus!' Shirley muttered, and then clutched Tom's arm. 'What was that?'

'A truck,' he explained. 'It missed us.'

'Man, that damn truck did be going too fast,' Harrison complained, increasing speed.

'You can let me go now,' Shirley suggested.

'I was going to count your grey hairs.' She wriggled free and huddled on the far side of the taxi. Water and mud sluiced past them as they left the town and began the drive to the airport. 'But there won't be any trouble flying in this?' Tom persisted.

'No, sir,' Harrison said. 'This cloud base is low, man. Five, six thousand feet there ain't nothing but blue sky.'

'It's getting up that high bothers me,' Shirley said.

To their surprise they reached Timehri without mishap, save for a chicken that attempted to cross the road at the wrong moment. 'You've killed it!' Shirley cried, looking out of the rear window at the tangled mess of flesh and feathers.

'Well, ma'am, I think that must be right,' Harrison agreed. 'It sure looking washed up.'

'Well, aren't you going to stop?'

'Why I should stop?'

'That chicken belongs to somebody,' Shirley pointed out. 'The owner must be told what has happened. And paid compensation.'

'Man, ma'am, he didn't have no business letting his chicken wander about the road so. If I stop and get out, I will get all wet.'

'Can't you make him stop?' Shirley whispered to Tom.

'I shouldn't think so. This is a different culture to Surrey. Or even Massachusetts.'

'Barbaric,' she said.

Timehri looked distinctly forlorn in daylight, a huge complex of streets and bungalows and offices and parkways and runways and hangars, carved out of the jungle that surrounded it as if waiting for the chance to reclaim it. The rain, added to the brown waters of the Demerara River flowing by a few feet from the amphibian's slipway, increased the feeling of desolation. But there were people in the huge hangar by the river's edge, into which Harrison drove with a fanfare on his horn.

'You got business?' asked a large man in overalls.

'Man, these people for Kaieteur,' Harrison explained.

'Yeah? Hey, Carl,' the big man called. 'Some more passengers.'

A black man, disturbingly young, but

113

wearing a pilot's uniform with the tie knot slipped down, came towards them, carrying a clipboard. 'Mr and Mrs O'Ryan, right?'

'Absolutely,' Tom said.

'I'm Carl.' He shook hands. 'These here are Mr and Mrs Dovey, and Jane.'

'Joe Dovey,' said the middle-aged American, who wore a floral shirt, Bermuda shorts and a panama hat. 'And this is Martha. Jane's our daughter.'

Martha also wore Bermuda shorts, which Tom considered an even bigger sartorial mistake than her husband's. Jane was about fourteen, he reckoned, at the awkward age, but with some promise in the small features and straight black hair. She also wore shorts, but her legs were much better than her mother's. 'Hi,' she said.

'My wife's American,' Tom said, and felt inane.

But the Doveys were delighted. 'Well, say, that's just great,' Martha Dovey cried.

'Say, Captain,' her husband said. 'We ready?'

'We have two more passengers,' Carl said, checking his clipboard. 'You all passed any cars on the road?'

'Not that we saw,' Tom said. 'Not that that means a lot. That rain is coming down.'

'Time of year,' Carl explained.

'We've heard about that,' Shirley said, and peered at the Grumman. 'How old is that

114

thing?'

'We've had it a while.'

'Jesus! Can you take off in it? I'm talking about the rain.'

'Don't make no difference to this plane,' Dovey shouted. 'It's an amphibian. Haw haw haw.'

Jane Dovey looked embarrassed.

'We'll just give them another ten minutes,' Carl said.

'You can wait as long as you like,' Shirley said. 'We're in no hurry. Maybe the rain will stop.'

'The rain ain't going to stop,' Carl explained. 'And I have a schedule. This looks like them.'

Another taxi was driving into the hangar, and two men got out. Both were middle-aged, somewhat overweight, wearing sodden panama hats and equally sodden white suits.

'You guys are over-dressed,' Dovey remarked.

'God, it's wet out there,' said one of the newcomers. From his accent he also was American.

'But you were in the taxi,' Tom pointed out.

'Had to stop. Our man drove over a chicken. He claimed it was already dead. But what the hell, had to do the right thing. Cost us twenty dollars.'

Tom and Shirley looked at each other, and

then at Harrison.

'Well, I got to be going,' Harrison said. 'You all take care now, and be sure you ask for me when you come back.'

'We'll do that,' Tom said. 'If only to find out if he's locked up yet,' he muttered.

'So, you're Mr Milton and you're Mr Glossop,' Carl was saying, ticking the names on his clipboard.

'That's us,' Glossop said. He did not bother to introduce himself to the rest of the group.

'Well, then, let's go,' Carl said. 'Now let's see how we're going to sit.'

'Your co-pilot hasn't turned up,' Shirley pointed out.

'I don't use a co-pilot, lady.'

'What happens if you have a heart attack?'

'I look as if I am going to have a heart attack? Tell you what. You can fly co-pilot.'

'I don't know anything about airplanes. Especially old ones.'

'I'll teach you,' he promised. 'Now, then, you two guys sit right behind us,' he told Glossop and Milton. 'Mr and Mrs Dovey, you next. Mr O'Ryan, I'd be obliged if you'd sit right in the back, with Miss Dovey. It's a matter of balancing the weight, see?'

Tom raised his eyebrows at Shirley, then got into the rear door. Jane Dovey followed. She sat beside him and strapped herself in. He supposed he had the pick of the travelling companions, if he couldn't have Shirley. And there was no prospect of that.

'Okay,' Carl said. 'Fasten up. Flying time about two hours.' He checked his instruments while the small aircraft trembled as the luggage was loaded aboard; there was more than just Shirley's and his, Tom realized; the additional gear included two outsize butterfly nets.

Carl got the thumbs-up sign from his ground crew, and started the overhead engines. The Grumman Mallard waddled down the slip and into the water with a slight splash. Then he raised his wheels and taxied to his take-off position. To either side of the river the trees clustered, save where the airfield made a huge gash in the green, while beneath them the river was flowing very fast.

'We're going backwards,' Shirley said.

'That's only so we can go forward faster,' Carl explained. Shirley took off her hat and scratched her head. Carl opened the throttles and the amphibian raced forward. Jane Dovey suddenly clutched Tom's hand. He didn't object, but a few seconds later they were airborne, and soaring over the river and the jungle.

Jane released him. 'I'm sorry. Flying scares me stiff. And this plane...!'

'Has been around a few years,' he agreed. 'So why are you here?' She made a face and nodded towards her parents.

'I'm with you.'

She was looking down. 'That is one big forest.'

'No place to come down.'

'You been here before?'

'I was born here.'

'Were you really? Oh, but...'

'I live in England now. My wife and I are honeymooning.'

'Say, that's great.'

He peered past the heads at the forward seats. Carl was talking animatedly, and waving his hands – presumably he had put the aircraft on autopilot – and Shirley appeared to be listening intently. 'Yeah,' he said.

They climbed above the rain clouds, which formed a visually impenetrable floor beneath them, then flew for what seemed a long time before the bright sunlight in which the aircraft was ensconced reached down to the ground, bringing a chorus of exclamations from the passengers. Below them the jungle was unending, broken only by the silver threads of the huge rivers and the numberless tributaries, save where a sudden outcrop of rock pushed its way high into the sky. 'Monkey Mountain,' Carl explained, and the word was passed back.

'Is it full of monkeys?' Jane asked.

The question was relayed forward. 'Don't know,' came the reply. 'Never been there. No one has.'

Jane hugged herself. 'That's uncanny,' she remarked to Tom. 'I didn't know there were any places like that left in the world.'

'Look ahead,' came the word from up front.

In the distance they could see the peaks of the Pakaraima Range, forming the border with Brazil; nestling amidst those mountains was the famous Roraima, the nine thousand foot high mesa that inspired Conan Doyle's *The Lost World*. Closer at hand they watched the trees seem to fall away into a deep gorge, swung to their left and stared at the water wall.

'Oh, gosh,' Jane gasped. 'That is *something*.'

Tom was inclined to agree with her. Although he had seen sufficient photographs of the Falls, this was the first time he had seen them in real life. There was something utterly primeval about the scene. The forest, below and all around them, clustering on the banks of the river. The slow-moving brown water, some three hundred feet wide, smooth and unbroken, reaching the lip without any change in surface demeanour, to plunge eight hundred feet into the valley beneath. He knew the sheer drop had been measured at seven hundred and forty-one feet; he wondered how they had done it, for the mist and spray cloud thrown up by the water had in itself to be a few hundred feet high.

For a moment his mind drifted back through time, as he envisaged the American Dakota, with its five drunken, happy passengers, possibly flying in this very position. But whereas Carl had now pulled back the yoke to send the amphibian soaring out of the valley and over the river, whoever had been piloting the Dakota had just kept on at this level, straight at the water, and then ... There would have been no sound to be heard by anyone watching, had anyone been watching or listening – the roar of the water would have seen to that. He wondered if Shirley was thinking the same thing.

Now they were descending again, a few hundred yards upstream from the Falls, which had disappeared behind them. The aircraft came down, water sluiced to either side, then they were taxiing into the bank, where there was a landing stage and a reception committee of a park warden and two guides. They were handed ashore while Carl greeted the locals, whom he obviously knew very well. Behind the landing stage there was some evidence of civilization: a small rest house and a jeep, parked on a track that led away into the forest.

'You all will go to the lip now,' Carl said. 'These guys say it may rain later.'

They followed a track, which in the first instance led away from the river and through the heart of the forest. The sun disappeared above the great overhanging trees, and their two guides had to show them the best way to go to avoid hanging creepers or twisted roots. Even so their feet sank into wet layers of fallen leaves, which had clearly been there a very long time. Birds whistled, and they were surrounded by rustling sounds.

'Isn't this something?' Shirley had fallen back to walk beside Tom, who was clutching his camera and camcorder to his chest. 'Makes you realize how unimportant we humans are.'

'You're starting to talk like a proper tourist,' he told her. 'Remember we're here to work. Did Carl teach you how to fly?'

'He suggested he'd like to.'

'Good thing we're staying for a day or two.'

'Did you find out how we get from here to Takdai?'

'I imagine we use that track back at the landing. We may even get a ride in the jeep.'

Now the roaring of the Falls was starting to make conversation difficult, and a few minutes later their guides parted the tree screen and they emerged on to a huge flat slab of rock, protruding into the river at the very spot where it went over.

'This ain't the place for anyone with vertigo,' the lead guide told them. 'Take it easy, now.'

They stood on the edge, the water flowing by only inches from their feet – the river was high – and watched it disappear. Then a couple of the bolder spirits, Shirley amongst them, went to the other edge, looking down into the gorge. Tom felt he should be with her, and followed, although he had a distinct feeling of instability. But the sight again took his breath away. The water flowed past about fifty feet to their right, falling vertical in a brown torrent, disappearing into the mist cloud rising from the foot, which seemed to be reaching up for them. Cameras snapped, Tom used his camcorder, and voices screamed comments, hardly heard above the roar. Tom retreated to the landward side and mopped his brow.

'You ever had someone fall over?' he asked the guides.

'Nope,' they replied. 'But we reckon it has to happen some day.'

They spent about an hour at the lip, while the midday clouds began to gather, and by the time they commenced their walk back it was drizzling. Kagools were unrolled and donned – umbrellas were a waste of time in the forest as they would continually have snagged on the overhead branches – and they plodded back, their feet rapidly soaked.

'Remind me not to put this on my list of favourite places,' Shirley muttered.

'Now, you must admit those falls were something,' Tom said.

'Oh, they were. Are. I'm quite willing to

believe they are the ultimate wonder of the world. But the climate...'

'That's what makes all the water. This is one of the wettest places in the world.'

At least the rest house was dry, and lunch was waiting for them, plain local food such as eddoes and plantains and yams, served with small, bony fish – 'haussa', their guide explained – and avocado pear and lashings of coffee. For dessert they had sour sop.

'Oooh,' Shirley said. 'That makes me feel all tingly inside.'

'I'm glad something does,' Tom remarked. 'They do say it's an aphrodisiac.'

Carl didn't eat with them, as he had gone into the settlement with the game warden, and as he did not immediately return they were able to relax in the wooden armchairs placed on the rest house verandah, and watch the rain, quite heavy now, teeming past the overhang and thudding into the ground. Milton and Glossop wandered off into the bush together.

'You reckon they're gay?' Shirley whispered.

'If a snake doesn't get them, they'll come down with bete rouge.'

'What's bete rouge?'

'If you ever get it, you'll know. It's a burrowing insect that itches like mad.'

Visibility had closed in with the rain, and they might have been isolated in time and space, with only the rustling water and the roaring sound, very loud even at a distance of half a mile, to keep them company.

'Spooky,' Jane remarked, sitting beside Shirley and Tom. 'Makes you feel you're going back to the beginning of time. Where are you guys going next?'

'We're staying up here for a day or two,' Shirley said.

'Here?' Jane looked left and right. The rest house was not the last word in comfort.

'In Takdai,' Tom explained. 'I imagine that's what Carl is doing now, seeing to our arrangements.'

'If he hasn't forgotten,' Shirley growled. 'No one has taken our bags out of the plane.'

'Good thing, too,' Tom pointed out. 'They'd have got soaked through.'

They both gazed at the aircraft, at the rain bouncing off the wings and the engine cowlings.

'Who's that?' Shirley asked, pointing at the man in the flight deck, standing up and reaching above his head.

'He's wearing overalls. Must be the local mechanic,' Tom said. 'Care for a stroll?'

'In the rain?'

'Well, it seems one hell of a shame to come all this way and find ourselves in the midst of all this jungle just to go to sleep.' He jerked his head at the Doveys, both of whom were snoring. 'With respect, Jane.'

'Oh, I agree with you,' Jane said.

'I wonder where the other two went,' Shirley said.

'God knows. Maybe they've gone back to the Falls. Maybe they went over.'

'Oooh, don't joke about it.' She got up, gathered her kagool around herself, adjusted the hood. 'Coming, Jane?'

'You're honeymooning,' Jane pointed out. 'Not in the rain.'

'I think I'd better stay here. Ma and Pa will go nuts if they wake up and I'm missing.'

Shirley hesitated, then went down the steps. Tom hastily followed.

'I'm sure we're both going to catch pneumonia,' she remarked.

'It's warm rain,' he pointed out. They were already out of earshot. 'Excited?'

'I'm not sure. What do we do first?'

'We settle ourselves in Takdai, act like real tourists and ask a few questions.'

'Such as?'

'Is it possible to get behind the Falls.'

'You know it isn't.'

'I only know they *say* it's impossible. But has anyone ever tried it? We have to have a go.'

'Through that mist, with a few thousand tons of water dropping on our heads.'

'We have to have a go,' he repeated.

'Hey, there's the jeep coming back.'

They squelched back through the soft

earth in time to see the jeep pull to a halt behind the rest house. Carl got down and hurried inside.

'Mr and Mrs O'Ryan?' he called.

'Here we are.' Shirley led Tom into the house.

'Right. Your accommodation is all arranged. Washington here will drive you in. You'll have company. Milton and Glossop are also staying over a couple of days.'

'Oh, no,' Shirley said.

Carl raised his eyebrows. 'Don't you like them? I thought you hadn't met?'

'She's a first-impression cookie,' Tom explained. 'I'm sure they'll be great company.'

Carl looked from one to the other, somewhat uncertainly, then shrugged. 'I'll pick you up Thursday.'

'Oh,' Shirley said. 'That quickly?'

'That's what my schedule says. You have to fly back to Timehri to make the flight into the Rupununi. It'll be a different aircraft.'

'Right,' Tom said. 'We'll expect you. Do we get to go back into town?'

'That's up to you.'

'Well, then, could you pick up some mail I'm expecting from the hotel and bring it up with you?'

'Sure.'

'What mail are you expecting?' Shirley wanted to know.

He winked at her. 'From my back-up, remember?'

'I thought you gave him my email address?'

'He may have decided to write if it's something lengthy.'

'Okay, folks,' Carl called. 'This is the big one. We take off over the Falls.'

'And we're going to miss it,' Shirley said.

'Don't be a goose,' Tom said. 'We'll see it the day after tomorrow.'

'It's been real great meeting you,' Jane said. 'I can't think of a more entrancing place to honeymoon.'

'Maybe when the rain stops,' Shirley agreed.

'But the rain makes it even more romantic,' Jane said.

She shook hands, as did her parents, and they got into the amphibian.

'Hey,' Tom said, suddenly remembering. 'What about our luggage?'

'Just getting it.' Carl opened the luggage compartment and took out the two carry-alls, then reached in again to produce the suitcases belonging to Milton and Glossop. Tom and Washington the park warden gave him a hand to lift the luggage into the shelter of the rest-house verandah, and Washington started carrying it out to the vehicle.

'Well, thanks for everything, Carl.' Tom shook hands.

'See you Thursday.' Shirley also shook

hands. 'And thanks for a lovely flight.'

'You all have fun,' Carl said, and climbed into the flight deck.

'You all coming now?' Washington asked.

'Hold on a minute. We want to see him take off,' Shirley said. No one else seemed very interested. In fact, only one of the guides was still around; even the mechanic they had seen earlier seemed to have disappeared. Tom resumed filming.

Carl started one engine and then the other. They both purred quietly, then the volume increased as the guide cast off the mooring warps and the aircraft moved away from the dock and turned to go up-river. The Doveys waved vigorously. Carl motored upstream to his chosen position, then turned the amphibian again. The engines were gunned, and the aircraft raced forward, almost hidden by the spray thrown up by its floats. It roared past the dock and the rest house, and Shirley clutched her throat.

'He always does wait till the last minute,' Washington remarked, having come back to stand beside them.

The machine hurtled at the lip of the Falls, then the nose came up and she soared over the cascading water, dropping for a moment almost out of sight before reappearing.

'Boy, that is really something,' Shirley shouted.

'Next time we'll be in it, looking down,'

Tom reminded her.

Then they stared in horror as the Grumman suddenly disappeared in a red ball.

Five

Shock

For several seconds no one spoke; the noise of the explosion, and any sound the aircraft might have made as it plunged into the gorge, was obliterated by the roar of the Falls. Tom stopped filming and slowly restored the camcorder to its case. Then Washington said, 'Holy Jesus Christ!'

The guide began running through the bush, to gain the lip. Shirley made to follow him, and Tom grabbed her arm. 'He won't see anything.'

'But...' she gazed at him, lip quivering.

'Yes,' he said. 'That was meant for us. Whoever planted that explosive didn't know we were staying over.'

'But Carl ... and that sweet kid...'

'Yeah,' he agreed. He looked at Washington. 'What's the drill?'

'We have to call town,' Washington said. 'There's a radio at the DC's office in Takdai.'

'Then let's get down there.' Tom helped Washington put the last of the gear into the back of the jeep; neither man now paid any attention to the rain.

Shirley had sunk on to a chair and was staring at the river, shivering.

'We have to go,' Tom said, and held out his hand.

She grasped it, tightly, allowing him to draw her to her feet.

'Listen,' she said. 'Those two men. Milton and Glossop. They're staying over. But no one knew that either.'

'You think they planted the bomb?'

'Who else could it have been?'

'Not them,' he said. 'They never had the opportunity to be alone on board. They were with us at the lip, and they went off into the bush without ever returning to the plane. Remember?'

'Then who could it have been?'

'That mechanic.' He turned to the impatiently waiting Washington. 'The mechanic. You know him?'

'What mechanic?' Washington asked.

'The man who was on the plane while Carl was in the village.'

Washington raised his eyebrows. 'There ain't no mechanic up here, mister. Carl does be his own mechanic. Did be,' he added.

Tom gazed at him for several seconds, then said, 'Let's go.'

★ ★ ★

Takdai was in the valley several miles away, reached by a bumpy road through the forest. The rain teemed down, the mud splashed up on to the bonnet and windscreen and the wipers whirred. Shirley, in the back with the gear, continued to hug herself and shiver; Tom thought she might well be coming down with something. But then he felt like doing some shivering himself. They had been warned that if they didn't get out of Guyana they would die. And now they were dead. As far as their would-be killers knew. It occurred to him that if this were a movie or something they'd be able to stay dead while they worked things out. But there was no chance of that. He glanced at Washington, face set, teeth gritted as he drove as fast as he could, downhill, skidding from time to time, coming close to smashing into a tree, but always regaining control. Washington knew what had to be done, and he was going to do it.

Which meant that the whole of Guyana, and then the whole world, would soon know that the amphibian had been blown up, and that they had survived. That would matter to only a handful of people ... The question was, what would they try next?

The road levelled off, and they saw houses looming through the trees. There was only one real street, and this was deserted as the rain pounded down; beyond, the road continued on its way into the forest and, presumably, the next settlement. Beside the village there was a stream, not very large but clearly an offshoot of the river coming over the Falls. There were no cars, only a couple of parked trucks and another jeep outside a slightly larger than average building, above which the red, yellow and green horizontal triangles of Guyana drooped damply. In a shed behind it, a generator rumbled.

Washington parked in front of the flag and got out. 'You'd best come in,' he said.

Tom looked at Shirley. 'You staying here?'

'No way. I'm coming with you.' Her tone indicated that she had no intention of ever letting him out of her sight again. At any other time he would have been pleased about that.

Washington opened the door and showed them into a neat office with two desks. There were two doors leading off, one closed and the other open to reveal a passageway, at the end of which was an empty cell. Behind one of the desks was a policeman, behind the other a female secretary. Both looked up at the three newcomers, from whom water was dripping on to the bare boards of the floor.

'Man, Washington, you are all wet,' the woman remarked.

'The commissioner in?' Washington asked.

'Sure he is in. You got a problem?'

132

'The Grumman,' Washington explained. 'It gone.'

The woman regarded him as she might an errant child. 'Back to Georgetown,' she agreed, and looked at Tom and Shirley more closely. 'You folks miss it?'

'No, no,' Tom said. 'We're staying here.'

'It gone,' Washington said again. He closed his fist and then opened the fingers, violently. 'Pouf! One big bang.'

'You must be Mr and Mrs O'Ryan,' the woman was saying, riffling through some papers in her in-tray. 'We did be notify—' Then she turned her head at the same time as the policeman stood up. 'What you saying?' she asked Washington, her tone sharp. 'You crazy, or what?'

'I'm afraid it's perfectly true,' Tom said. 'It blew up.' As if his words had activated an unthinkable memory, Shirley's knees gave way and she sank on to the one vacant straight chair in the room.

'You mean it did crash?' asked the policeman, picking up his cap.

'It crashed,' Tom said. 'But it blew up first.'

The secretary turned to look at the inner door, which now opened to reveal a small black man wearing an open shirt and horn-rimmed spectacles as well as a considerable amount of gold jewellery draped round his neck.

'Man, Mr Rimmer,' she said, 'these people

saying the Grumman blown up.'

'I heard,' the commissioner said. 'You are...?'

'Tom O'Ryan,' Tom said. 'My wife, Shirley.'

District Commissioner Rimmer peered at Shirley. 'She don't look too good.'

'She isn't feeling too good,' Tom pointed out. 'And she's soaked through. I need to get her to the hotel. But we thought we should tell you first.'

'You damned right,' Rimmer said. 'Where this happen?'

'At the Falls,' Washington said. 'It took off and went over the lip, and then, boom.'

Rimmer looked from face to face. 'How this happen?'

'We think it was a bomb.'

'A bomb?' The district commissioner, his secretary and the policeman spoke together.

'It just blew up,' Washington repeated.

'How can it have been a bomb?' Rimmer demanded.

Shirley recovered. 'There was a man in the aircraft, just before it took off.'

'What man?'

'We don't know,' Tom said. 'He was there. We thought he was a mechanic. Then when we looked again he was gone. We didn't think anything of it.'

Rimmer looked at Washington. 'Carl had a mechanic?'

'No, sir, Mr Rimmer,' Washington said. 'That he didn't.'

'I must get out there,' Rimmer decided. 'Washington, you come with me and show me where this happen.'

'You won't see anything,' Tom told him. 'The wreckage fell into the gorge.'

'That is a fact, Mr Rimmer,' Washington said. 'It just went boom, and disappeared.'

'I am going out there,' Rimmer said again. 'I must see for myself. You.' He pointed at the constable. 'Get on the radio to Georgetown and tell them what happen. You.' He pointed at Tom. 'Stay here until I get back.'

'Look, we're all wet through,' Tom protested. 'Can't we go to the hotel? We'll be there when you get back.'

Rimmer hesitated, then nodded. 'All right. You go to the hotel. And stay there, mind.' He pointed again. 'And don't tell nobody what happen, eh?'

'Right,' Tom agreed.

'But...' Shirley protested.

Tom squeezed her shoulder. 'Let's do as the commissioner wants, darling. He's the boss.'

Washington and Rimmer dropped them off at the hotel, a small building further down the street, which also flew the Guyanese flag.

'I going see you later,' Rimmer promised them.

Tom carried their bags into a front room, where there was a desk and a potted palm. On the desk there was a bell, and this he rang, several times.

'Now, why you making all this noise?' A large black woman wearing slippers and a dressing gown emerged from a door behind the desk. 'This is sleeping time, man. You Mr O'Ryan? Carl did say you was coming in, but he didn't know when.'

'Well, here we are,' Tom said brightly.

'Carl did say you was honeymooning,' the landlady remarked, looking at Shirley somewhat pessimistically; water continued to drip from her hair, even her nose.

'That's absolutely right. We got caught in the rain.'

'Yeah,' the landlady agreed. 'I putting you in number four thousand and three.'

'Did you say four thousand?'

'You ain't liking that? Four thousand and three is ma bridal suite.'

Shirley opened her mouth, but Tom beat her to it. 'That sounds great. Does it have a bathroom?'

The landlady surveyed him as if he were a beetle. 'How it going have a bathroom?'

'Ah,' Shirley said. 'We need a bathroom. We'll have the room with the bathroom.'

'The bathroom is at the end of the passage,' the landlady informed her, clearly placing her also in the beetle category. 'What you think this is, the Hilton?'

'Our mistake,' Tom said humbly. 'May we go along there now?'

The landlady opened a drawer in the desk and took out a key. 'Is the second on the right, through there.' She pointed to a doorway on the other side of the lobby. 'Man, man, you know you dripping all over ma floor? I just done polish that floor, this very morning.'

'Oops,' Tom said. 'We'll get along to the room.' He picked up the bags.

'The other two men,' Shirley ventured.

The landlady opened a book on the desk. 'Mr Milton and Mr Glossop,' she said. 'They ain't come in yet. When you dry, you sign this, right?'

'Absolutely,' Tom said, pushing Shirley through the door into a gloomy corridor, off which there opened four doors.

'Tom...' Shirley began.

'Don't say it. Don't even think it. Don't think anything. Four thousand and three.' He unlocked the door, showed her into a surprisingly large room, which seemed larger than it was, because apart from the bed, which occupied the exact centre of the floor and was a four-poster that had surely once housed a Dutch timber merchant and his wife and all of their children, and the washstand with white china basin and ewer decorated with blue flowers, a matching slop bucket on the floor beside it, there was no furniture, not even a carpet.

'My God,' Shirley commented.

'Look on the bright side.' Tom placed the carry-alls on the floor, opened a door in the wall. 'Walk-in cupboard. And it has shelves.' He went to the one window and peered through the screen at the rain, which was still teeming down. 'And we're screened, so hopefully there'll be no bugs.'

'Then what's that, looking at me, waving its whatsit?'

'Proboscis,' Tom explained, crossing the floor and stamping on the two-inch long cockroach that had incautiously emerged from beneath the skirting board.

'I am not going to sleep in that bed with those things crawling all over me.'

'Darling, the natives in these parts are prepared for everything, and always expect the worst. If you will look at the bed, you will see that each leg is standing in a bowl of water. That is because cockroaches do not cross water. Neither do ants or any other creepy-crawlies. So your bed is inviolable.'

'Well, what are you going to do about that?' She pointed at the crushed insect.

'All taken care of,' he said. Shirley gazed at the sudden swarm of ants that had also emerged from beneath the skirting board, and were now lifting the cockroach and carrying it off. 'Dinner,' Tom explained.

'Why did I come,' she asked. 'Why did I *come*?'

'Because it has been your lifelong ambition to spend your honeymoon with me in the middle of a jungle. And to find out what happened to your grandad, of course. What you need is a hot bath. I'll just go check it out.'

'You're not leaving me alone here!'

'I'm going the length of the corridor, darling. Back in a tick.' He went outside, wondering if she really was on the verge of a nervous breakdown. He couldn't blame her; he didn't like thinking about what had happened, and had so nearly happened to them, had been intended to happen to them, any more than she did. He opened the bathroom door, looked inside, frowned and returned to four thousand and three. The door was locked. He knocked.

'Who is it?'

'Me.'

The key turned and she allowed him in. 'Well?'

'The good news is that the bathroom is vacant, so I suggest you occupy it. The bad news is that there is no bath. But there is a shower. And a towel.'

'And I suppose there is no hot water.'

'I think it would be optimistic to expect that, yes.'

She opened her carry-all, delved into it,

located clean clothes and her washbag and departed. Tom also removed his wet clothes and wrapped himself in his dressing gown, then sat on the bed to think. He had no doubt that the bomb had been planted by the man they had seen in the plane. Takdai was a very small place. It should surely be possible to pin the fellow down. Trouble was, he wasn't sure he would recognize him, having only seen him at a distance and through the glass of the cockpit windows. He wasn't even sure whether he was an Amerindian or a black man.

Equally, there were several other villages in the vicinity. The man could have come from any of them. But he had been there, when presumably he, like everybody else in the community, should have been someplace else, doing ... whatever it was they did. Something to put to Rimmer.

'Aaaagh!'

He leapt to his feet and ran along the corridor to the bathroom. Predictably the door was locked.

'Tom!' Shirley shouted, 'For God's sake ... Tom!'

'Open the fucking door,' Tom shouted.

Hands scrabbled on the inside of the door and it swung in. Tom stepped inside, for a moment losing all sense of urgency as he surveyed a naked Shirley retreating across the bathroom in a flurry of water, the shower still dripping.

'Do something!' she shouted.

Reluctantly he accepted that her idea of what he should be doing was different to his, and he peered into the square of concrete that composed the shower stall. Scrabbling around the plughole there was a large scorpion.

'When the water went down, that came up,' Shirley gasped, now flat against the far wall, hands clasped in front of her.

'I'll need a stick,' Tom decided.

'Man, but you is noisy people,' remarked the landlady, coming along the corridor and peering censoriously at Shirley. 'Lady, you ain't got nothing on. That ain't decent.'

'She always takes her clothes off to shower,' Tom pointed out. 'She's funny that way. What about him?'

The landlady peered at the scorpion. 'You need a stick.'

'*We* need a stick,' Tom told her. 'Have you got one?'

'Yeah. I going fetch it. Why you don't turn off the water? It wasting.'

In view of the steady pounding on the roof that did not seem a vital point, but Tom obligingly turned off the water, at which the scorpion, who had apparently been enjoying his bath, reared up and waved his sting at them.

'Jesus!' Shirley muttered, pushing past him

and fleeing down the corridor.

'But where she gone?' the landlady enquired, returning with a broom and peering at the shower as if Shirley might have gone down the hole.

'She's scared stiff,' Tom said. 'Here, give me that.'

'Mind you don't break it,' she admonished. Tom upended it and struck the scorpion several times as hard as he could. The broom handle cracked. 'Man, that is going on your bill,' the landlady said.

'Then you can deduct the scorpion,' Tom told her. He turned on the water again to flush the corpse down the waste pipe, and returned to the bedroom.

At least Shirley hadn't locked the door, but she was in bed, sheet pulled to her chin, slowly turning sheer with wet.

'Have you any idea what the dragon will say when she discovers you have gone to bed soaking wet?' Tom asked.

'Fuck off,' she suggested.

'Ah, well, my motto has always been if you can't beat them, join them.' Tom took off his dressing gown and got into bed beside her.

'You touch me and I am going to break your arm,' she warned.

'I was intending to warm you up.'

'Think again.' She got out of bed, towelled herself dry and began to dress.

'Do you have any objection if I borrow the

towel and have a shower myself?'

'Best of luck,' she told him.

By the time he returned Shirley was fully dressed. Rather incongruously, while she was wearing a frock she was also wearing thick socks and her walking boots.

'Clump clump,' he remarked. 'Guess what: the rain is stopping. It generally does late afternoon. We could take a walk in the moonlight, suitably coated with insect repellent, of course. Then when we kiss we'll go slither, slither. Doesn't that sound like fun?'

She stood at the window, peering out, but made no reply.

'Have I been sent to Coventry?' he asked. 'It's a long way away, and, you know, I didn't create either the cockroach or the scorpion. They were just God's creatures trying to get on with their lives.'

She turned to face him, arms folded. 'What are we going to do?'

'There's not a lot we can do, till we've been interviewed by Rimmer. But I have an idea I know exactly what he is going to say.'

'I am saying that plane was blown up,' Rimmer announced, standing in the middle of the hotel lounge and looking important. The word lounge was perhaps an exaggeration, Tom considered, as the room contained four chairs, a low table and another potted palm. But there were some mats on the floor, and in the far corner there was a bar, judging by the few bottles on the shelf behind the counter, which was the most encouraging sight he had seen since arriving in Takdai, if he excluded Shirley in the shower.

'Is that a fact,' he commented.

They had been joined by Milton and Glossop, who had turned up, wet and bedraggled, a few minutes earlier; apparently they had been walking in the bush, and been caught by the rain. 'Butterflies,' Milton had explained. 'We're after butterflies. They have some whoppers up here.'

'But you didn't catch any,' Shirley had remarked, disagreeably.

'What I am saying is,' Rimmer declared, 'that this is a police matter. I have been on the radio to Georgetown,' he added, more importantly yet, 'and they are sending up a special squad to investigate. There ain't nobody to leave Takdai until that squad get heah.'

'They can't suppose we had anything to do with the disaster,' Glossop protested. 'We could have been on that plane.'

'But you weren't,' Shirley pointed out.

'Neither were you,' he riposted.

'When will the police get here?' Milton asked.

'Well, it going take them about four days,' Rimmer said.

'Four *days*?' Shirley was aghast.

'Well, you see, Mrs O'Ryan, that was the only amphibian. Now, if we had an airstrip, they could come up by turbo-prop. I am saying to those people in Georgetown, time and again, that we should have an airstrip up heah, but they are saying it is too expensive. They always have money for their own projects, mind.'

'Aren't you from Georgetown?' Tom asked, innocently.

'I am from New Amsterdam, Berbice,' Rimmer said, with dignity.

'But ... four days!' Shirley said again.

'I think we could all do with a drink,' Tom said. 'Do you suppose Mrs ... do you know, I never did catch her name.'

'Is Smith,' Rimmer told him.

'I thought that might be it. Well, Commissioner, do you suppose Mrs Smith would object if we helped ourselves to a drink from her bar?'

'Not so long as you putting it on the slate.'

'I will do that.' Tom went behind the bar. 'Now, what have we here? One half-bottle of dark rum. Several tins of what looks like orange juice. One bottle of tonic water. One quarter bottle of gin. Half a dozen assorted tins of beer, none refrigerated. And a half-bottle of red wine.' He looked up.

'G and T,' Glossop said.

'And me,' said his friend.

'I can't offer you ice and lemon, because there isn't any.' Tom poured 'Shirley?'

'I'll have the wine.'

'Right you are. I'm afraid the glasses are a bit dusty, but it all helps the ambience. Commissioner?'

'I am on duty,' Rimmer pointed out.

'Right. Well, I will have a warm beer.' He wrote it all down in the notebook lying on the counter and handed the drinks out. 'Now, Commissioner, we can't just sit around waiting for the police to arrive. I think we should endeavour to help them.'

'How we going to do that?'

'Well, we can start collecting clues as to what happened.'

'You have clues?'

'Not on me. But there are bound to be clues at the scene of the crash. I suggest we go along there tomorrow morning.'

'Man, there ain't no wreckage.'

'There must be something left.'

'Maybe. But it went down the Falls. We can't go there.'

'Why not?'

'Because it ain't possible. We would drown.'

There was a sudden explosion of sound, and all the men turned sharply to look at Shirley, who had just spat out her first mouthful of wine. 'Jesus!' she gasped. 'How long has that stuff *been* there?'

'I did notice there was no bouquet,' Tom agreed. 'Have a glass of warm beer instead.'

She raised her eyes to heaven. But she was interested in the line he was pursuing, which was why she had absently drunk the wine.

'Now, Commissioner,' Tom said, 'the river goes over the lip, and falls eight hundred feet. It hits ... what does it hit?'

'How I am knowing that?'

'Doesn't anybody know? What about the people who live here? They must know.'

'Nobody knows,' Rimmer said. 'It must be rock or something. They got a lot of water down there. The river goes on, see? Caused by the water coming down.'

'Right. So there is a river at the bottom as well. Now, when all that water hits the rocks, or whatever is at the foot of the Falls, it throws up a lot of spray, right?'

'You seen it, man.'

'Only from the top. Surely it's possible to get close to it, into it, maybe, at the bottom?'

Rimmer shook his head. 'No way. That spray is solid water.'

'You're telling me that no one, not even one of the locals, has ever penetrated to the floor of the Falls?'

'No one still living,' Rimmer grinned.

'Now there's another point. There were four people in that plane. Three of them were Americans. Americans like to bury their dead in their own cemeteries. If you don't get those bodies out, PDQ, you are going to have the entire state of wherever the Doveys came from descending on you.'

'Could be good for business,' Glossop remarked.

'We have got to find that plane,' Tom insisted. 'Would you object if I asked about?'

'You go ahead,' Rimmer said, magnanimously.

'Thank you. I'll start on that tomorrow. And would you have any objection if we went into the gorge and saw how close we can get to the foot of the Falls?'

'I ain't objecting, man. But mind you be careful. I don't want no more deads on my hands.'

'We'll be careful,' Tom promised.

'You know what?' Glossop said brightly. 'How about damming the river?' They all stared at him. 'Well,' he said, 'if we were to dam the river, the flow would stop, see, and then the foot would be exposed.'

'Man, you crazy or what?' Rimmer asked. 'That river is a hundred metres wide, and a lot of feet deep. You know what damming it would cost? And anyway, the Falls are sacred.'

'Eh?'

'The Indians, what they calling Native Americans, used to think it was a god. One time they pushed people over it in a canoe, to make the gods happy. Nowadays they have got all confused with the Christianity thing, but they still wouldn't like to see it go.'

'Stuff the Indians, or Native Americans or whatever. I think it's a brilliant idea,' Shirley said. 'Think what you might uncover if that water flow stopped.'

'Like what?' Rimmer asked.

'Well...' she glanced at an anxious Tom. 'I have no idea. But it would have to be something. What about anything that might lie *behind* the Falls?'

'Like what?' Rimmer asked again.

'Well ... there must be something there.'

'There'll be a huge cave,' Glossop said. 'Eaten away by the water over the centuries. There's a cave behind almost every big waterfall.'

'I don't know nothing about that,' Rimmer said. 'Now I must go along. You all have a nice night, now.'

'There's just one more thing,' Tom said. Rimmer paused in the doorway, impatiently. 'It looks like being a lovely night, now the rain has stopped,' Tom said. 'My wife and I thought we might take a walk after dinner. Is it safe?'

'You don't go near the water,' Rimmer recommended.

'Anywhere else is safe?'

'Sure, man. No problem.'

'What about that man?'

Slowly Rimmer came back into the room, while Milton and Glossop stared at Tom; if they weren't innocent bystanders, they were giving a very good impression.

'What man?' Rimmer enquired.

'We read in the newspapers that a man from these parts was attacked by some kind of beast, only a few months ago. And killed.'

'And we read that a young woman disappeared about three months before that,' Shirley said. 'And several others before then.'

Tom mentally cursed; now Rimmer's expression was definitely hostile. 'You don't want to believe everything you reading in them newspapers,' he advised. 'Anyway, that girl was from Kagerama. Not heah. Good night.'

'What about the mechanic?' Shirley shouted.

Rimmer checked again. 'What mechanic?'

'The man we saw in the plane, just before it took off.'

'*You* saw him,' Rimmer pointed out. 'And your husband. Who else?'

'Well ... the American girl, Jane Dovey. She saw him.'

'And she is dead,' Rimmer said. 'You watch out.' He stamped out of the room.

'Well!' Shirley commented.

'Like the man said, you watch out,' Tom

recommended. 'I think he has it in mind that it may have been one of us planted that bomb.'

'You guys care to explain?' Milton asked. 'Seems to me we're all in this together.'

'We saw this man fiddling about in the plane, not long before Carl returned for take off,' Shirley explained.

'Holy shit!' Glossop said. 'But you didn't do anything?'

'We thought he was a mechanic. No one told us there wasn't a mechanic.'

'And you reckon he was planting a bomb,' Milton said thoughtfully. 'Now why should he do that?'

'He wanted to—'

'Blow the plane up,' Tom interrupted. 'I don't suppose we'll ever know why. Until they catch him.'

Shirley glared at him, but she had to understand they didn't want the whole world to know they had been the intended victims.

'You all eating or what?' Mrs Smith demanded from the inner doorway. 'Dinner been ready this half hour.'

The food was strange to Shirley. 'What is that?' she whispered, as Mrs Smith produced a huge earthenware pot, placed it in the centre of the table and began ladling helpings on to soup plates with a large spoon. It was clearly some kind of stew, but whatever the meat was it was turned black by the heavy and pungent sauce with which it was covered.

'This heah is pepper pot,' Mrs Smith explained.

'But why is it black?'

'That is the casseripe. Is a preservative, see? I make this three weeks ago.'

'Three weeks?' Shirley's voice went up an octave.

'Some people keep a pepper pot going for months,' Tom said, unhelpfully. Shirley stared at him with her mouth open.

'Months?' Mrs Smith said scornfully. 'Man, I knowing people what keep one for ten years.'

Shirley put down her knife and fork.

'It won't poison you, really,' Tom said.

'It's just that I'm not very hungry,' Shirley said. 'I'll just have some rice.'

'Try it,' Tom insisted.

She hesitated, then cautiously took a spoonful of the black meat and gravy, masticated with the air of a woman on the block. Then gasped.

'Is hot,' Mrs Smith agreed. 'That is what preserve it, see? Drink some water.'

Shirley drank some water, breathed more easily, and cautiously took another spoonful of the stew.

'What it will probably do,' Tom said, 'is

give you the runs.'

'You all going walk?' Mrs Smith enquired after dinner. 'Well, you watch out, eh?'

'For what?' Shirley asked.

'Stay away from the water.'

'But there is water everywhere. You mean there may be alligators and things?'

'Alligators don't cause no trouble at night, chil'; they sleeping. They is daytime creatures. But them comoodi now, they is always awake. If they gets hold of you, you got trouble. Heah.' She bustled into her kitchen and reappeared with a machete, four feet long, of which three and a half were a slightly curved, razor-sharp blade. She handed this fearsome weapon to Tom. 'You take this, and if a comoodi gets hold of your wife, whap him.'

Tom took the machete gingerly. 'Whap him where?'

'He head, man. Right behind the eyes.'

'You mean he won't be biting Mrs O'Ryan?'

'No, man.' Mrs Smith was contemptuous. 'He going use he tail, for wrapping round she legs to drag she into the water. So you want to cut off he head, then it all relax like. Right?'

'Right,' Tom agreed, grasping the machete with suitable determination.

'And you take care of that cutlass, eh?' Mrs Smith said. 'Is the only one I got.'

'Absolutely.'

'Can't we just go to bed?' Shirley asked, as they went outside.

'I never thought I'd ever hear you make a proposition like that,' Tom said.

'Look, it's been a pretty goddamned traumatic day,' she told him. 'We could be dead. We should be dead. And you want to go chancing your arm again...'

'No risk, as long as I have this little winkle-picker.'

'And I suppose you have your revolver as well.'

'Of course. So you see, you have nothing whatsoever to worry about, and we really do need to have a chat, without being overheard or interrupted.'

She followed him out of the hotel and down the street, avoiding the puddles left by the rain. People stood in doorways, half shrouded in the flickering lights of oil lanterns, gazing at them and mostly greeting them. Dogs barked. The local pub, known accurately as a rum shop, was packed – presumably with people discussing the drama that had so suddenly entered their lives.

'They're a nice friendly lot,' Tom suggested.

Which was more than could be said for the insects that swarmed out of the forest to either side, and kept them slapping and scratching.

'Damn,' Tom said. 'We forgot the citronella or whatever.'

'What a fucking country,' Shirley remarked.

'Listen.'

They were clear of the houses, standing where the track led into the jungle, presumably to Kagerama or some other village. They were several miles from the Falls, but they could hear the roaring of the water as it crashed into the gorge.

'I'll never be able to hear that sound again without seeing that plane going over,' Shirley said.

'Well, learn to live with it, because we're going to be here for a few days. But we'll never have another opportunity like this. Rimmer has virtually given us carte blanche to do a little investigating on our own. So we start tomorrow.'

'Doing what?'

'I think our first priority must be to find that wreckage. Or, at least, try to do so. That's logical. We can apply for help from the locals, see if anyone has any idea of how close we can get to the foot of the Falls, even hint that the wreckage may have somehow gone behind the water, and see what kind of a reaction we get.'

'And you really think we can get behind the water?'

'If there is anything living behind there, and it can get out, then we can get in.' He squeezed her hand. 'You're not going to come over all chicken on me now, are you?'

'No,' she said. 'No.'

'We can also see what we can pick up regarding strange goings-on, especially that murder. We have to talk to the companion of the dead man, who apparently can describe the creature that attacked them.'

'Who is he?'

'It shouldn't be difficult to find him. Then we have to make it somehow related to the crash.'

'Um,' she said. 'Okay. You really are being very determined, Tom. I'm sorry I've been such a wimp. It was that plane going over ... my God!'

He put his arm round her shoulder to give her a squeeze. 'You're going to be all right. And we're going to get to the bottom of this whole thing. Believe me.'

She turned up her face, and he thought she might be ready to be kissed, but before he could make up his mind to do it their ears were assailed by an unearthly noise from behind them: a huge roaring sound, accompanied by a chorus of terrified screams.

Six

Critters

'My God!' Shirley shouted. 'What's that?'

'Could be what we're looking for. Come on.'

Tom grabbed her wrist and dragged her through the bushes in the direction of the noise, the machete thrust in front of him. She muttered curses as various thorns and branches tore at her flesh, but he refused to let her go. There was noise from the village, where the screams had also been heard. But from in front of them there was now no sound, save for a low gurgling. Tom kept heading in the direction of this, continuing to drag Shirley, panting and swearing, behind him. They burst through another tree fringe and reached a clearing where there were two people. If they were people.

One was, certainly: a young woman, the woman who had screamed, presumably, but who had now lost her breath, as she was being dragged by the ankle across the clearing and towards the bushes on the far side.

She had been wearing jeans and a shirt, but while the shirt remained intact the jeans had been pulled entirely off one leg; the other limb flailed on the water-soaked earth.

'Hey!' Tom bellowed, releasing Shirley to charge after them. As to who or what the other person was he couldn't be sure in the gloom. He got an impression of a lot of hair. Then the man, or beast, whatever it was, released the woman's leg and disappeared into the darkness.

Tom started to follow, swinging his machete, and was checked by a shout from Shirley. 'You stay here!'

He stopped running and went back to the two women. Shirley was kneeling beside the stricken girl, pointing in horror at the huge scratches on her thigh. Tom knelt beside her.

'Jesus!'

The girl continued to scream in a high-pitched wail, but now there were noises bursting through the undergrowth, and a moment later they were surrounded by people, headed by District Commissioner Rimmer, who was accompanied by the police constable, three women, Mrs Smith and several other men.

'You assaulted this woman?' Rimmer demanded.

'Don't be daft,' Tom said. 'We rescued her.'

'From what?'

'I don't know.'

'It looked like a big monkey,' Shirley said.

'We don't have big monkeys up here,' said the constable.

'You have to lock them up,' said Mrs Smith. 'They ain't caused nothing but trouble since they got heah.'

'Well, I like that,' Tom remarked. 'We have been model guests.'

'Listen here,' Rimmer said. 'We got to get this girl to hospital.'

'You mean you have a hospital?' Shirley asked.

'No, we ain't. But she got to have first aid, anyway. You and you...' he waved at the men. 'Carry she to my office. Tell Claretta to do the first-aid thing. Hurry now. And you had best call Washington.'

The girl screamed again as two of the men lifted her and began carrying her through the bush.

'And handle her good,' Rimmer shouted. An ambiguous instruction, Tom thought.

'You knowing she mark for life?' Mrs Smith enquired.

'How I am going to prevent that?' Rimmer demanded.

'I assume she has a name?' Tom asked.

'Yeah. That is Monica.'

'Nice name, Monica. Now what would she have been doing, walking out here by herself in the dark?'

'She got a man,' Mrs Smith suggested,

knowingly.

'Then where is he?'

'It ain't he assault she? I never did trust that boy.'

'Not with fingernails five inches long.'

'Listen here,' Rimmer shouted, again endeavouring to take control of the situation. 'You are saying you saw what was attacking Monica?'

'Only briefly.'

'Well, describe him.'

'It wasn't necessarily a him,' Shirley said.

'Absolutely,' Tom agreed. 'It could have been a her. Kinky, don't you know?'

Rimmer scratched his head.

'It was an it,' Shirley declared.

'You sticking with this monkey story?'

'It wasn't human,' Shirley insisted. Rimmer did some more scratching.

'Listen,' Tom said. 'We can follow it.'

'Now?'

'He, she, it, was hurrying. Half the people up here are Indians. They must be capable of tracking.'

'Maybe,' Rimmer said. 'Some time back. There ain't much cause for tracking nowadays.'

'Don't they hunt for game or whatever? Meat?'

'They get their meat in tins from Georgetown,' Rimmer pointed out. 'Anyway, we can't track in the dark. Tomorrow.'

'We'll be there,' Tom promised. 'You know what, Mrs Smith, what we would like is a nice cup of Horlicks or something, before we go to bed.'

'You can have cocoa,' Mrs Smith told him.

'God, what a day.' Shirley cleaned her teeth. She was clearly upset, because she hadn't even sent him out of the room while she undressed. 'To think that this time yesterday...'

'We were already involved in a murder,' Tom pointed out, taking his place beside her. 'If you're going to indulge in reassuring nostalgia you have to go back at least a week. Like before we ever met up in that hotel.'

'I wish we hadn't.'

'I shall take that as evidence that you are on the verge of an hysterical breakdown. I am going to the loo. Kindly do not lock the door on me.'

'Hold on,' she said. 'I'm coming too.'

'Why, Shirley, you make the most delightful propositions.'

'I need to go, and I'm not going alone.'

'Even if I promise you there won't be any apes in the bathroom?'

'What about scorpions?'

'Ah.'

They opened the door, and discovered that the corridor was in darkness.

'Mine hostess is a thrifty wench,' Tom said.

'Hold on.' He went back into the bedroom to fetch his torch, and had just picked it up when the bedroom lights went off as well. 'That's going a bit far.'

'Listen,' Shirley said out of the darkness. The night was absolutely quiet, or as quiet as a tropical night could be, with various insect noises snapping away, and the roar of the Falls ever present in the background. 'That engine has stopped.'

'Of course. The generator.' He went to the window and peered through the screen. 'That blacks out the entire village, save for the odd oil lamp.'

'Then that thing could come back and do whatever he likes. You should have shot him.'

'You said it was an it. Did you spot a whatsit?'

'Oh, really, Tom.'

'You mean you don't look out for things like that on naked its? Ah, well, maybe we'll get a closer look tomorrow. Come along now.' He stood in the dark of the corridor and shone the torch round the door while she did what she had to do, then she did the same for him. 'We are going to have a lot to tell our grandchildren,' he suggested.

'Chance would be a fine thing,' But she held his hand as they returned along the corridor and locked the bedroom door.

'Listen,' she said. 'What about our butterfly hunters? They weren't around tonight.'

'Are you suggesting they have a monkey suit in their luggage?'

'I just find them suspicious. Turning up out of the blue like that...'

'Insisting upon paying for the chicken they think they killed. I know. Doesn't fit, does it?'

'Oh ... brrr.' She got beneath the sheet and he joined her. Their thighs touched. Then suddenly she turned and was in his arms.

'I'm so scared, Tom.'

'With me around? What the hell. Didn't I dispose of your scorpion? And your monkey it?'

'I can feel evil, all around us,' she muttered, nestling into his chest, and apparently not noticing that he wasn't wearing anything. But then, he realized, as he slid his hand over her thigh, neither was she. Her flesh was like velvet, faintly clammy with sweat. She was absolutely there for the taking, in her present mood. But it had to be mutual; he had grown to like her too much.

He kissed her forehead, and, when she moved her head back, tried her mouth. That was good. 'Do you want this?' he asked.

'Does it matter, to you?'

'As a matter of fact it does. To me.'

'I want something,' she said. 'What have you got?'

He had, in the early days of their relationship, thought she might be a virgin, and was relieved to discover she was not. More importantly, she did not appear to have any hang-ups whatsoever; she knew what she wanted and when and where she wanted it. As for his other suspicion ... But perhaps she was omnivorous.

When at last she rolled off him, she lay on her back, staring into the darkness. 'I needed that.'

'I knew it from our first meeting,' he pointed out. 'And have been trying to rectify the situation ever since.'

'I do not go to bed with any Tom, Dick or Harry,' she said. 'I need to know my men. Very well. You grew on me. Slowly.'

'I spotted that, too. So, from here on, we're totally committed. To unearthing the it, I mean.'

'Are we really going to do that?'

'Isn't that why we're here?'

'I'm half inclined to forget the whole thing and just holiday. Wouldn't you like that?'

'I can think of nothing I'd like more. But it's an old family custom never to quit. We're here, and we're going to get to the bottom of this business. Anyway, the argument against quitting is now stronger than ever; once it gets about that we survived the crash, don't you think our friends are going to try again?'

'I don't usually like masterful men,' she remarked, snuggling against him again. 'But for you I'll make an exception.'

She was asleep in seconds, but Tom was not. It was very pleasant, lying there with a naked woman in his arms. He just wished he didn't have quite so much on his mind. What had started out as a promising caper with perhaps a story at the end of it had suddenly become very serious. He had gathered that when those two thugs had paid a visit to his flat. But even then, while he had accepted that the woman Lynette might have been carrying something of great importance all those years ago, he had not really taken to the monster theory. He had never believed in yetis, or bigfeet, and he knew there were no large apes in South America. But tonight he had seen one. Or had he? Maybe he was hallucinating. But if he had been, so had quite a few other people, including Shirley.

No doubt the girl Monica would be of some help, once she got over her shock. Following the beast had a high priority, but he also felt he should get in touch with Lionel Gifford, and see if he could turn anything up. Because maybe there was the answer to the whole business.

He awoke to rain thudding on the roof, so heavily that it sounded as if he was inside a drum. He blinked sleep from his eyes, felt around himself and discovered that the bed was empty. Then he saw Shirley standing at the window, still not wearing anything;

silhouetted against the dawn light she made an entrancing sight. He gave a sigh of relief. For a moment he had wondered if their romance was going to be too short to be remembered.

'Hi,' he said. She turned and came back to the bed, sat beside him. He put his arms round her and kissed her stomach. 'Sleep well?'

'Like a log. Tom ... did we really...?'

'You mean you don't remember?'

'Oh, I remember. But it all has a sort of dream-like quality...'

'I think we'd better try it again.' He brought her down on top of him.

'I think it's time to get back to Gifford,' Tom said, when they were dressed. 'Now is no time for him to forget about us.'

'There may be a problem with that. In case you haven't noticed, this place has no telephones. I'm talking about the village, not the hotel.'

'But you can log on through your mobile, right?'

'Mobile? Ah ... you mean cell phone. I left my cell phone in Georgetown.'

'You what?'

'The battery was low, and we never had the time to look for a new one.'

'Then why did you bring the laptop?'

'Because it has all my notes in it.'

'Shit!' He kissed her. 'But I love you any-way.'

'Some goings-on, last night,' Milton said at breakfast, which consisted of sliced avocado pear and some kind of fresh fish, together with thick black coffee; the meal was actually referred to by the locals as coffee, breakfast being the name for lunch.

'I'm surprised you didn't turn up,' Tom said. Despite his inability to contact Gifford, he was feeling on top of the world. Well, who wouldn't be? he asked himself.

'We were on the other side of the village,' Glossop explained. 'We heard the rumpus, but by the time we got back it had been sorted out.'

'Save for that poor girl,' Shirley pointed out. She was also looking fairly pleased with herself, which made Tom very happy. 'Do you know if she's all right?' she asked Mrs Smith.

'They saying she gone clean out of she mind,' Mrs Smith said, placing a pot of marmalade and a loaf of home-made bread on the table.

'What about her boyfriend?'

'That Washington? He never did get there,' Mrs Smith said. 'He was late. Men is always late.' Her glance took in her three male guests.

'Couldn't it have been him attacked her?'

Glossop asked. 'Maybe he has long nails.'

'Now why he going do that?' Mrs Smith enquired. 'He got she whenever he want, right? Anyway, he did be with his mommie until just before she was attacked. They was talking wedding, see?'

'Oh, what a shame,' Shirley said.

'Now she gone out of she mind,' Mrs Smith repeated, aggressively.

'Well, first thing we have to find that critter,' Tom said, brightly. 'When do we begin?'

'You seeing that rain?' Mrs Smith asked.

'We still have to track him.'

'Man, you going get lost yourself.'

Tom looked at Glossop and Milton. 'I take it you guys are in on this?'

'In on what?'

'Shirley and I know exactly where the attack took place. So does everyone else. The beast or whatever it was ran off when we appeared. There have to be tracks.'

'In this rain?' Mrs Smith remarked, contemptuously.

'Well, we are going to look,' Tom said. 'Come along, Shirley.'

Shirley drank the last of her coffee. 'Do you think a kagool would be any use?'

'Bring it along.' He wore one himself, although it was easy to deduce that he would soon be as wet with sweat inside as with rain outside.

'Man, you all is crazy,' Mrs Smith observed.

Milton and Glossop were showing no signs of accompanying them. 'Well, bugger them,' Tom muttered, as he led Shirley on to the porch. They had both opted for heavy trousers and boots as safest for tramping through the bush, but these were almost immediately soaked by the rain, which was striking the street and, while reducing it to a river of mud, was also splashing back up some eighteen inches.

'What a climate!' Shirley complained.

They waddled and waded along to the commissioner's office, stamped up the steps and then stamped on to the verandah.

'Man,' remarked the secretary, Claretta, 'but you are *wet*.'

'The commissioner in?' Tom asked.

'Oh, sure, he is in.'

'Well, we're ready for the off.'

'Off the what?'

'Oh, for God's sake. Listen, we'd like to speak with the commissioner.'

'Well, you can't come in,' she said. 'Not with all that mud and thing.'

'Then would it be possible for him to come out?'

She considered for a few seconds. 'I going see,' she announced.

Rimmer emerged. 'Man, you are wet,' he announced, and regarded Shirley. 'You too,

Mrs O'Ryan.'

'It happens to be raining,' Shirley pointed out.

'That is a fact. And it don't look like it is going to stop, neither. This time of year is something terrible. Nobody can't get nothing done.'

'I meant to ask you about that,' Tom said. 'What exactly do these people do?'

'The men working in the goldfields. But in this weather they can't get home, so the women ain't happy.'

'I can appreciate that. But the weather can't be too good for monsters, either. Are you ready?'

'To do what?'

'Go and track the beast,' Tom said, with a rising sense of alarm.

'That ain't possible, in this weather,' Rimmer said.

'Why not?'

'All them track must be going wash away.'

'But we won't know until we go and have a look.'

'Listen,' Rimmer said. 'All them tracks will be wash away. I am saying this. What we have to do is question Monica. She will tell us what attacked her.'

'Mrs Smith says she's gone out of her mind.'

'That is true. Well, when you have a monster jumping out at you, sudden like, it must happen.'

'Then what help can you expect from her?' Shirley asked.

'She going get she mind back,' Rimmer explained. 'I have called Georgetown. They going send the doctor with the police what is coming up. He is the one what came before.'

'Before what?'

'He is our regular doctor. He does come every two months, anyway.'

'And he'll be able to help Monica's mind?'

'Oh, yes. He did come up to see that Elias Martindale. He did see the creature,' Rimmer explained. 'When Jonas O'Brien did get kill.'

Tom managed to stop himself asking if Jonas O'Brien had had Irish blood. 'He's a man we would like to speak to,' he said, 'Elias Martindale.'

'Why?'

'Well, to compare notes. He saw the monster. So did we. We could put two and two together.'

'Well, he ain't heah.'

'Ah. Where would we find him?'

'In the madhouse in Georgetown. He went clear out of he mind. It was something terrible.' He peered at Tom. 'You ain't gone out of your mind?' It was less a question than an accusation.

'I've been seeing monsters all of my life,' Tom assured him. 'But that was the first time when reasonably sober.'

'Yeah,' Rimmer said, obviously uncertain whether or not he was having his leg pulled. 'Anyway, you can talk to the police when they come up. They say they was going to hurry. And they going bring the doctor.'

'But we're talking about days before they get here,' Shirley cried.

'Well, where that critter going go, Mrs O'Ryan?'

Shirley scratched her head and dislodged a good deal of water.

'Meanwhile, he's prowling about waiting to spring out on some other woman,' Tom said.

'I have issued instructions,' Rimmer pronounced. 'No woman is to leave the village without an escort. Until further notice,' he added.

'Suppose the critter is into men?' Tom enquired. As on the previous day, Rimmer looked at him as if he were a beetle. 'Just an idea,' Tom said. 'All right, commissioner, you think it's a waste of time looking for tracks. You have any objection if Mrs O'Ryan and I see what we can find? You said we could, last night.'

'You don't get lost, eh,' Rimmer said, and returned to his office.

'So much for official cooperation,' Shirley remarked, as they surveyed the rain. 'I gather I am not counted as a woman.'

'You happen to have an escort. Me.'

'So, are we going?'

'You bet. But we need a few things first. I had assumed that we were going to be part of a posse, but as we're not...' He led her back to the hotel.

'You can't come in heah with all that mud and thing,' Mrs Smith informed them, blocking the doorway.

'I need to go to our bedroom to fetch something,' Tom explained.

'Well, take them boots off for a start.' Tom obeyed, wondering how far she intended to go. But it seemed to be only the boots that were bothering her. 'Just don't drip,' she recommended.

'We're going into the bush, you see,' he said. 'And I thought we might be able to borrow your machete, again.'

'Machete? What is this, machete?'

'The big knife you lent us last night,' Shirley reminded her.

'You talking about ma cutlass.'

'I see. Well, can we borrow it?'

'Who you going chop in the day? It ain't no use against alligators.'

'We are going to chop leaves and branches that may get in our way,' Shirley said wearily. 'And, of course, we may well chop the monster, if we can find it.'

'Listen here,' Mrs Smith said. 'I don't want no blood messing up ma cutlass, eh? And no bluntness, neither.'

'We'll take good care of it,' Shirley promised.

Mrs Smith regarded her for a few more seconds, as if sizing up the risk of again allowing her the use of what was apparently her most prized possession, then she waddled into the house.

'Back in a tick,' Tom whispered. 'I'm just getting my gun and my camera.'

For once she didn't object, and he saw why when he returned a moment later, the revolver tucked into the back of his pants: Shirley was brandishing the cutlass. 'What do you reckon?' she asked.

'I apologize. For anything I may have said, or done, or even thought.'

'With this thing,' Shirley said with some satisfaction, 'I'd feel safe even walking the streets of New York alone at night.'

'That monster doesn't know what's coming at him. Just one point: suppose he turns out to be your long lost grandad?'

'Shit,' she commented; she hadn't thought of that.

The village was giving a good impression of being uninhabited, although people were certainly watching them from behind half-closed jalousies. They plodded up the street and reached the track leading up to the Falls. On their left the stream gushed by, noisily.

'That looks as if it's getting ready to flood,' Shirley remarked.

'Be optimistic,' Tom recommended.

The rain, as Rimmer had suggested would be the case, had quite obliterated their footprints from the track, as it had even the wheel prints of the jeep; but not even the incessant wet could remove the evidence of several people rushing through the bush. They found their way quite easily to the little clearing where the assault had taken place.

'Now observe,' Tom said. 'To our left, the stream, an offshoot of the river coming over the Falls, right?'

'Right.'

'Ahead of us, the Falls, right? I mean, the drop.'

'I suppose so.'

'And the critter made his attack here. So they have got to be connected. Right?' Tom was parting several broken branches. 'He went through here. He...' he dropped to his hands and knees, careless of the mud. 'What do you think of this?'

Shirley leant over him. 'It's a footprint.'

There were several footmarks, but most had been washed away by the water. This one happened to have been protected by a large overhanging leaf, and remained fairly clear, although it was obvious that it, too, would dissolve if the rain kept up.

'Yes,' Tom said. 'It is the print of a bare foot.'

'So, a lot of the people around here don't wear shoes.'

'That print cannot be older than last night, or it would have been washed away. And no one was out here last night, not after that attack.'

'You think it's the monster?' She shivered, looked around her at the sodden forest, then peered at the print. 'I suppose it's big enough.'

'It is a perfectly ordinary human footprint.'

'Well...' She stooped to look closer.

'Okay, it's a little distorted by the water. But those are toe marks, not claws. And the weight is on the ball of the foot, with the heel hardly visible, just as a human would make if running.'

'But that shaggy skin...'

'May just have been a shaggy skin. Anyway, it looked to me more like a lot of hair than shaggy skin.'

'Jesus,' she muttered. 'You mean this creature is human?'

'Well, I can think of quite a few humans who aren't really human, if you follow me. But it goes with our theory.'

She shivered. 'You going to get Rimmer out here?'

'Chance would be a fine thing. Let's see if we can find another print.'

'If we don't show him this print now, it'll have dissolved and we'll have no proof.'

Tom opened his camera case and took several photos. 'Now he'll just have to believe us. But he'll believe us even more if we turn up something else. Here.' He pointed to a broken branch and pushed past it. 'Here!' Another branch, this time un-broken, but with a small tuft of hair hanging from one of its offshoots.

'Now this really is evidence.' Gently he detached the hair and peered at it.

'Ugh!' Shirley commented.

'It doesn't smell. In fact, I'd say it's very ordinary hair. Most likely human.' He put the hair in his pocket, peered into the forest wall. 'Hm. No more broken branches. Our friend must have got his, or her, nerve back and stopped hurrying. But I'd say we go towards the Falls.' Which could clearly be heard, roaring in the distance, even above the steady pounding of the rain.

'I don't think I have ever been so wet in my life,' Shirley complained. 'Not even in a swimming pool.'

'That way.' Tom pointed, and, as he did so, the rain stopped. 'Well, holy hallelujah.'

'Now we catch cold,' she pointed out.

'Take off your kagool and you'll dry,' he suggested.

They took off their waterproofs and looked up. The trees weren't all that thick here, and

177

they could see the sky, which was suddenly blue; a moment later the sun appeared. And a moment after that, it seemed, they were immersed in a thick mist that obliterated trees, sky and sun.

'What do we do?' Shirley asked.

'Make for the Falls.'

'You're sure we're not there?'

'This is the sun sucking up all the moisture so that it can rain again later on,' he pointed out. 'When we get to the Falls we'll know about it. If you don't intend to use that winkle-picker, you'd better let me have it. This stuff is quite thick.'

She gave him the machete and he began hacking at the foliage in front of them. It was difficult to maintain any sense of direction in the mist, but the sound of the Falls loomed ever louder as they made their way through the bush, until Tom stepped into a stream.

'Shit!' he said as he lost his footing on the muddy bottom and sat down, up to his neck in the rushing water.

'Tom!' Shirley screamed.

'I'm all right.' He pushed himself up. 'But my fucking camera isn't. So much for that print.'

'Piranha!' she shouted.

'Eh?' He scrambled out. 'Where?'

'You don't see them.'

'Is that a fact? Well, I don't think they'll be in that water, except by accident.'

'You've dropped the machete.'

'Shit!' He looked at the stream. 'Ah, well, I'm wet already.'

'You're not going back in? What about the piranha?'

'I've told you, I'm sure there won't be any. They'd have had to come over the Falls, and I don't see any self-respecting fish willingly dropping eight hundred feet. Anyway, who'd you rather face, a piranha or Mrs Smith when we tell her we've lost her cutlass?'

She peered into the swiftly flowing brown water. 'Something's gleaming.'

'That's it.' Cautiously he slid down the bank.

'Oh, Tom, be careful.'

'Was that a note of love I heard in your voice?'

'Get on with it.'

The stream was deeper in the middle than at the side, and he had to put his head under as he reached for the machete. But he got his fingers on it and straightened, waving the weapon in the air. 'Excalibur!'

'Now get out.'

He scrambled up the far bank.

'Noodle,' she shouted. 'Now we're separated.'

'No we're not. You have to come across.'

Again she peered into the water. 'I'll get all wet.'

'Darling, you are all wet. Put your kagool

179

back on.'

She stuck out her tongue at him, slid down the bank and splashed across with enough noise to frighten off any fish that might be in the vicinity. He grasped her wrist to pull her out on the far side.

'There. Nothing to be afraid of.'

'I can feel my hair turning white. Is your camera really ruined?'

'It's oozing water.'

'So we've lost our proof.'

'So we just have to find some more. Onward. Listen!'

The noise of the rushing water was by now very loud. They advanced towards it for another few minutes, then the trees and the undergrowth suddenly ended and they were standing on the banks of the lower river, surrounded by a thick wet mist as solid as rain. In front of them the mist was ever thicker, and now the roar was so loud they had to shout.

'Now what?' Shirley asked.

'We keep going.'

'Into that? You're nuts.'

'We're still a long way from the actual Falls,' he said.

'Okay, so we get closer. We can't see a goddamn thing. So what are we proving?'

Tom chewed his lip. She had a point. Even in the remote chance that there was a way through behind the pouring water, they'd never find it in the mist, save by the merest accident. But to have got so close ...

'Lunch,' Shirley suggested. 'It'll take us an hour to get back to the village anyway.'

'Yeah,' he muttered.

'And a nice strong rum punch,' she added winningly.

'Yeah,' he agreed, and turned away, then checked as a wailing scream came through even the roar of the water.

'Oh, Jesus!' Shirley caught his arm.

'Over there!' He plunged into the bushes, tripping and falling, feeling his kagool being torn to pieces.

'Hey!' Shirley shouted. 'Don't leave me behind.'

He found himself on his hands and knees, panting, and she fell over him. 'Ooof. What brought that on?'

She rolled on her back. 'What are you doing, crawling about the place?'

'I tripped, if you must know. Listen!' There was sound coming through the forest, loud enough to be heard even above the roar of the Falls.

'Oh my God!' Shirley clutched his arm. 'What do we do?'

'Hold our ground. Here.' He gave her the machete, drew his revolver and presented it, held in both hands as he had seen the experts do.

'It's coming closer!' Shirley screamed.

'It's...'

...An enormous butterfly net, torn to pieces by the jungle, but held in front of himself like a weapon by a clearly terrified Glossop.

'Stop right there!' Tom commanded.

Glossop stopped and promptly fell to his knees, panting. He had lost his hat and his wet hair was plastered to his head. 'Help me!' he screamed. 'That thing!'

'What thing?' Tom asked. Glossop continued to pant.

'There's nothing there, really,' Shirley told him.

Slowly, fearfully, he looked over his shoulder. 'It was there!'

'Can you describe it?'

'Billy! Where's Billy?' Glossop scrambled to his feet. 'Billy!' he wailed.

'I assume Billy is friend Milton,' Tom suggested. 'He was with you, right?'

'We were together. We'd seen this magnificent red butterfly. We were going to get it, when this thing suddenly appeared. We ran. Billy must have gone the other way.'

'Then we'd better go find him.'

'Back there?'

'Look, he's your friend, right?'

'He's probably back in the village by now,' Shirley suggested.

'We still need to know where this thing appeared from,' Tom said.

'It just appeared.' Glossop's teeth were chattering. 'Like out of the ground. Just appeared.'

'Show us,' Tom insisted. 'Don't be scared. We're armed.' He grinned at Shirley. 'Don't worry, darling. If it's your grandad I'll shoot him in the foot.'

He went forward. Whence Glossop had come was fairly obvious from the broken branches.

'After you, Mr Glossop,' Shirley said.

The big man hesitated, then shambled behind Tom. Shirley brought up the rear.

'Stay close,' Tom shouted over his shoulder.

They were definitely approaching the Falls, because the noise was ever louder. They went forward for about ten minutes, then Glossop said, 'Here! It was here.'

Tom looked around him. Maybe there were more broken branches here than before, and the ground was trampled, but there was nothing distinct. The heavy moisture continued to settle over everything, and it was obvious that any marks there were would have disappeared in a couple of hours.

'So where did the creature appear from?'

'I don't know,' Glossop moaned. 'We were looking at this butterfly, like I said, and suddenly there it was.'

Tom hunted around, looking for some kind

of lair from which the creature might have emerged, and which might just be linked to some passage leading behind the Falls, and saw nothing but thick bush and thicker mist.

'So where's Billy?' Shirley asked.

'I don't know,' Glossop wailed. 'Oh, he's gone. I know he's gone. Poor dear Billy.'

'Didn't Kenneth Grahame write a poem about poor dear Billy?' Tom asked. 'I think he went thataway.'

Again the branches were broken. Tom went forward more cautiously now, still holding his drawn revolver. He had gone about fifty feet when he tripped and fell, again landing on his hands and knees, and found he was looking down on Billy Milton's body.

Seven

A Glimpse of Eternity

'Billy!' Glossop screamed. 'Oh, Billy!' He fell to his knees beside his partner's body. 'Billy, speak to me!'

'I don't think he can do that,' Tom said. Talk about having your throat torn out, he thought, as he gazed at the great bloody mess where Milton's windpipe had been.

'I think I'm going to be sick,' Shirley said, and turned into the bushes.

'Just don't get out of sight,' Tom recommended. He was now also looking at the bushes, the broken branches leading away from the dead man. His instincts were to follow, but his sense of duty told him this latest tragedy needed reporting.

'Is he really dead?' Glossop was asking, tears mingling with the moisture rolling down his cheeks.

'He doesn't look too good,' Tom said, trying to calculate his options. They were at least a couple of miles from the village, and this was the South American jungle. If Milton's body was left where it was for even a few hours it would virtually have disappeared – already there were ants investigating the corpse.

And the beast had to be close, so close. But he couldn't go after it and leave either Glossop or Shirley, or both, here alone, just in case the creature doubled back; he didn't think Shirley's machete was really going to be a lot of use, as handled by Shirley.

'What are we going to do?' she asked. She hadn't actually been sick, but it looked as if it could still happen at any moment.

Tom sighed. 'We have to get back and report this.'

'We can't leave Billy here,' Glossop moaned. 'He'll be eaten by snakes and things.'

'Ants,' Tom said, and pointed. 'He'll be eaten by ants. But I promise you he won't feel a thing. And the sooner we get people out here the better. Right?'

Glossop stood up, looked left and right. 'That thing...'

'I'll protect you,' Tom promised. 'Let's go.'

'Where?' Shirley asked.

'We'll follow these broken branches back to the stream, and follow the stream back to the village.'

'Which stream?'

'Oh, shut up,' he recommended.

'A dead?' Mr Rimmer enquired. 'You got another dead?' He was incredulous.

'Well, he looked that way to me,' Tom said, defensively. It had taken them four hours to find their way back to the village, and he was both exhausted and hungry – and given Mrs Smith's inflexibility, he was pretty sure they had missed breakfast. He had also had to put up with Glossop's wailing for all of that time; the big man was now sitting on the top step of the commissioner's office, still crying. Shirley was sitting beside him; she was more exhausted, emotionally and physically, than either of the men.

'Man, you knowing what?' Rimmer demanded. 'In the past three years we have had one dead up heah. You all arrive, and now there is five within twenty-four hours.'

'With respect,' Tom said, 'you've had several young women disappear in that time.'

'I ain't knowing they are dead. They could be anywhere.'

'And the woman, Monica or whatever, who was attacked yesterday?'

'She ain't dead,' Rimmer snapped.

'She would've been, if we hadn't turned up.'

The two men glared at each other.

'Well,' Tom said, 'are you coming out to fetch this body back, or not?'

'You going lead us?'

'As well as I can. As soon as I've had something to eat.'

'You can eat on the way,' Rimmer told him. 'Claretta, make this guy some sandwiches.'

'I'll need something to drink as well.'

'And a bottle of beer,' Rimmer shouted. 'And fetch my revolver.'

Neither Shirley nor Glossop felt up to returning to the scene of the murder; both, in fact, went to bed. By now the village was buzzing with the news, and there was no lack of volunteers for the trek back to where Milton's body might be found. Rimmer recruited his policeman, and was accompanied by Washington and several other apparently unemployed young men, while even some of the women tagged along. The noise they made as they ploughed through the jungle and splashed through the various streams was enough to frighten King Kong, Tom reckoned; certainly there would be no chance of the creature hanging about.

'Man, you know, I ain't never been so close to them Falls?' Rimmer remarked, taking off his pith helmet to wipe his brow. 'Shit, what a racket. And all this water ... you know we could get drowned?'

'We won't,' Tom assured him, desperately searching for broken branches. Actually, the trail was reasonably easy to follow, they had made such a mess coming out. The question was... 'Right about here,' he said.

Rimmer pushed back his helmet and took off his glasses to polish them, not that he achieved much, as they were immediately steamed up again. 'I ain't seeing no body. Or nobody, neither.' Clearly he regarded himself as a wit.

'It was here,' Tom insisted.

'Yeah? Well, he couldn't have been as dead as you said he was. He's probably back at the hotel by now, eating.'

'I got some blood,' Washington said. They crowded round.

'That is blood?' someone asked.

'Well, it got some water with it,' Washington pointed out. 'But it look like blood to me.'

Rimmer and Tom both peered at it. 'That

188

is definitely blood on that leaf,' Tom said. 'And I reckon this is blood on the ground here, as well.'

'Yeah? Well, where is the critter that is doing all this bleeding?' Rimmer asked.

'This isn't the creature's blood. This is Milton's.'

'Hey, Mr Rimmer, look here.' The constable had moved a little way away from the main party.

'What you see?' Rimmer asked.

'All these bushes broken down, like.'

The party shifted to the new point of interest.

'That's it,' Tom said. 'I didn't think he would, but the creature came back after we left, and took away the body.' He felt quite shivery to suppose that all the time he and Shirley and Glossop had been standing by Milton's body, the creature, or the murderer, could have been a few yards away, watching them.

'Now why he would want to do that?' Rimmer asked.

'Maybe he don't want our jungle littered up with deads,' Washington suggested. Rimmer gave him a dirty look.

'He took it away...' Tom drew a deep breath. 'To eat.'

The six men stared at him with their mouths open. 'To *eat*? You saying this thing eats human flesh?' Rimmer drew his revolver.

'I certainly think he needs human beings, for some reason or other.'

'And them girls,' Washington said, rolling his eyes.

'Jesus,' Rimmer said. 'Well, that is it. If we got some fucking cannibal roaming these woods, I am putting this gorge out of bounds, until the police get heah. And we having an armed guard in the village, too.'

'But...' Tom was aghast. 'Aren't you going to follow him? He can't be far. And if he's dragging or carrying Milton's body he'll have left one hell of a track.' He looked left and right. 'You can't just let him walk away. Who'll come with me?'

They all looked at Rimmer. 'My boys doing what I say,' Rimmer said.

'All right,' Tom said. 'I'll go on my own.'

'And wind up dead? You listen here, Mr O'Ryan. I am responsible for the lives of everyone up heah, and I am saying no one is going after that critter until the Georgetown people get heah. That includes you. And if you try to buck me I am going to put you in the lock-up for that time.'

Tom glared at him, then looked at the trampled bushes.

'If he is there,' Rimmer said, 'we going get him. When we got the men and the fire-power. Right?'

★　★　★

190

'We were so *close*,' Tom muttered. He lay on his back on the bed and stared at the rafters; there was no ceiling, which was why the rain always sounded so loud. 'I almost felt I could touch him.'

'I'm glad you didn't.'

Shirley had eaten, had a shower and washed her hair, and was sitting up in bed with a towel wrapped round her head, obviously feeling much better.

'I'm inclined to agree with Rimmer, believe it or not,' she said. 'We'll go after whatever it is when we have some serious reinforcements.'

'You reckon? When those serious reinforcements get here, we are going to have to tell them what we know.'

'Do we know anything?'

'You're saying this is not some relative of yours, turned into a wild animal by all those years living behind the Falls?'

'I'm not really keen on including creatures that tear out people's throats in my family tree,' she pointed out. 'I just want him, it, her, whatever, caught and put away.'

'In a zoo? Where people can come and stare at it? And say, "That's Shirley Richards' cousin"?'

'Unless we tell them, they won't know that. I agree, it's a ghastly thought. But it's better than tearing out people's throats.'

'Well, Rimmer or no Rimmer, we are going

out there tomorrow to see what we can find.'

'No way. I'm not having my throat torn out by any creature, relative or not. And neither are you.'

Tom considered for a few minutes. 'Are you actually suggesting that we spend the next three days just making love?'

'I'd have supposed that would appeal to you.'

'It does,' he said. 'Oh, it does. I just never supposed I'd hear you say it.'

Actually, even if they had planned to go after the creature they wouldn't have been able to do much about it, because that evening the rain set in again and it didn't stop for the next two days. The village street flooded, and then most of the houses, rain coming in through the roofs as well as up through the floors, even if they were all built on stilts for just such a situation. The flow over the lip was increased, as was the level of the various streams beneath the Falls, the whole area turned into a vast lake.

'Man, I ain't never seen rain like this,' commented Mrs Smith. 'This is like something out of the Bible. You believe this is something out of the Bible, Mr Glossop?'

She had taken the big butterfly hunter under her wing, since his terrifying distress at the loss of his partner.

'We'll all be drowned,' Glossop agreed. 'We

192

all deserve to be drowned.'

'Well, I ain't saying that,' Mrs Smith said. 'Only some of us.' She cast a disparaging glance at Shirley and Tom, who were sitting at the table in the corner drinking beer and playing gin. And then looked up with even more distaste as there was an explosion of mud and water through her front door.

'Man,' she bawled. 'You ain't know I cleaned this floor this morning?'

'Blame the weather,' Rimmer told her. 'I got news.'

Tom and Shirley both got up; Glossop did not respond.

'The first thing is, that girl Monica talking.'

'Geronimo,' Tom said. 'What is she saying?'

'Now that's just about what she is saying,' Rimmer said, astounded.

'She's saying Geronimo?' Shirley asked, no less astounded.

'Well, is that kind of noise. What they call gibberish.'

'Big deal.' Tom sat down again. 'So she can't help us.'

'She talking,' Rimmer insisted. 'Sooner or later she going say something we can understand. The other thing is, I get a call on the radio, right? Them police is coming up. They going be here tomorrow.'

'In all this rain?'

'Well, they coming up the road from

Bartica, see? Now they saying the road damn near wash away in places, but they still coming. That Simpson, when he going someplace, nobody and no weather better try to stop him.'

'I beg your pardon,' Tom said. 'Did you say Simpson?'

'Yeah, man. Is himself. Man, a plane blowing up is big time.'

'I'm sure it is. Talking about that, what about that mechanic?'

'What mechanic?'

'The man Miss— my wife and I saw inside the Grumman only a few minutes before it blew up. Have you made any attempt to trace him?'

'Nobody else saw him,' Rimmer pointed out.

'Are you calling my wife and me liars, Mr Rimmer?'

'I ain't saying that,' Rimmer protested. 'But is a fact nobody else saw him, right? And is a fact we ain't got no mechanic about heah, right? Well, how I going to find somebody who don't exist?' He chuckled. 'Maybe it was the creature.'

'There are other villages pretty close,' Tom said, keeping his temper. 'The man must have come from one of them. I think you should at least try to find out.'

'Superintendent Simpson going to do that,' Rimmer said. 'When he gets heah. And when the rain stops, eh?'

'Is Simpson coming good or bad news for us?' Shirley asked.

'Some of each, I should think,' Tom said. 'He appears to be a good policeman, so maybe he'll get something done. On the other hand, he also appears to run a very tight ship, so we're going to lose some of our freedom of action.'

'What freedom of action?'

'When the rain stops...'

It stopped the next morning. The sun came out and scorched down, and the entire village was enveloped in thick mist.

'This going burn off by midday,' Mrs Smith informed them. 'You listening?'

Shirley, eating avocado pear, put down her spoon. 'A car horn.'

'More than one,' Tom said. They all went outside, to peer into the mist. The entire village had turned out to welcome the reinforcements; Tom thought of Lucknow, although there was no one blowing the pipes. But he had to admit that the sight of Cal Simpson's huge uniform emerging from the leading jeep was most reassuring; sadly, having been brought up in the best traditions of British policing methods, he was not wearing a gun – although Tom assumed he had one handy should it be needed. With him were four policemen, none of them armed either – although there were various weapons stacked in the back – and a man in plainclothes whom Tom assumed to be the doctor.

Cal and his people did not immediately come to the hotel. The policemen disappeared into Rimmer's office with the commissioner, and the doctor was escorted to see Monica by an enthusiastic Washington.

'He'll be along,' Tom said.

And, sure enough, half an hour later Cal stamped up the steps of Mrs Smith's establishment.

'You two guys sure attract trouble,' he remarked, shaking hands.

'Now we'd like to unattract it, really,' Shirley said.

'You making any headway with Claude Diamond's death?' Tom asked.

'Nope. I reckon when we get the people who blew up the plane, we'll get the people who killed Claude. Now, Rimmer has put me in the picture as he sees it. Let me recapitulate. You and the rest of your party went to look at the Falls. You were not the only people not going back to town; two butterfly hunters were also staying.'

Tom nodded. 'Glossop and Milton. Milton is the one who got killed.'

'Let's take things in order,' Cal said. 'So you waved the rest of the party off, and boom. Rimmer tells me you claim to have seen someone on board the plane just before take off.'

'We *did* see someone,' Shirley said, bristling.

'But you can't describe him.'

'Well...' she flushed. 'He was ... well...'

'He was dark skinned, and we all look alike to you. But surely you can tell the difference between a Negro and an Indian? Did he have long hair?'

Shirley looked at Tom.

'He was wearing a hat,' Tom said. 'I think.'

'God help us all if I ever have to put you two in the witness box,' Cal remarked.

'He was there,' Shirley said, sulkily.

'If he was there,' Cal said, 'we'll find him. Okay, so someone, or someones, blew up the aircraft. I have to tell you that we don't have all that many planes blown up in Guyana, but that could be because we don't have all that many planes. I also have to tell you that we didn't have *any* planes blown up until you guys got here.'

'You accusing us of something?' Tom enquired.

'I'm not accusing you of anything,' Cal said. 'I'm stating simple facts. Now let me give you some more facts. You and Miss Richards decide to come to Guyana on holiday. Your holiday has something to do with what is happening up here. Okay, so you're a journalist, and maybe Miss Richards is, too. I can't blame you for hunting up a story, if there is one. Within twenty-four hours of your arriving in Guyana one of our most respected journalists is dead. So you didn't kill him. But somebody did, and assuming that you agree with me that it had to do with your visit to Claude that afternoon, that somebody had to have known you were coming and be keeping an eye on you from the moment you landed. And that's not all. You fly up here. This is only two days after arriving. And the moment you get here someone plants a bomb on your aircraft, under the mistaken impression that you are on a day trip. There is no way that bomb could have been planted in Georgetown and not gone off until after you had landed here and taken off again. I believe someone did go on board and set it up. But then, you see, he also had to have known you were coming. That is to say, we have two men, at least, in different places, knowing all about you and prepared to kill you and anyone around you.'

'The killers must have been in radio contact,' Tom suggested.

'Sure they were,' Cal agreed. 'But now we're talking about a conspiracy. A gang. A group. We don't like to think there are such things in our country, Tommy. That's bad news, especially when we now have five deaths, and counting.'

'Six,' Shirley muttered. 'You've forgotten Mr Milton.'

'You say he's dead. Rimmer says he's disappeared.'

'Look, we saw the body,' Tom said.

'Okay, six. That makes it worse. Not that I'd say Milton's death or disappearance is connected to the others. It's them I'm interested in. I think you guys have got to come clean to me, and tell me just what you're after.'

Tom looked at Shirley, who shrugged. 'I think it's getting a bit too big for us to handle.'

'Thank God for some common sense.'

'Okay,' Tom said. 'There were these two men in London, who called at my flat. They had discovered we were coming out here to look for Shirley's grandad, but they felt that was a cover. They thought we were looking for something else.'

'Something being carried by one of the women on the aircraft,' Cal said.

Tom frowned at him. 'How did you know that?'

Cal grinned. 'You'd be surprised what I know. Tell me about these two goons.'

'There isn't much to tell. One was white, one was black. Both were British, by their accents. I don't think they were very important, but were working for someone.'

'And you couldn't tell them what they

199

wanted to know. Or could you?'

'I couldn't. Because I didn't have a clue what they were after. Then they suggested that if I didn't know, Shirley did, and that I had better get the info out of her or they would start beating people up. Meaning her. So, as Shirley didn't know what they were after either, we decided to do a bunk, and came on down here a couple of days earlier than we had planned.'

'But as soon as they discovered you'd left they were on to their people here.'

'Quicker than that. When we arrived in our hotel room there was a death threat waiting for us.'

'Like I said, we are talking about a considerable conspiracy,' Cal said. 'But you took what these people had to say seriously, even before you got here to death threats and murders.'

'Well, I wouldn't say we took it that seriously,' Tom said. 'If there was a woman carrying something of value, that was more than sixty years ago.'

'Then why did you contact a journalist acquaintance of yours, Lionel Gifford, and ask him to see what he could find?'

Tom raised his eyebrows. 'How the hell do you know that?'

Cal reached into the breast pocket of his tunic, and took out an envelope. 'This came for you just before we left Georgetown.'

Tom took the Special Delivery envelope slowly. It had been slit open.

'This is marked Private and Most Confidential.'

'That is a fact. But murder generally overrides considerations like that. You and Miss Richards have been holding out on me, so I reckoned it was every man for himself.'

'So you've read what's in this?'

'I have.'

'Why didn't he email us?' Shirley asked.

'Maybe he felt it was too important to risk, in case somebody accessed your computer. Tell us, Tommy.'

Tom glared at him, then sat down and unfolded the sheets of paper.

You owe me one, or two, or three, Gifford had written.

Although maybe it'll pay for itself. Thank God for the Internet. Lynette Marshall was a WAAC officer, as you described her, one of the secretaries of General Andrew Hopewell. Hopewell was seconded to General Auchinleck's staff in Cairo in early summer 1942 to coordinate the American plan for helping out in North Africa. Operation Torch, the proposed American landing in Algiers and Morocco, was, of course, top secret at that time, and it was felt only personal contact would suffice. Hopewell was a bit of an antiquarian, and, luckily for us, he kept a diary, which is now in the Library of Congress. This tells us that, having time on his hands, he paid a visit to the Oasis of Siwa, down in the south-west of Egypt. This used to be called Ammonium, and was the seat of the Temple of the Oracle of Ammon, the supreme god of the Ancient Egyptians. It was here that Alexander the Great visited in about 332 BC, and when he left it he declared himself a god.

Hopewell didn't go that far, but it would seem certain from his entries that when he returned from Siwa he was in a highly elated and agitated state. In his cups, he confided to two or three people that he had found what man has been looking for since time began, the secret of eternal life, something he apparently bitterly regretted – telling anybody, I mean, although apparently they just laughed at him. However, it would appear that he actually had this elixir in his possession, or at least a formula for creating it.

He seems, however, to have had sufficient brains not to make his discovery public knowledge; he would probably have been certified. And, this apart, he seems to have been a reasonably sensible chap. By the time he got back from Siwa things had hotted up. The first battle of El Alamein was being fought, and there was every possibility of Rommel breaking through. Hopewell knew he couldn't leave his post without permission from Washington. But he was determined to send whatever he had back to the States for analysis and possible use. He gave his precious discovery to Lynette Marshall, and told her to deliver it personally to her namesake and US military supremo, General Marshall. I have no idea if Lynette knew what she was carrying. It seems unlikely, other than that it was a substance or formula of the greatest secrecy and importance.

Hopewell then contrived to get himself killed while observing the battle; his diary was found amongst his private papers after his death. Now, as you may recall, it was shortly after the end of this battle that Auchinleck was replaced by Alexander and Montgomery. So things were in an even greater state of flux, while Lynette Marshall took off on her journey back to Washington, and by the strangest of fates wound up crashed into Kaieteur Falls. As for the other informed and interested parties, our only clues lie with the people with whom Hopewell was intimate when in his cups, as mentioned in the diary. As far as I have been able to ascertain, he had three particular cronies in Cairo. One was a British officer, Major James Birt. He was killed in action in Normandy in 1944. I have spoken with his grandson, and his family know nothing of

Hopewell or any elixir of life. The second was Peter Garth, an officer in British Intelligence. He is still alive, believe it or not, a sprightly eighty-seven. He remembers the incident well, but as a joke. Mad as a March Hare, is his description of Hopewell. This, incidentally, appears to have been the opinion of the people who went through Hopewell's papers after his death, which is why they were simply filed and forgotten.

The third was a Jason Falby, one of Hopewell's staff. Thus an American. The only information I have on him is that he retired from the army, with the rank of colonel, in 1947. Then he dropped out of sight, and I haven't had the time to probe too far in that direction. He would be eighty-nine years old by now, if he is still alive. There may of course have been others whom I have been unable to trace.

However, my money would be on Falby, or a descendant of his, being in possession of at least part of the information you are after, for this reason: a team of American antiquarians visited Egypt in 1951 and spent some time at Siwa Oasis. Falby's name is not connected with this expedition, but if our reasoning is correct there is a strong possibility that he was part of it – maybe even its leader. As to whether he found what he was, and you are, looking for, I cannot say. So there you have it. Let me know if you would like me to follow up the Falby angle. Also let me know if you happen to catch up with Lynette Marshall, and what she was carrying. Could be a story.

Tom gazed at Cal. 'We need to get in touch with him.'

'Done.'

'What's in the letter?' Shirley asked.

Tom gave it to her. 'What do you mean, done?'

'I'd like to find this fellow Falby, too, or whichever of his descendants is still looking. So I wired your friend to continue the search. Oh, I signed your name.' He grinned. 'And put it on your hotel bill.'

'Shit!' Tom commented.

'Oh, my,' Shirley said, having read the letter. 'You think Falby is behind all this?'

'Or one of his descendants, certainly. It's our best lead.'

'But ... how? I mean, how did they cotton on to us?'

'I agree it's pretty sinister. Figure it this way. The first Falby obviously believed Hopewell's claim. There was nothing he could do about it while the war was on – presumably conditions made it impossible for him to get down to Siwa himself – and of course no one in Washington at that time knew Lynette Marshall was on her way, much less what she might be carrying. But,

205

with Hopewell dead, once the war was finished Falby started to probe. So he returns to Egypt and goes to Siwa. And finds nothing. But then he learns that the plane, or a plane, carrying Lynette Marshall went into the Falls only a week or so after Hopewell's discovery. With her went the formula for the elixir, or whatever. So that's the end of that. Save that elixirs of life, by their very definition, don't dry up and disappear. Now, I checked up on our records, and discovered that there was a so-called scientific expedition up to Kaieteur in 1952.'

'And it was headed by Falby,' Shirley said, excitedly.

'It may have been, but there was nobody named Falby in it, but he could have changed his name after he got out of the army. But it was an American expedition, just like the one to Siwa the previous year, which is why I'm backing your friend's hunch that we're looking for Falby's descendants over either of the Englishmen.'

'And, of course, it's still a wild goose chase,' Tom said.

'Most sensible people would agree with you. Your correspondent friend certainly seems to,' Cal said. 'On the other hand...'

'Look,' Tom said. 'Old Alexander the Great came back from Siwa calling himself a god. Now, I know there were compelling political reasons for him to do this. On the other hand, he was also claiming immortality. But he died only a few years later. QED.'

'It's a point,' Cal agreed. 'However, as long as this character Falby, or whoever is acting on his behalf or has taken over from him, believes in it, it seems he is going to kill to get to it, or stop others getting to it, so the first thing we need to do is track down who is doing the killing. I'd say your mechanic is at the top of the list of sub-killers, if you like. What are the chances of your identifying him if we bring him in?'

'I'm not too sure about that. As we said...'

'All dark faces look alike to you. But we'll have a go. Just tell me who else was around just before the plane went up.'

'Well,' Tom said, 'there was Shirley and me, and the Doveys, of course, but they went up with the plane. Then there was Washington ... but he only came out with Carl. There was no way he could have planted the bomb.'

'What about Milton and Glossop?'

'They wandered off into the bush when we'd been to the lip. But...'

'If it'd been one of them you'd have recognized him,' Cal agreed. 'Who else?'

'Well ... nobody else.'

'Save for the mystery mechanic, eh? Okay. Who was about when you landed? Apart from the people on the aircraft?'

'Ah ... there was Washington and the two guides.'

'And what happened to them?'

'The guides came with us to the lip. They had to take us through the forest. After we returned to the rest house they left.'

'They came back to the rest house with you?'

'Well...' Tom frowned, trying to remember. 'I'm not sure they did. We were so busy chatting I didn't really notice.'

'Of course they did,' Shirley said. 'They served us lunch. Or breakfast, or whatever they call it. I think they went off after the meal.'

'And the park warden?'

'Ah ... he wasn't there.'

'You just said he was.'

'He was when we landed. But, as I said, he went off with the pilot and came back with him after lunch.'

'I believe in it,' Shirley said suddenly. Both men looked at her. 'You're overlooking what really matters,' she said. 'The creature, the man, the woman, who is living behind the Falls. Or the group, perhaps.'

'Now, Shirley,' Cal said, 'I hate to say it, but that has got to be rubbish.'

'What about the hair?' Tom took it from his pocket. 'We found this attached to a branch, close by where that girl Monica was attack-ed.'

Cal peered at the tuft, then sniffed it. 'I would say this is human hair.'

'That's what we think.'

'But I'll have to have it analysed. Mind if I keep it?'

'Sure, if it'll help things along.'

'I'm not sure it will,' Cal pointed out. 'It could well have come off anybody.' He looked speculatively at Shirley, but her hair was yellow, and the hair he had in his hand was reddish brown.

'Listen,' Tom said. 'You have had a number of strange disappearances over the past few years. Check your records. I'd say there have been strange disappearances up here for the past sixty years or so.'

'People disappear, especially in jungles. But, as far as I know, young girls disappear pretty regularly even in your so-civilized England.'

'And what about Milton? His throat was torn out. And then his body was carried off.'

Cal gazed at him for several seconds. 'You are saying that there *is* an elixir of immortality, which works, and that someone, or more than some one, survived the plane crash and has been using this elixir to stay alive.'

'Either that or, more realistically, if the survivors were a man and a woman, and...' Shirley suggested.

'Biblically speaking,' Tom said, 'they got to know each other, and begat.'

'And maybe their children and descendants as well.'

'Sawney Bean,' Cal muttered.

'Hey,' Tom said. 'You know about him?'

'I'm a policeman. I know about crime everywhere. But what you're saying doesn't make sense. Sawney Bean lived in a cave on the seashore. He had easy access, when the tide was out. And he had all the fish he could catch, even if he seems to have preferred human flesh. Even supposing, just supposing, it might have been possible for someone, or two people, to have survived a crash through the Falls, that would still have been it. There is no way of getting behind that water. Therefore, there is no way of getting out from behind that water. What have these people lived on, these past sixty years, unless they used that elixir?'

'I don't believe the elixir exists,' Tom said.

He looked from face to face, studying their expressions. 'That is quite horrible,' Cal said.

'You're a policeman,' Tom reminded him.

'There has got to be a way out from behind that water,' Shirley said. 'There has to be.'

'And if there's a way out, then there's a way back in,' Tom said.

'Yeah. Well, we could spend the rest of our lives looking for it,' Cal said. 'Like you keep reminding me, Tommy, I'm a policeman. I came up here to investigate the blowing up of the Grumman, and the resulting murder of Carl Lemmon and the Dovey family. I am damned sure that crime is linked to the people who killed Claude Diamond and who are getting after you, and *that* is linked to whatever Lynette Marshall was carrying when that plane went in. Therefore, by doing my job, I am helping all of us, right? Now, the only lead on the ground that we have is this mechanic you saw in the plane. He is what I am going to concentrate on, and when I have found him I believe we are going to be able to unravel this entire shitting mess. With respect, Miss Richards.'

'And Milton? And the monster behind the Falls?' Shirley enquired.

'If he pops out again, we'll nab him. Now tell me this: do you people require police protection?'

Tom looked at Shirley, who gave a quick shake of the head. 'We can manage,' Tom said. 'And you did say you couldn't spare us any.'

'That was before I knew we were all going to wind up here. Okay. I'm not going to put any restrictions on your movements. But I strongly recommend that you stay close to the village.' He grinned. 'After all, you're my only witnesses, right?'

'He's growing on me,' Shirley said. 'Think he'll find that mechanic?'

'I think he probably will. Although I think

he's being optimistic in supposing that will solve the case. Meanwhile...'

'Meanwhile,' she said, 'we are going to find our way behind that water.'

Eight

Snakes

'And just how do you propose to do that?' Tom asked.

'We're going about it the wrong way,' she said. 'That's obvious. The way in and out can't be at the *foot* of the Falls. There's simply too much water. It has to be at the top. Someplace close to the river, perhaps. An opening that could lead down to the cavern behind the Falls. As Milton said, there has to be a cavern.'

'Fanciful,' Tom commented. 'And you're talking about searching a huge area of forest. That could take years.'

'I don't think so,' Shirley argued. 'This is rainforest, right? They have some of the heaviest rainfall in the world up here. Everything gets very wet and soggy. It stands to reason, therefore, that if there was what you might call an ordinary way down to the cavern, it would be covered in mud.'

'Which doesn't do much for your theory.'

'Which narrows the area we have to search,' Shirley said. 'We are looking for some rock formations that might include caves, at ground level.'

'Finding one of those will be just as tedious as finding a hole in the ground. We don't know where to start looking.'

'Hey, you all coming for breakfast, or what?' enquired Mrs Smith from the doorway.

'Just coming,' Shirley said. 'We'll find out, shall we?'

'I ain't knowing you is friends of Mr Simpson,' Mrs Smith remarked, benevolently, as she served them fish surrounded by rashers of bacon.

'We went to school together,' Tom said.

'Is that a fact? Well, glory be. You eating, man?'

Glossop had been staring morosely at his plate. 'How can I eat?' he moaned. 'My friend, eaten by a monster...'

'Well, we ain't knowing that,' Mrs Smith pointed out. 'He done just gone, right?'

'His throat was torn out,' Shirley said, unable to decide whether to eat the bacon separately or treat it as surf and turf.

'Well, that could be anything,' Mrs Smith said, equably. 'Mr Simpson going get to the bottom of it, you see. Now,' she said, pouring coffee, 'if there is anything you all wanting, anything at all, mind, you just have to say.'

Being a friend of Cal Simpson was apparently as much an asset up here as it had been in Georgetown.

'I suppose you've lived here all your life, Mrs Smith,' Shirley said, chattily.

'Well, not all of it,' Mrs Smith confessed. 'I did come up heah when I marry that damn Smith. I was just a girl, then.' She sighed, heavily.

'What did your husband do?' Tom asked, politely.

'This hotel, man. He build this hotel. And I did cook and thing, even then.'

'That being...' Shirley encouraged.

'Oh, twenty year ago now,' Mrs Smith said. 'But then he get sick and die, and I am taking care of everything.'

'You never thought of marrying again?'

'Eh? What I am going marry again for? Husbands are just one load of trouble.'

'Absolutely,' Shirley agreed, smiling at Tom. 'Twenty years. You must know the area pretty well.'

'Why I am doing that?'

'Well ... don't you go for walks? Explore? Haven't you been up to the Falls?'

'I did do that one time when we first come here,' Mrs Smith said. 'But if you mean I must be see them monster things, that is one reason for not walking, eh?'

'How long have you known about the monsters?' Tom asked.

'Oh, they saying things ever since. And before.'

'And people have been disappearing?'

'I ain't knowing about that.'

'But some have disappeared from this very village.'

'That is a fact.'

Shirley was showing signs of impatience; they were not getting anywhere. 'What we are looking for, Mrs Smith,' she said, 'is a cave, or caves, fairly close to the river. Above the Falls. If there are caves, there must be rocky soil. Outcrops of rock, perhaps. Do you know of any?'

'Now how I going be knowing that?' Mrs Smith enquired.

'We saw some, on the day of the explosion,' Glossop said. All heads turned to look at him. 'Billy and I...' Glossop paused while tears rolled down his cheeks. '...After we looked at the Falls, we went for a walk to-gether.'

'So you did,' Tom said. 'I remember.'

'It was so beautiful,' Glossop said. 'Walking through the forest, with the rain slanting through the trees...' He sniffed, and dried his eyes.

'And you saw some caves?' Shirley re-frained from commenting that anyone who would enjoy walking through the forest in the rain had to be a nut.

Glossop shook his head. 'We saw some outcroppings of rock.'

'Where was this?'

'Above the rest house.'

'How far?'

'Oh ... half a mile, maybe.'

'That would make it more than half a mile from the Falls,' Tom said, looking at Shirley.

'That's not so far; we don't know how far the cavern behind the Falls stretches. And it's all we have. Could you show us these rocks, Mr Glossop?'

'Well ... yeah, sure. I can show you them. You think they could have something to do with that critter that attacked Billy?'

'I'm sure of it.'

'You want to be careful,' Mrs Smith recommended. 'You don't want to go getting near no monster.'

'We'll be careful.' Shirley finished her coffee. 'When can we start?'

'After our siesta,' Tom recommended. 'And we'll need transport. It's a good hike up to the rest house. If we try walking it we won't get there and back before sundown.' He turned to Mrs Smith. 'Any chance of borrowing a jeep, or something? Just for the afternoon?'

'Well, the only jeeps around heah is the one belonging to Mr Rimmer, and the one

216

Washington does drive.'

'Do you think you could get hold of Washington for us, and negotiate the use of his jeep for this afternoon?' He gave her his best smile. 'We'd be ever so grateful.'

'Mind you,' Mrs Smith said, 'now they got all them police jeeps...'

'We'll stick with Washington,' Tom said. 'After our siesta. Can you do it?'

'Well, maybe I could have a word.'

'You're an absolute treasure, Mrs Smith. See you around, Mr Glossop. Three o'clock suit you?'

'I don't see why we don't go now,' Shirley grumbled. 'This siesta thing is for the birds. I'm not going to sleep a wink.'

'Of course you're not. We're going to have sex,' he explained.

'I suppose it passes the time.'

'Listen,' she said later. 'Do you really believe that American colonel found the elixir of life?'

'No.'

'But you do believe there's someone, or something, living behind the Falls, and able to get in and out at will.'

'It seems likely.'

'Supposing we do find a cave or something, what is our plan?'

'To search it, and see if there is a succession of caves leading downwards.'

217

'You, me and Glossop?'

'I think you and me. I can't see Glossop being a great deal of help.'

'You don't think we should have a back-up? Or at least some weapons?'

'I'm going to carry my gun, and you can borrow Mrs Smith's cutlass again.'

'I don't think she'd go along with that. You mean you're not going to tell your friend Cal anything about it?'

'Let's find the cave first,' Tom suggested. 'And make the big decision afterwards. If we tell Cal and have him and his bluebottles come out there with us and there is nothing there, he's going to regard us as even more of a nuisance than he does now. While if we do find your grandad Cal will immediately want to arrest him for murder. Right?'

'Mm.'

She went to shower, and obviously did some thinking.

'That creature...'

'Your grandad.'

'Don't excite me. That creature attacked Milton at the *foot* of the Falls, not the top. In broad daylight.'

'You're arguing against yourself. This is a sparsely populated jungle, and he probably knows it better than anyone.'

'Or she,' Shirley said, even more thoughtfully.

'Could be. We'd better make a move.'

'Flashlights. We'll need flashlights.'

'I have my torch.'

'That little thing? We need a proper flashlight.'

'I think, as I said, my dearest girl, that we should first of all establish that there is a cave that possibly leads to the cavern behind the Falls, and then equip ourselves with all the necessary gear. And *maybe* even Cal and a couple of heavily armed policemen. But establishing the fact comes first.'

When they got outside they found Washington waiting for them, with his jeep parked at the foot of the steps. Glossop was already there, as well as Mrs Smith, and a somewhat small, pleasant-looking white man wearing a jacket and tie and sun helmet.

'This heah is Dr Willard,' Mrs Smith said proudly. 'He is staying in ma hotel.'

Willard raised his hat. 'Pleased to meet you, Mr O'Ryan. Mrs O'Ryan.' He spoke with a faintly American accent. 'Cal Simpson was telling me you're scientists trying to discover if there is a way to get behind the Falls.'

'It's an intriguing thought,' Tom said.

'Absolutely. One often wonders what might lie behind the great waterfalls, Niagara, Victoria ... But there's none so tall as Kaieteur, of any size, anyway. And have you had success?'

'We're still looking,' Tom explained.

219

'You're not Guyanese, are you?'

'Well, by adoption. I was born and educated in Ohio. But I came out here on a visit, oh, twenty years ago, and liked it so much I decided to hang out my shingle, as it were.'

'Twenty years?' Shirley asked. 'Wasn't that during the civil war?'

'No, that was thirty years ago. I came afterwards,' Willard said.

'We'd better be on our way,' Tom said, before Shirley really let her hair down and told the doctor where they were going that afternoon – which would probably be immediately relayed to Cal.

'You all mind how you going, eh?' Mrs Smith recommended.

'Is the rest house, nuh?' Washington enquired.

Tom nodded. 'Retracing steps and that sort of thing.'

He sat beside the driver; Glossop and Shirley were in the back.

'You all come back for dinner, eh,' Mrs Smith shouted.

'I think she's becoming quite fond of us,' Shirley suggested, as they drove out of the village.

'Even since she discovered we knew Cal,' Tom agreed. 'What is the superintendent at this afternoon, Washington?'

'Well, boss, he done drive over to Kagerama to talk with the people there.'

220

'So he doesn't know about this little expedition.'

'Well, boss, he going know about it when he come back.'

'When it'll be too late for him to stop us,' Tom said.

'We going some place he shouldn't know, boss?'

'Oh, no, no,' Tom said. 'But you know what policemen are like.'

Washington digested this, possibly *not* knowing what policemen were like.

'How is Monica?' Shirley enquired, politely. 'Or should I have asked the doctor?'

'Well, all she can say is that thing coming at her,' Washington replied. 'But the doctor saying she will soon get back to normal.'

'When were you planning to get married?' Tom asked.

Washington gave him an old-fashioned look; clearly he was having second thoughts about that. They bounced up the track to the rest house, conversation limited by the roar of the Falls to their left. The rest house itself was deserted.

'It's not locked,' Shirley commented, opening the door.

'What they going lock it for?' Washington enquired. 'If someone want to get in and it locked he going just bust down the door, eh?'

'Now,' Tom said, 'we are going to take a

walk up the river a little way. You coming, Washington?'

Washington considered. It wasn't actually raining, and was in fact quite a pleasant afternoon. 'I might do that,' he agreed.

'Show us those rocks,' Tom told Glossop.

The big man began walking up the river bank, following a fairly well-defined path, although sufficiently overgrown to hamper their progress. Glossop was equipped with a stout stick for pushing aside the under-growth. Tom followed, wearing a bush jacket despite the afternoon heat; his revolver was tucked into his waistband in the middle of his back, concealed by the jacket. Shirley came next. She had not asked Mrs Smith for a further loan of her cutlass, but had also equipped herself with a stick, and had tucked her jeans into her boots. Washington was last, clearly amused by the whole expedition but equally clearly enjoying watching Shirley's somewhat tight jeans undulating in front of him; he carried a large knife in a sheath hanging from his belt.

The river whispered by on their left, brown and inscrutable. Occasionally they saw a drifting tree branch – called tacabas by the Indians – but there was no sign of life, although Shirley had no doubt that there *was* life, certainly as they moved away from the Falls; as Tom had said, not the most vicious piranha or alligator or water snake would risk getting too close to that tumbling water.

'I reckon it was just about here,' Glossop said, after they had walked for fifteen minutes. 'In there.'

On their right the jungle was thick, the great trees rising out of the undergrowth in their search for sunlight, reaching heights of seventy and even a hundred feet.

'Where in there?' Tom asked. 'Once we leave the river we'll be lost in seconds. What were you doing in there, anyway?'

'We were chasing a butterfly. Magnificent thing. I'll swear it was six inches across. We chased it, and Billy all but had it...' He burst into tears.

'How do you know it was here?' Shirley asked, embarrassed.

'There was that nick in the bank, over there.' Glossop sobbed. He was pointing across the river, where there was a definite indentation in the bank.

'That's as good a marker as any,' Tom agreed. 'How far in did you go?'

'Haven't a clue,' Glossop said, drying his eyes. 'When we got to the rocks we lost him.'

'But you found your way back to the river easily enough, right?'

'Well, we could hear it.'

'Fair enough. But we're going to do this sensibly. Washington, I'd like you to stay on the bank, right here, look at your watch, and every five minutes give us a shout. One of us will reply. Right?'

'Right,' Washington agreed.

'Off you go, Mr Glossop,' Tom invited.

Glossop used his stick to push under-growth left and right; here there was no semblance of a path. Tom and Shirley stayed close behind – Tom hadn't been joking when he had suggested that once they left the river they could lose sight of each other in seconds.

'How far did you chase this butterfly?' Shirley panted.

'Not far.' Glossop was also panting.

'Halloooo!' Washington's voice wailed through the trees.

'You answer him,' Tom told Shirley.

'Why me?'

'Because you're staying here, to make up the next link in our chain.'

She made a face, but threw back her head and uttered a responsive wail.

'Right,' Tom said. 'Now when he shouts again, you answer, and we will answer you. Okay?'

Shirley looked around at the trees and bushes, clustering close. 'How long are you going to be?'

Tom looked at Glossop. 'We must be very near, now,' Glossop said. 'I told you, we could hear the river, and that's just about faded here.'

'Then it'll be a couple of minutes, and a

couple of minutes to have a look around, and we'll be back. Would you like my gun?'

'No, I would not,' Shirley snapped. 'Just hurry.'

Glossop was already parting the bushes, and in fact they had only advanced a further twenty feet from where Shirley was standing when he pointed. 'There.'

There was a sudden clearing in the forest, where there was a cluster of boulders; they all seemed firmly anchored in the earth. Tom went forward, passed between two of the rocks, each considerably taller than himself. Beyond the boulders there was a larger outcrop of rock, centuries old, judging by the rain erosion on the top, but still rising some twelve feet out of the forest floor. Close to the ground was a roughly rectangular patch of blackness.

'Eureka!' he said.

'That what you were looking for?' Glossop enquired.

'Could be.' He parted the bushes to get to it.

'Do be careful, now.' Glossop had stayed by the boulders.

'Just checking.' Tom took out his pocket torch, shone it at the blackness. It was definitely an opening. He got up to it, knelt, peered in. The hole extended some distance into the rock. If there was a way down ... He placed the torch between his teeth, crawled forward, looked up and found that the roof was some feet away. He couldn't stand, yet, but he thought he might be able to a short distance further along. And the hole, which now could be called a tunnel, went down, and then, so far as he could make out in the single beam of light, bent to the left.

'Eureka,' he muttered again, and heard a sound behind him, a heavy slither.

'Glossop?' He turned, surprised at how far he had come into the cave. The beam of light did not reach the opening, but there was certainly nothing between him and it. At eye level, anyway. Yet he could hear the stealthy sound, growing louder; someone was crawling about in this cave with him. Or some *thing*! The throbbing of his heart quietened as his nerves regained control. He drew his revolver. 'Stand up,' he said.

The movement stopped. Tom was sending the torch beam to and fro, but still had not picked anything up. Then the movement began again, and sweat started out of Tom's forehead. The movements were too deliberate for a human being. Now it was very close. He thrust both revolver and torch forward, and at last saw it. It stared at him from the floor, its head rising up the better to look at him. It looked sleepy, bewildered. It was orange and brown in large, rectangular patches, and it was six feet long, sprawled across the floor. Memories, descriptions, pictures crowded through his brain. Too big for a rattlesnake, too small for a comoodi, too bright for a grass snake...

The bushmaster moved with startling speed. It slid across the intervening space before Tom could pull the trigger. He jerked backwards, his shoulder struck the wall of the cavern and he swayed forward again. He shouted, what he never knew. He squeezed the trigger and the gun exploded with a frightening roar in the confined space. He slapped at the creature with the barrel as the head came closer, again moving with frightening speed. A numbing jab entered his left thigh just above the knee, a spurt of pain followed by insensibility throughout the limb. Bushmasters never stop striking, he remembered desperately, and threw himself to one side. Orange and brown reared above him, and he fired again. And again. And again. And again. Then a click, and silence. But the echoes of the reports rolled around the cavern, and faintly he heard a thrashing noise. Using his arms he propelled himself backwards into the gloom. The heavy thrashing followed him, then there was a clang, a stifled ejaculation, more thrashing, then a series of heavy blows on the floor of the cave. Fear began to swell upwards within him as he fancied he could feel the poison spreading through his system; a bushmaster's venom could be fatal in minutes.

He felt at his thigh, squeezed the flesh between his hands, above the bite, and gazed at Glossop. 'Did you kill it?' he whispered.

'You did. I just finished the job.'

'It bit me.'

The big man knelt beside him, fumbled in his pocket and struck a match. With this light he found the dropped torch. Then he drew off Tom's belt, pulled down his pants, already torn by the bushmaster's fangs, and strapped the belt round his thigh; slowly he drew it tight enough to constrict the poison-carrying veins, loose enough to leave the arteries free, then buckled it. Anything less like the man who had collapsed into tears at the sight of his dead partner, and had wept periodically ever since, could hardly have been imagined. As he seemed to realize. 'We have snakes in the States, too,' he said. 'Maybe none as bad as this. But I've done my first aid. Now lookee here: I'm going to have to cut you.'

It seemed unimportant. Tom lay back on the floor of the cave. He was drowsy. It had been a long day. 'Is it bad?' he asked.

'A bushmaster is never very good.' Glossop knelt beside him, and from his pocket drew a Swiss army knife; he struck another match and used this to burn the edge of the blade. A trickle of sweat crept out from his hair, reached the end of his nose and dropped.

'Tell me when,' Tom suggested. Glossop

didn't reply, and a moment later Tom felt heat searing his thigh; he realized Glossop had cut into him, and he had felt no pain. In fact, the throbbing seemed to abate a little. Glossop whipped the knife out and cut again, firmly, pressing deeply, making a cross above the mark of the fangs. He laid the knife on Tom's other leg, and placed his lips against the oozing blood; Tom saw the lips hollow and then bulge, but still he felt nothing. Glossop spat into the darkness, then struck another match to sterilize the blade yet again.

'Again?' Tom asked.

Glossop nodded. 'Perhaps many times. Don't worry, you'll lose little blood until the poison is gone, then I can bind you up.'

Footsteps and panting breath. 'I heard the shots,' Shirley gasped. 'Oh my God! Oh my *God*!' She dropped to her knees beside Tom.

'Sssh,' Glossop recommended. 'Snake bite.' He unbuckled the belt, moved it an inch higher, tightened it again.

'Is it spreading?' Tom asked.

'It always does.'

'Snakebite,' Shirley whispered, and looked left and right in the gloom.

'It's dead,' Glossop said, and cut again, with quick, economical movements, sucked again, spat again and sat down heavily.

'What can I do?' Shirley asked. She was weeping, just as Glossop had done over

Milton, Tom thought, his brain seeming to work very slowly and over aeons of time.

'A brief prayer might be a good idea,' Glossop suggested. 'Then get Washington in here.'

'Can you stop it?' Shirley asked.

'If it can be stopped.'

'You've done this before?'

'Yeah,' Glossop said. 'Get Washington.'

Shirley hesitated, squeezed Tom's hand, then left the cave. From a million miles away he could hear her shouting. Glossop was cutting again. Tom forced a smile. 'My leg won't bear looking at.'

'So what's the odd scar?' Glossop bent his head to suck, and Tom caught his breath; the pain came sharply, unexpected after the numbness of the previous cuts.

Glossop looked up and grinned at him. 'Did I hurt you?'

'I'll say you did.'

'Then you're a lucky man.' He sucked another mouthful of blood and poison, and spat over his shoulder. 'You'll be all right. I knew a man once had to be cut seventeen times. But he lived.'

Tom gave a little sigh, and fainted.

He gazed at a handsome face, hovering above him. 'You guys are getting to be more trouble than you're worth,' Cal said.

Tom blinked. 'Where am I?'

'In Mrs Smith's best room. And she don't want you bleeding all over her sheets.'

'But ... Shit, I passed out. I have never fainted in my life before.'

'It ain't the macho thing to do,' Cal agreed. 'On the other hand, I'll bet you ain't never been shot so full of poison before. You owe that fellow Glossop your life.'

Tom sighed. 'I thought he was one of the bad guys. How did I get back here?'

'Glossop and Washington and Shirley carried you back to the jeep. Quite a trek, I gather.'

'Am I all right, Cal?'

Cal looked at the doctor, standing beside him.

'You have to just lie there and let your system take care of what poison's left in it,' Willard said.

'Shit,' Tom muttered.

'Sure I know it's a bind,' Cal said. 'More for me than for you. I have an identity parade all lined up. Now I guess your Shirley will have to do her bit.'

'Where is Shirley?'

'I'm here,' Shirley said, and knelt beside the bed. 'Oh, you great oaf. Fancy tangling with a bushmaster.'

'Correction,' Tom said. 'He tangled with me.'

'I don't suppose either of you guys is going to tell me what you were doing out there?'

Cal asked.

'Hunting butterflies,' Tom said. 'Glossop wanted company.'

'I see.' Cal accompanied Willard to the door. 'One day you are going to find yourself up shit creek without a paddle, Tommy. Now, Shirley, one hour, eh?' He closed the door behind him.

'Oh, Tommy,' Shirley said again.

'Listen,' he said. 'I think I've found that underground passage.'

'You joke.'

'Never was more serious in my life. There's certainly a fault in the rocks, leading down.'

'Holy shit. And the bushmaster was down there?'

'No. I think it followed me into the cave.'

'You think we should tell Cal?'

'Not yet. Nothing has changed. He has enough to keep him busy for the moment, anyway, especially if you can identify that mechanic.'

She gave a little shiver. 'I'm not too good at pointing the finger. And we didn't get a good look at him.'

'Well, if you can't, Cal will just have to keep looking. Anyway, it seems as if we are going to have to hang about here for the next few days, legitimately. No one can expect me to move too soon after being bitten by a snake. So we just sit it out, and as soon as

I'm fit to move we'll have a look at that hole.'

Shirley looked doubtful. 'You're not going to be fit for a week, at least.'

'I'll be up and about in two days,' he promised her.

The door opened. 'You ain't bleeding?' Mrs Smith enquired.

'Not a drop,' Tom said. 'I'm all bound up.'

'I did tell you,' Mrs Smith said. 'Don't go messing with no snake.'

'I wish everyone would get their facts straight,' Tom said. 'I didn't mess with no snake. The snake messed with me.'

'It coming to the same thing. You wanting anything?'

'Scotch,' Tom said.

'We ain't got no Scotch people round here.'

'I'm talking about the drink, not the people, who, by the way, are known as Scots, not Scotch.'

Mrs Smith looked puzzled. 'You want to drink Scotch?'

'Whisky, woman. Whisky.'

'Ah. Maybe they got some in the store. I going see.' She paused at the door. 'Mind you ain't bleeding on that sheet.'

'I'm going to give her a chapter to herself in my memoirs,' Tom said. 'Now you hustle along and identify our mass murderer.'

Willard came back in as Shirley left. 'How're you feeling?'

'I've felt better.'

'That chap Glossop did a great job. Were you really chasing butterflies?'

'Isn't that what Glossop says?'

'He says you were looking for a cave that might lead to a way under the Falls.'

Tom blinked at him. He did owe Glossop his life, but damn the man.

'Did you find such a place?' Willard asked.

'I found a snake, Doc. That put an end to further investigations.'

Willard grinned. 'So it did, Mr O'Ryan. Just remember, I'm on your side, when next you feel like help. Now, I'm just going to give you a shot, to make you sleep.'

Shirley felt she was the cynosure of all eyes as she walked up the street to the commissioner's office. It was dark by now, but it was Saturday night – had they really be in Guyana only a week? – and the street was certainly crowded; just about the entire population of the settlement, not including the chickens and dogs – fifty odd people, including most of the husbands back from the goldfields – was present, as it appeared that there had never been an identity parade in Takdai before, and most people didn't know what was going to happen.

Glossop joined her. In the strangest way, she realized, they had had a role reversal, and he was now shepherding them.

'Nervous?'

'Yes.' She glanced at him. 'Don't tell me: you've been on identity parades before, as well.'

'Some.'

'To look someone in the eye, and say he did it ... gives me the creeps.'

'If they do it right, there won't be no looking in the eye,' Glossop pointed out. 'They won't see you at all.'

'This ain't the NYPD,' she reminded him.

As even Glossop realized when they were shown into the commissioner's office, which glowed with light. A screen had been erected, but it didn't reach the ceiling, and anything that was said was clearly audible throughout the building. Beyond the screen there was much muttering and shifting of feet; on her side of the screen Shirley had the company of Cal and two of his policemen, as well as Rimmer and his secretary; Glossop was also allowed in.

'Now all you have to do is walk up and down in front of the men in there,' Cal said reassuringly. 'Take your time. And when you see the guy who was in the aircraft, touch him on the shoulder.'

'Jesus,' she muttered. 'What will he be doing?'

'Standing still,' Cal said, 'because I will be at your shoulder, and I have told them that if anyone moves I am going to kick him in the balls. So, you ready?'

Shirley drew a deep breath. 'I suppose so.'

'Thank you, Mr Rimmer,' Cal said. Rimmer and his secretary folded the screen and pushed it against the wall, and Shirley found herself staring at six men, of all shapes and sizes, and races, too. 'Take your time,' Cal repeated. 'Start at the left.'

Shirley swallowed, and faced the first man. He was an Amerindian, short and squat and sweating, with lank and long black hair. She didn't think the man on the plane had had long hair. The second man was black, tall and heavy. She didn't think the man on the plane had been that heavy. The third was another Amerindian, and she dismissed him without hesitation. The fourth was mixed race, she supposed; he had black skin but Caucasian features and hair. He was of average height and build, and his face was relaxed, although he stared at her with great intensity, so that she stepped back and had her arm gripped by Cal. But he said nothing, and after a moment she went on to the other two. But neither of them fitted her idea of the man on the plane, either.

'All right, Sergeant,' Cal said. 'Take them to the cell.'

'Man, you holding us?' enquired the big black man. 'Why you holding us?'

'Just for half an hour,' Cal assured him.

The policeman led them out.

'Ledden, right?' Cal asked. 'Number four. You scared the shit out of him.'

'Well...' Shirley bit her lip. 'I can't be sure.'

'You stopped in front of him.'

'Well ... he was the only one I thought could possibly be it. But I couldn't swear to it.'

'Good enough,' Cal said.

'What do you mean? You can't use me as a witness.'

'Maybe not. But I'm arresting him anyway. He's from Kagerama, where he runs a motor repair shop. Outboards, mainly. But he's a mechanic. And he was away from the village last Tuesday afternoon. He was gone several hours; long enough to have walked over here, planted the bomb and walked back.'

'Doesn't he have an explanation for why he was away all that time?'

'Sure. He says he went fishing. But he didn't catch anything. He's our man. Now, all we have to do is persuade him to tell us who he was working for.'

'And how do you propose to do that?'

Cal grinned. 'We'll think of something.'

'Does this mean you'll be going back down to Georgetown?'

'In a few days. You coming?'

'I have to stay here until Tom is able to move. And what about this yeti? And the elixir of life?'

'If either of them exists.'

'The creature exists,' she snapped. 'We saw it. And so did that poor girl, Monica.'

'Yeah. Well, my first business is finding out who blew up that plane, because, like I said, my bet is it's the same lot who killed Claude Diamond. And who, you want to remember, have you and Tom in their sights. When I've sorted that out I may have the time to think about your friend.'

'Oh for God's sake, you can't just go off and leave things the way they are.'

'Like I said, we'll be around for a few days. Thanks a million, Shirl. You've been a great help.'

She didn't believe that. But Cal seemed so sure. On the other hand, Cal always seemed so sure. She intended to tell Tom about the so-called identification parade, but he was fast asleep. 'I give him the whisky,' Mrs Smith explained. 'Right after the doctor give him a shot.'

'You gave him a glass of neat whisky just after he'd had a sedative? Did the doctor approve of that?'

'Well, he didn't know about the whisky. He done left when I gave it.'

'For God's sake.' Shirley sat beside Tom, peered at him. His breathing was heavy, but it was regular, and his pulse was only a trifle slow. 'He could be out for hours. Days.'

'Best thing for him,' Mrs Smith opined.

'The doctor change he bandage, too, without messing the sheet.'

'He's a professional.' She moved to sit in the chair Mrs Smith had thoughtfully brought in and put beside the bed. She felt thoroughly out of sorts. Part of it was sheer fright, she knew. She had really thought Tom was for it. And that snake...! But part of it was also irritation. She didn't suppose she could blame Cal. He had been given a job of work to do, and he was doing it to the best of his ability. Finding the people responsible for blowing up the aircraft, and for murdering Claude Diamond, clearly was far more important to the Guyanese government than chasing after a creature that, from their point of view, might or might not exist.

But from her point of view the creature was far more important. If in some way her grandfather had managed to survive, or even a descendant of his ... and, besides, the possibility of his survival was what had triggered this whole thing, including the several murders that had accompanied her investigation. There was the true answer. And they were so close. If Tom really had discovered a cave that might lead beneath the river and behind the Falls ... But he continued to sleep. So much so that she went to see the doctor herself; as he was there, he was conducting a surgery, which was something else everyone in the village felt they

239

should attend – Shirley had to wait an hour to get to him.

'There is undoubtedly some poison still in his body,' Willard said. 'It would have got up there before the first tourniquet was applied. Obviously there is not sufficient to kill him, and given time the body's own antibodies will defeat the poison. But while that is happening, complete rest is the best thing for him.'

'Just so long as you're sure he's going to wake up.'

'Oh, there is no doubt about that, Mrs O'Ryan.'

'Did you know he had a slug of whisky immediately after your sedative?'

Willard raised his eyebrows. 'No, I did not.'

'But you're still confident?'

'He will be all right,' the doctor asserted.

Shirley hoped he was right, especially next morning when Tom continued in a deep, apparently dreamless sleep. 'I think we should feed him coffee,' she suggested to Mrs Smith.

'The doctor say to let him sleep,' Mrs Smith pointed out. 'He going be all right.'

'Oh...' She decided to go out before she was rude. And found Washington parking his jeep at the foot of the steps.

'Well, hi, Mrs O'Ryan,' Washington said. 'How is your husband today?'

'Still sleeping.'

'Best thing for him,' Washington suggested.

'Don't you start, for God's sake. What about Monica?'

'Well, that is the thing. She talking sensible.'

'Is she? What is she saying?'

'Well, she saying she did be waiting for me, and she heard this sound behind her, and she turn round...'

'And what did she see?'

'The eyes, ma'am. The eyes.'

'Only the eyes?'

'That is what she saying, before she fainting. The eyes.'

'I don't think that's going to get us very far.'

Shirley spent the day playing chequers with Glossop, who was surprisingly good. And surprisingly good company, too; he seemed fully recovered from his grief at Billy Milton's death. It being a Sunday, both the hotel and the village was quiet; everyone, including Mrs Smith, had gone off to church in Kagerama. But Shirley's mind was elsewhere.

When she went to bed, Tom was still sleeping. He woke up next morning, but wasn't very coherent. Dr Willard came, and took his pulse, and seemed as confident as before.

'He'll be all right in a couple of days, but

241

I'll keep an eye on him.'

'You're not going back to town with Cal?'

'I'm staying here for a day or two longer. I only get up here every other month, and some of these people are quite ill. And then there's Monica.'

'I thought she was being taken to town for psychiatric care?'

'She needs extensive psychiatric care, to be sure. Her hallucinations are quite startling. But I'm not sure she's physically up to the journey as yet.'

'You're sure they're hallucinations?'

'Oh, absolutely. Monsters! We don't have monsters in Guyana, Mrs O'Ryan. She was attacked by someone, maybe someone she knew. Maybe she's too afraid to admit, even to herself, who it was. That's something I have to try to get to the bottom of, bring her mind back to normal. Simpson, of course, is hoping her attacker will turn out to be Ledden, the man he has under arrest. That would tie things up very neatly.'

'I'm sure it would,' Shirley said. 'But you know something, Doc? I'm damned glad you're staying.'

Never had she felt so frustrated, even after a good night's sleep. Everyone around her seemed determined to treat what had happened with the utmost logic and common sense. Whereas she knew better. As did Tom.

But Tom was lying there virtually helpless, mentally as well as physically, and would remain like that for the next few days. While Cal and his people were taking off tomorrow. She had to make them stay, as well as follow up *her* line of thinking. Make them ... she chewed her lip, then went to the window. It was another beautiful day. The rain really seemed to have gone away, at least for a while.

She was sure she could find the cave again. And Tom was sure the cave led somewhere. If she could prove that, Cal would have to do something about it. If she could.

She dressed, pulled on her stout boots. Snakes! Where there had been one bushmaster there might well be others. Carefully she took Tom's revolver from his pocket, reloaded it. Thank heavens they had left the undressing of the unconscious man to her, and thus Cal had not found out about the gun; Glossop had not mentioned it, but then he probably had one himself – he was turning out to be a man of hidden talents. Just to be safe, she wrote a note, which she folded and left on the washstand.

She tucked the gun into the back of her pants, the way Tom always did, added a light jacket to conceal it, pocketed his torch, put on her hat and went outside.

'I'm just taking a little walk, Mrs Smith,' she said. 'I'll be back for breakfast.'

'You ain't taking coffee?'

'No, I won't today, thank you.'

'Well, don't get bit by no snake,' Mrs Smith recommended.

Glossop was not yet about, to her relief, and the village was only just waking up. There were one or two people, who gave her their usual pleasant greeting, then she was at the end of the street and facing the walk up to the rest house. She drew a deep breath and set out. In the absence of rain it continued to be a glorious day, although there remained enough moisture in the forest to cause some of it to fall from overloaded leaf or branch every so often. Again, in the absence of rain, there were sounds she had not noticed before, rustlings in the undergrowth to either side of the path, bird calls that ranged from the plaintive wails of the yellow-headed kiskadees – so named for their cry, a corruption of the French phrase *qu'est ce que tu dis*? – to the always distant but incredibly loud squawk of the huge-beaked toucan, a cross between a howl and a bark, high and penetrating.

The track led away from the river. But the water continued on her left, the roar of the Falls growing louder by the moment, so that it eventually obliterated all other sounds. She tried studying the marks left on the track during the rain, which had solidified into mud, but they were mostly the wheels of

Washington's jeep. Now she was climbing quite steeply, and had to pause from time to time to catch her breath. By the time she reached the rest house she was exhausted, and sat down. It was just after eight, and she had been walking for two hours, uphill.

She fanned herself with her hat while she gazed at the slow-moving brown water. Impossible to remember that she had sat right here, with Tom, only six days ago, to watch the Grumman take off. She shivered, got up, put on her hat and followed the path along the river bank. Look for the indentation on the other bank, she told herself. But it was nearly nine before she saw it.

Obviously she was not going to get back for breakfast. But that might be no bad thing, if it caused Mrs Smith to open the note and have Washington, or, even better, Cal come looking for her. Now she faced the jungle. If she were to get lost in there ... But the path she and Tom and Glossop had hacked through the undergrowth was clearly visible. Yet she proceeded slowly, and carefully, looking from left to right and pausing every so often to listen. The sun was quite high now, and gaining in heat; the forest was steaming and visibility was down to about thirty yards. She was sweating profusely, both from the long walk and climb and from the sudden heat, but the noise of the Falls was dulled and distant.

She had walked for about ten minutes, and was almost inclined to turn back, when she saw the rocks. Now she hurried, tripped over an exposed root and fell to her hands and knees. Her hat came off and she crammed it back on her head, gazed at the aperture. Tom had said the snake followed him in. She looked left and right, followed several of the rocks and boulders right round, peering into their damp overhangs, but saw nothing.

She returned to the aperture, stooped and entered the cave. Now she drew the revolver with her right hand, held the flashlight in her left and sent the beam to the back of the cave. Or as far as it would reach. Cautiously she advanced, then paused again to listen. There was no immediate sound. Distant sound was obliterated by the roar of the Falls.

She followed the beam of the flashlight. The cave was definitely descending. And turning, although she had not been aware of it; when she next stopped and looked back the opening was lost round a corner, its presence signified only by a faint glow of light. She turned back again, her nostrils suddenly afflicted with an unpleasant smell. She crept forward, the beam penetrating the now quite intense darkness in front of her, and suddenly there was nothing beneath her feet.

Shirley plunged into blackness.

Nine

The Cavern

Shirley actually did not fall all that far, and landed on a fairly soft surface. But she was totally winded, and had lost her flashlight. The darkness was intense, the only faint glimmer of light coming down the passage she had followed, but the entrance was now far away, and several corners distant, and it was no more than a glimmer. The roar of the Falls was deafening. She knew they had to be at least half a mile away, but in the confined space it was like being inside a bass drum.

She pushed herself up, feeling her arms and legs to make sure she had not broken anything, and realized that she had also dropped Tom's revolver. She scrabbled about in the darkness and gradually understood that she was in some kind of a rubbish dump, which gave off the offensive smell she had noticed earlier. Desperately she rose to her feet, and fell down again as she lost her balance. Then she became aware of movement from above her. It was stealthy movement, but too disconnected to be that of a snake. It made her heart pound, and when she tried to lick her lips they were dry.

She tried to estimate the distance to the lip of the passageway from which she had fallen, and made it about eight feet. She fumbled against the rock wall, but it was too smooth to contemplate climbing in the darkness. So she wasn't going to get out of the pit without help. Thus she either sat tight, in these distinctly unwholesome surroundings, and waited for someone to come and get her, which might not be for several hours, or she attempted to contact whatever was above her. But the thought of who, or *what*, that might be was stomach churning.

The movements had stopped, but she heard a series of barks, as of wild animals communicating, loudly, because of the noise. Wild animals? But the sounds were vaguely intelligible, and the intelligible parts were English! Her cousins? Her flesh came up in goose pimples. Whoever it was knew she was there! They were asking each other who, or what, was in the pit. She took a deep breath.

'Hello!' she called. 'Is anyone there?'

The shouted conversation ceased. These creatures, if they were creatures, had been responsible for the death of Billy Milton, and heaven alone knew how many others over the years. Not to mention the abduction of various people – for what purpose she didn't care to think about. But they could be her relatives.

'Hello,' she called again. 'I don't mean you any harm. I'm unarmed. I just want to speak with you. Can you help me get out of this pit?'

The conversation resumed, but they spoke quickly, and in the noise she couldn't make out what they were saying. 'Listen!' she shouted. 'My name is Shirley. My grandfather's name was Donald Wishart. Does this mean anything to you? Donald Wishart! He was on the airplane that crashed here, sixty-two years ago. Donald Wishart!' She paused, panting, listening.

There was again silence, then more movement. She waited. Still the Falls roared in the distance, setting up a continuous rumble within the cavern. Then something landed beside her. The thump was heavy, and startling. Taken by surprise, she blinked into the gloom and saw only a pair of eyes, well above her own, while the scent of humanity – she hoped it was humanity – grew very strong. But the eyes ... that was what Monica had said: the eyes, gleaming at her.

They made her think of cats' eyes, and she understood why; these eyes could see in the dark. Dimly she took in the shape in front of her. The man, if it was a man, was very large. He was also naked, she estimated. But almost entirely covered in hair.

She couldn't be afraid. Or, at least, she couldn't show her fear, even if she was trembling and sweat was pouring out of her hair.

'I'm Shirley,' she shouted. 'Shirley.'

'Shirley,' he shouted in reply.

'Oh, thank God!' she cried. But then the creature moved forward, with startling speed. Shirley could only gasp as his arm went round her waist and in the same instant he put up his other arm. Instantly she was whisked upwards, and she understood that they were being lifted, all on the strength of his right arm, and the immense power of whoever had hold of his hand. A moment later she was again on firm ground, on the inner side of the pit.

And now she was surrounded, by four of the creatures, two of them women, she thought, as they came close to finger her clothes and her flesh. All were naked, and all were shrouded in hair.

'Shirley,' she said desperately. 'Shirley Wishart. Your grandfather is mine.'

They gabbled, perhaps at her, perhaps at each other. Then her arms were grasped and she was being half pushed, half carried down the sloping floor of the inner passageway. The walls were close on either side, and the noise of the Falls grew louder by the moment.

'Listen,' she said. 'I would like to help you. Help you.'

'Wishart,' one of the creatures said.

Shirley was utterly taken aback. The woman pronounced the word uncertainly. But she had definitely said Wishart. 'I guess you don't talk much,' she said. 'Maybe you don't have too much to talk about. I can help you. Really I can. We're cousins.'

She was thrust forward and her arms released, so suddenly that she fell to her hands and knees, and only then realized that the passageway had debouched into a large chamber, faintly lit by phosphorescent outcrops of rock. But she could see, and caught her breath in horror. Stalactites hung from the roof, and stalagmites rose from the floor; this was to be expected, but hanging from the rocks to either side were large chunks of meat, most of it high. Was any of it human? She couldn't be sure. But most of the carcasses were of animals.

She turned her head left and right, able at last to see her captors – for she had so to consider them at the moment – clearly for the first time. They were, as she had estimated, two men and two women. They were certainly human, although, as their hair did not appear ever to have been cut, this needed a second look to be certain. Both men and women had tumbling locks, which would, if allowed, have reached their ankles, but they each had gathered it up and wrapped it several times round their waists, from which it hung down like a sort of skirt, giving them much of their animal-like appearance. The men also wore moustaches, drooping past their chins, and long beards. The hair was dark with streaks of red. For the rest, however, they seemed perfectly normal, although the women as well as the men had extremely well-developed muscles, and they ambled rather than walked, shoulders hunched. And carried their heads thrust forward, an indication of the conditions in which they lived, either in the low-ceilinged passage-ways of their caves or in the jungle itself. The men, certainly, were clearly interested in their female prisoner.

'I'm your cousin,' she said. Not that she supposed they would be put off by the thought of incest.

Something tugged at her trousers, and she turned, sharply, to discover that she was surrounded by five children, aged between about four and eight, she estimated. Like their parents – as she had to presume the adults were – they were naked and their hair was already very long. They were shouting at her, but again she had difficulty in deciphering what they were saying. They were also dragging her across the floor of the cavern.

She looked at the adults, but they didn't seem to object, so she allowed herself to go with the children, wondering if she was about to be sacrificed to some forest god. Suddenly they stopped moving, and she found herself gazing at two other people, whom she had not noticed when she had first entered the cavern.

One of them was a young woman, who did not look in the least like any of the others, either in feature or colouring, while her hair, though long, reached only as far as her thighs. Shirley guessed immediately that she was the girl abducted from the village several months earlier; this horrendous thought was confirmed by the fact that she was heavily pregnant. She stared at Shirley with her mouth open, but didn't speak, and Shirley was too busy taking in the other person to attempt to start a conversation.

This was a man, seated on a slab of rock. He was as naked and as shrouded in hair as any of the others, but much older; his hair was quite white, and his body emaciated. But the greatest surprise was when he spoke.

'You are not from the villages,' he said, in perfect English, with a strong American accent.

Shirley swallowed. 'No,' she said. 'I am from the States. America. I came to find you. I'm Shirley Wishart. You are my grand-father.'

The old man gazed at her for several seconds, his eyes sliding up and down her body. At last he asked, 'Shirley Wishart?'

'Wishart,' said the woman standing at Shirley's shoulder. She then spoke very quickly, but ended with the word Wishart again.

Shirley guessed she was telling the old man – was he also her grandfather? – that Shirley had claimed the name when first captured.

'Listen,' Shirley said, 'Don Wishart was my grandfather. Lieutenant Don Wishart, jg.' She drew a deep breath. 'Are you him?'

The man she was facing could easily be eighty-plus. 'Don Wishart,' he said. 'Lieutenant, jg. You cannot be his granddaughter. Don Wishart never married, or had a child, in America.'

'No,' she said. 'He did have a child. He left Marge Cowan pregnant. Okay, so my name isn't Wishart. I was trying to establish myself, right? My name is Richards. But I am Marge Cowan's granddaughter, by Don Wishart. He ... you ... are my grandfather.'

Another long stare. 'It may be possible,' he said at last. 'But why have you come here? How did you get in here?' He looked at her captors. One of the men mumbled something unintelligible. 'That is bad,' the old man said. 'Very bad. It must not happen again.' He looked at Shirley. 'You were on that airplane that exploded?'

'I had been on it,' Shirley said. 'You mean you saw that?'

'We heard it, even above the water,' Wishart said. He looked at the two men. 'Michael was very upset. He went out and killed. Why did you bring this trouble upon us?'

'I came here to find you, Grandpa.' Shirley took a step forward, and checked, as the people, the children included, seemed to close around her, while Wishart, if it were he, made no sign of welcome.

'Why?' he asked.

'It is something I wanted to do. I have wanted to do it all of my life.'

'Are you alone?'

'There is a man with me.' The people at her shoulders stirred. 'But he is in bed with a snakebite,' Shirley explained hastily. 'I am alone, now. But ... he, or others, will come looking for me if I do not return by this evening.'

'Evening,' Wishart said, as if he was not sure what time of day that was.

'Listen,' Shirley said urgently. 'Come back to the village with me. You can't go on living like ... like this, for ever.'

'Go close the entrance,' Wishart told the young men. 'And don't ever leave it open again.' Immediately they hurried off. 'No one will find you, now,' Wishart said, with some satisfaction.

'You don't understand,' Shirley said, refusing to accept the very real fear that was starting to attack her mind. 'I don't want to harm you. Nobody wants to harm you.'

'They hunt us,' Wishart said. 'As you hunt us.'

'That's not true,' Shirley shouted. 'They don't understand you, that's all. I can make them understand you. Oh, there may be some trouble over the people you have abducted. But I'm sure we can sort that out.'

'And the people we have killed?' Wishart asked.

Shirley bit her lip. 'Why did you have to do that?'

Wishart shrugged. 'My grandsons wish to prove they are lords of the forest. The forest provides us with women. We do not wish the men. But when they see us, they wish to attack us. Then, the explosion ... I told you, it excited them.'

Shirley decided against pursuing that line of conversation, or bringing up the matter of Billy Milton, until she could get out.

'Listen, the policeman in charge up here is a friend of mine. I know he'll understand.'

'You are a stupid woman,' Wishart said. 'Woo-woo was a stupid woman.'

'Woo-woo,' Shirley said. 'Yes. She was one of the people on the plane. You mean she survived the crash?'

'Come,' Wishart said.

He got up and walked towards the back of the cavern, moving more freely than Shirley had expected of so old a man, and she was pushed behind him by the two women, while the children again clustered around to pull at her clothes, urging her onwards. She glanced at the Amerindian girl, but she didn't move. Half pulled and half pushed she followed her grandfather, as she now knew him to be, deeper into the cave, which suddenly bent to the left. She stumbled over the uneven surface, and paused in utter consternation.

The noise had been growing ever louder, and now they were in a very large cavern indeed, stretching some two hundred feet ... and ending in a wall of tumbling water. The Falls. Seen from the *inside*! The noise was quite ear shattering. But between them and the pouring water there was the wreckage of an aircraft, partly burned out.

'My God!' Shirley muttered. 'You did come through the water!'

'Smailes,' Wishart said. 'He was a fool. And he was stale drunk.'

'But you survived,' Shirley said.

'And the women. We were in the cabin, and we got out,' Wishart said. 'Lynette, Woo-woo and me. We got out before the plane caught fire.'

'And you've been here ever since?' Shirley asked. 'But...' She looked left and right at the women and children. 'How have you lived?' She wasn't sure she wanted to be answered.

'We couldn't get out through the water,' Wishart said. 'But we knew we had to find a way out, or die. It took us more than a fortnight to find the way up.'

'But ... how did you live for that time?' she asked again, and bit her lip.

'We pulled Harry and Smailes out as well,' Wishart said.

'Oh my God,' Shirley said. 'Oh my *God*!'

'They were already dead,' Wishart explained. 'There was no means of burying them.'

Shirley's legs gave way and she sank to the floor of the cavern. Sawney Bean, she thought. Sawney Bean! And she had supposed that a macabre legend.

'Woo-woo,' she muttered.

Wishart stood beside her. 'Woo-woo cracked up,' he said. 'She had been behaving oddly since we found the way out. Then when we got out she ran off. Lynette and I looked for her, but we couldn't find her before she reached some men. We watched from the trees. She started to tell them about the plane crash and the men we had eaten. But she was naked, and they didn't listen. They threw her on the ground and they raped her, one after the other. Then they strangled her. There was nothing Lynette and I could do. When they were finished with her, they came looking for us. We got back into the cave and they never did find us. But they were going to murder us, too. Then we knew we couldn't come out.'

'But ...why wasn't she dressed?' Shirley asked, unable to grasp the extent of the tragedy.

'Our clothes got all messed up in the crash, and after. Anyway, who needs clothes in this climate?' He eyed her shirt and jeans speculatively.

Keep talking, Shirley told herself. While she tried to think, to come to grips with both the fact that her quest had ended, successfully ... and, horribly, that this man *had* become more of an animal than a human. 'And you and Lynette...'

Wishart smiled. 'There wasn't much else to do, down here. And once we had found the way in and out we were able to gather food, vegetables as well as meat.' He smiled, reminiscently. 'We had no knives so we used our bare hands, for everything'.

Shirley looked at the long, sharp nails, and shuddered. 'You have lived like ... like animals, for more than sixty years?'

'Why not? We raised a family.'

'And started attacking the villages.'

'Well, the boys wanted more than their sisters. From time to time. Anyway, those were the bastards who murdered Woo-woo.'

Shirley took several deep breaths 'These...'

'Are my grandchildren, and their children,'

Wishart explained. 'We had a sickness some years back, and all my children died. Lynette too.' He sighed. 'I sure was fond of that girl.'

'And that Amerindian girl...?'

'She'll be giving birth some time soon,' Wishart said.

'And the others...' she licked her lips.

Wishart smiled. 'We didn't eat them, Shirley. We've no taste for that any more, when there's animal meat available. When they'd produced and the boys were tired of them, we pushed them out through the Falls. Same as we buried Lynette and the kids. They're down there, at the bottom, waiting for the rest of us. Waiting for me.'

Shirley couldn't believe her ears. 'You mean you just murdered them?'

'We got rid of them,' Wishart said, carefully. 'They weren't family. They didn't integrate.'

'Is that the way you'll get rid of me?'

Another quick smile. 'You're family. I think the boys will like you. And we'll be getting some good old American blood back into the family. That's what we've lacked these last few years. You can see it in the great-grandchildren.'

Shirley looked at the children, who were all looking at her, almost expectantly. I'm going to be sacrificed, she thought. First sexually, and then ... And somehow they'd blocked up the cave entrance, or thought they had.

'Come,' Wishart said, and led her back to the inner cavern, where the noise was slightly abated. Shirley stumbled behind him, the two women always at her shoulders, not speaking, but clearly her gaolers. The children followed, still excited by their new toy.

'The girls are called Lynette and Margaret,' Wishart said over his shoulder. 'We always have a Lynette.'

Lynette! Shirley thought. If she could distract him, and his grandchildren, sufficiently ... 'Grandpa,' she said. 'Do you mind if I call you Grandpa?'

'I'd like that,' he said, and seated himself on the flat rock where she had first seen him.

She knelt at his feet. 'Tell me about Lynette.'

'She was a sweet kid.'

Shirley drew a deep breath. 'Was she carrying something back to the States?'

Wishart frowned. 'Now how did you know that?'

'I found out. Was she? What was it? Did she tell you?'

'It was a phial containing some kind of liquid.'

'Didn't she know what it was?'

'Nope. She thought it was some kind of new gas the Germans had invented, and her boss in Cairo had got hold of a sample and wanted it analysed.'

'And is it ... did it survive the crash?'

'Oh, yes. She carried it in a special belt inside her clothes. The phial itself was lead, so although it got knocked about a bit it survived. Say, did that war ever end?'

'Years and years ago. But the phial ... do you still have it?'

'God knows. Somewhere, I guess.'

'Somewhere in here?'

'I guess.' He was utterly uninterested.

'Didn't you ever open it, to see what was inside?'

'Lynette reckoned it might be dangerous. Highly toxic, or explosive if mixed with air. She wouldn't ever open it.'

'May I see it?'

'Shit, Shirley, I have no idea where it is. Lynette stashed it somewhere over sixty years ago. How come you're so interested in it? Whatever it was, it will have evaporated or just disintegrated long ago.'

Not if it's the elixir of life, Shirley thought. But she decided against saying it.

'It could be valuable.'

'You mean, money wise? What have we got to do with money? Money is a waste of time, when you have everything that money can buy, anyway.'

It was a philosophy to which she would have subscribed, in any other circumstances. But right now ... She heard movement behind her, and turned to watch the two men emerging from the upward-sloping corridor.

'All taken care of?' Wishart asked.

'Yeah'm,' one of them said.

'They don't talk all that well,' Wishart explained. 'Well, they don't have all that many people to talk with, right? You talk to them, Shirley. It'll do them good. This here is Lyle, and that one is Michael.'

'Hi,' Shirley said. The man called Lyle stepped up to her and ran his hands over her shirt. 'Cut that out,' she said, and made to step back, only to find her arms grasped by Michael. 'Make them stop,' she asked Wishart.

Who gave one of his smiles. 'They think you are beautiful. Well, you are beautiful, Shirley.'

'Me'um too,' Lyle said.

'Sure,' Wishart agreed. 'He wants to fuck you,' he explained. 'After me, of course.'

'After *you*?' Shirley shouted. 'You're my grandfather, for God's sake!'

'I can still do it,' he asserted. 'Who do you think fathered all these kids?' Shirley looked left and right at the great-grandchildren. 'They get the women when I'm done,' Wishart said. 'They'll have you when I'm done. And right now I feel it coming over me.'

Shirley could see that. My God, she thought, I am about to be raped by my own grandfather. 'Listen,' she said. 'If I'm not back at the settlement by this evening...' she

263

looked at her watch. It was just on eleven. They'd be sitting down to breakfast. And they should have found her note by now, too. She had to survive until they reached her. 'They'll come looking for me. Men. Policemen, with guns.'

'Because you have disappeared? Several people have disappeared over the past few years,' Wishart pointed out.

'I'm not several people,' Shirley shouted. 'I'm me, Shirley Richards. I told you, I'm up here with the police. Listen! I came to find you, sure. But the others are after what is in that phial. They'll kill to get it.'

He was at last interested. 'You think it's that valuable?'

'They think it contains a recipe for immortality. The elixir of life.'

'The elixir of life?' Wishart spoke slowly. 'That is a ridiculous dream.'

'Maybe. But there are people out there who will do anything to get hold of it. You say you heard that plane crash a few days ago? There was a huge explosion, and then it went down in the gorge.'

Wishart looked at his grandsons.

'Bang,' Michael said. 'We hear'm.'

'We heard it,' Wishart said. 'Like I told you, it upset Michael.'

So that he went out and attacked Monica and then tore out poor Billy Milton's throat, Shirley thought. But at least she had their attention. 'That plane was blown up, deliberately, by the people who are after that phial,' she said.

'They cannot reach us here,' Wishart said.

'They will, you know. They'll find that entrance, and if necessary they'll blow it open.'

'To find you? Or the phial?'

'I left a note, telling them where I'd gone. We found the cave entrance two days ago. But then my partner was bitten by a snake. So I decided to have a look on my own. But I left the note. They'll have found that by now.'

'And they want the phial,' Wishart said thoughtfully. 'If they find the phial, they will go away and leave us in peace.'

Shirley bit her lip; she had overplayed her hand. 'They'll want me as well,' she said. 'The police will.'

'They want the phial,' Wishart said. 'They have no interest in you. Save as another missing person. Then we must make sure they get the phial and will go away again. Search,' he told his grandchildren. 'Seek and find.'

'What?' asked Lynette.

'A little bottle, made of heavy metal. About this big.' He extended thumb and forefinger.

'Where?' Margaret asked.

'Start where Grandmother Lynette used to sleep,' Wishart said. 'All of you, now. Find 'that phial.'

'I'll help them,' Shirley volunteered.

'You stay,' Wishart commanded. She hesitated, watched her cousins disappearing down a side passageway. To her relief, the children went, too, chattering excitedly, but so did the Amerindian girl, leaving her alone with Wishart. But he was an old man.

'Come here,' Wishart said.

He was ready for her now, hairy, naked and aroused. Her grandfather!

'Listen,' she said. 'Grandpa. I don't want to have to hurt you, but let me tell you, if you lay a finger on me I am going to kick you in the balls.'

He smiled and stood up. 'You think you can fight me? You? A mere girl? Strip.'

Shirley took a step backwards. There was no sound coming from any of the others, lost as they were beyond the rumble of the Falls. Nor did she think they'd hear Wishart shout. But after she had laid him out, as it now appeared she was going to have to do, what then? Had they really blocked the entrance? But even if they had, it had to be a block removable from the inside, or they would not be able to get out again. He was right up to her now, reaching for her, his face twisted in a mixture of lust and anticipation.

'No,' she said. 'Please, Grandpa.'

He touched her hair, and his hand slipped round to the nape of her neck. His other hand suddenly moved down her shirt front, ripping away the buttons. Only then did she realiz how strong he was. Far too strong for an old man. Because he had lived all his life using his muscles. She turned away sharply, still reluctant to fight with her own grandfather. Having opened her shirt, his fingers caught in her brassiere, and now the hand on her neck moved back to her hair and twined fingers in it. Shirley gave a gasp of pain and struck backwards with her elbows. It was his turn to gasp, and his grip slackened. She jerked her head free, felt her bra strap popping as his other hand tightened its grip. She threw herself away from him to the sound of ripping material, landed on her hands and knees naked from the waist up, thrust herself forward and felt his hand close on her ankle.

He was shouting now, a continuous high-pitched roar which didn't seem to contain any words. And he was pulling her back to him. Shirley kicked with her free leg, and got him somewhere, for there was a shout of pain amidst the roar. But the grip on her ankle remained unbroken, and now he was turning her over, on to her back, kneeling between her legs, teeth gleaming in the darkness. Billy Milton had had his throat torn out. Jesus! She thought.

'You fight me, I'll tear you apart,' Wishart said, releasing her ankle, but only to slide his hand up her pants leg, while his other hand closed on her belt, fumbling at the buckle. His face was close to hers as he leant over her, both hands now sliding over her crotch, releasing the belt and fumbling for the zip. She would have to hurt him, after all. She struck up at his face, slashing at his cheeks with her nails. Blood spurted, and he gave a truly animal howl of pain and anger. But for the moment she was free. She dug her heels into the stone floor and propelled herself backwards, out of his reach, turned on to her hands and knees and scrambled to her feet.

He was still kneeling, roaring and scraping the blood from his face and eyes. Shirley looked left and right. There were four possible exits from the cavern. One led back to the outer cave and the Falls, and was clearly a dead end. The one on the right was where the family had gone, to search for the phial. That, too, was out of the question. The centre passageway, she was sure, led back to the entrance. Which was now blocked? The fourth led into the rock wall; she had no idea where it might end up.

She chose the centre passageway. Not only was it more familiar than the others, but she was sure it would still enable her to get out, somehow. It sloped upwards, as she remembered, and she ran up it for some distance. Here it turned a corner, again as she remembered, and here, too, the darkness once again became intense as the phosphorescence was left behind.

She paused, panting, and listened to heavy footsteps behind her. He was following. She ran up the slope again, trying to remember how far she had been brought after they had lifted her from the pit; she couldn't afford to fall in there again.

Staring into the gloom, she ran on a few feet, then paused. Still the sound was following her, but he was of course moving more slowly than she. Now she had to slow to a walk, trying to get her breathing back under control, and still coming on the pit sooner than she had expected. Her boots scrabbled at the edge as she forced herself back against the wall. The crevasse wasn't more than a few feet wide. It should be possible to jump across it – supposing there was nothing solid on the other side to throw her back. If she missed ... at the very least she would probably break something. But the alternative...

The sound from behind was now very close. Shirley retreated several feet, drawing great breaths and tensing her muscles, and heard him roar as he saw her.

'Bitch!' he bellowed. 'I am going to make you hate the day you were born.'

She had forgotten: these creatures could see in the dark as well as any cat! She raced forward, reached the edge of the pit and hurled herself across it. She cleared the opposite lip by a couple of feet, landed on her hands and knees with a jar that seemed to crack every bone in her body and fell to her face, panting and groaning. But she was across. The open air was only a few feet away now. Sunlight, and, hopefully, people. She pushed herself up, and there was a thump behind her. She turned, still on her knees, to stare in horror at Wishart. He hadn't jumped, but had crossed the crevasse by holding on to a dangling vine and swinging himself over. She hadn't noticed the vine before.

Now he had released the vine and was standing above her. She saw his teeth gleam.

'Granddaughter,' he said. 'I am going to break every bone in your body before you go over the Falls.'

Shirley turned away from him, ran round the corner and heard the hissing of the snake.

Ten

The Search

Tom blinked at Cal. 'I need a drink,' he muttered.

'And you shall have one,' Cal assured him. 'Jessie! A glass of water for Mr O'Ryan. And then some coffee.'

'Jessie?' Tom asked. 'Is that her name? Jessie?'

'That's it. How're you feeling?'

Tom scratched his head. 'Would you believe it if I said almost human?'

'That figures. You've done hardly more than sleep for the past forty-eight hours. Doc Willard says you can get out of bed today. But you have to take it easy. He's leaving you some medication, pills and the like, just in case the fever comes back. What's your temperature now, by the way?'

'How the hell should I know?'

'Shirley was supposed to take it, last thing at night and first thing in the morning.'

'I don't remember her doing it. You'll have to ask her.'

'I will, when she comes back.'

'Where's she gone?'

'For a walk, I believe. Now, there's some-one here I want you to meet.'

Tom had been aware all along that there was another person in the room, but for the moment he was too grateful for the glass of water that Mrs Smith produced, together with the steaming mug of coffee.

'Man, but you is looking one whole lot better,' Mrs Smith remarked. 'I did think you was going to die.'

'I felt like that myself,' Tom agreed.

'This is Professor Fuller,' Cal said.

Fuller was a white man, tall but thin, wearing a crushed white suit; he even had a tie, which drooped from his neck like a piece of string. 'I've been hearing a lot about you,' he remarked.

Another American. Tom looked at Cal.

'I told you about him, remember?' Cal said. 'Dr Fuller is an anthropologist. He's interested in the theories you and Shirley have.'

'Came right up,' Fuller said.

'What theories?' Tom asked.

Fuller frowned. 'You're not suffering from amnesia, I hope?'

'I'm not suffering from amnesia,' Tom said. 'But there are several theories knocking about.' Once again he looked at Cal.

'Like I said, the doc is an anthropologist.

He's interested in Shirley's idea that her grandad could have survived that crash and then could have fathered a family living behind that waterfall. That right, Prof?'

'That's right,' Fuller said.

'Even if you don't see how that could be possible, eh?' Cal added, meaningfully, so that Tom would understand that he had not told Fuller about the elixir.

'All things are possible, I guess. Feel up to a chat, Mr O'Ryan?'

Tom drank coffee. 'What I really feel like is some breakfast,' he said.

'I'll get Jessie on to it,' Cal said. He went to the door, checked. 'I'll want a decision from you as to whether or not you and Shirley are coming back to town with us. We leave at dawn tomorrow morning, and Doc Willard says you're fit enough to travel.'

'You're leaving as soon as that?'

'Well, we have our man. I want to get him to town and charge him properly, and see if he'll tell us who's paying him. Your being along might help.'

'I'll ask Shirley,' Tom said. He was trying to get his thoughts under control, to separate reality from the various extreme nightmares he had endured over the past forty-eight hours. But that cavern had been real. If it hadn't been, if there hadn't been a snake, he wouldn't be here now. That really meant there was no way they could abandon the search now, when they were so close.

'Ahem,' Fuller remarked.

'Oh, sorry,' Tom said. 'I drifted off.'

'May I ask you a few questions?'

'Certainly.'

'Would you mind telling me just how you got involved in this? I mean, what information led up to your expedition.'

'Expedition?' Tom grinned. But he supposed to someone as wrapped up in scientific probes as this man obviously was it had been an expedition. He told him about Shirley's advertisement, his reply, their meeting in London and their decision to come to Guyana. He did not mention the two heavies in his apartment, or the death threats.

'Hm,' Fuller said. 'Rather a wild good chase, in my opinion. But there has to be more to it than that. What about this plane blowing up?'

'That's Superintendent Simpson's territory. I'm just glad we weren't on it.'

'I'll say. And you don't think it had anything to do with you? The locals here seem to think it did.'

'Well ... why should anyone want to blow us up, Professor Fuller?'

'Why indeed,' Fuller agreed. 'So, what have you managed to unearth since getting here?'

'We seem to have activated the creatures, whatever they are. There have been two attacks since we arrived, one of them fatal.'

'And the superintendent is investigating these, too?'

'No, he's not, at the moment. You heard him. He's more interested in the blowing up of that plane. He reckons he has the man who planted the bomb. All he wants now is to find out who paid him.'

'And he's ignoring a murder?'

'Well, you see, Professor Fuller, the problem is that he's not sure there's been a murder. Shirley, that's my partner, and Mr Glossop...'

'I've met Glossop.'

'Well, the two of them and myself found the body of Glossop's friend Milton. Trouble was, when we went back to it with the commissioner it had gone. Unfortunately, people do tend to disappear in this jungle, without necessarily having been murdered.'

'But there was also a girl attacked, I'm told.'

'Sure there was. Again, the only people who saw the attack were Shirley and me. The girl can't remember anything about it that matters. And Cal has the idea that Shirley and I are so obsessed with her possible relatives that we're seeing bigfeet behind every bush.'

'Hm,' Fuller said. 'Well, let me ask you something straight out, Mr O'Ryan: *did* you see something?'

'Yes, we did, Professor. And we found

tracks. And the tracks were those of human feet. I also found a piece of hair.'

'Now that is interesting,' Fuller said. 'May I see it?'

'Cal has it. I believe he means to have it analysed.'

'Hm. So, you genuinely believe that there is a creature, or a nest of creatures, with human characteristics, living behind the Falls. Who are able to get in or out at will. Now, how do you suppose they can do that?'

Tom considered the man. But Fuller seemed prepared to believe him, where Cal was not. And Cal was in any event returning to Georgetown in the morning.

'I think we've found out how,' he said.

Fuller's eyes narrowed. 'You serious?'

'How do you think I got this snakebite?'

'You are saying you have found a way to get behind the Falls?' Now he was sounding doubtful. But also excited.

'We think we have. We found the entrance to a cave beyond which I am certain there is a passage into the ground, in the direction of the river and the Falls. Trouble is, as I entered the cave I was attacked by that goddamned snake. Well, Glossop saved my life, and he and Shirley and the game warden got me out, but naturally that put an end to the idea of exploring the passage, for the time being. But as soon as I am on my feet again, which could be today...'

'Your breakfast ready,' said Mrs Smith, from the doorway.

Fuller sat with Tom while he ate, and they were joined by Glossop, and Dr Willard also came in; he had been holding another surgery.

'Do any of you have any idea where Shirley is?' Tom asked.

'She gone for a walk,' Mrs Smith said, serving.

'She seems to be gone a long time.'

'Now where...' Glossop looked at Tom, not sure whether or not Fuller was in his confidence.

'Christalmighty!' Tom said. 'That silly girl.'

'You reckon she went back to that cave?' Fuller asked.

'Shit!' Tom exploded. 'What time did she go out, Mrs Smith?'

'You mind your language,' Mrs Smith admonished. 'I told you, she went out early. Must've been before seven.'

'And now it's eleven. Four hours.'

'If she was walking, it'd take her about that long to reach the cave,' Glossop said.

'She's a strong, fit woman. More like two.'

'Then you reckon she may have gone inside?' Fuller asked.

'I don't know what she's done. What we have to do is go after her. Mob-handed. Glossop, would you get hold of the superintendent? I'm going to get dressed.'

'You reckon you're strong enough to go out there?' Glossop asked.

'Yes,' Tom snapped, drank the last of his coffee and limped back to his bedroom.

Glossop hurried out of the building.

'Will somebody please tell me what's going on?' Willard asked, following Tom. Tom obliged while he dressed. Willard scratched his head. 'You mean you really did find a way to get under the Falls?'

'I don't know that. I found what I thought was a passageway, and then that goddamned snake found me. I have an idea Shirley has gone back to have a closer look.'

'But if she has ... holy smoke,' Willard commented. 'What about that snake?'

'That snake is dead,' Tom pointed out. 'We didn't see any others. I'm more worried about what else she may have found. If she managed to get in there.'

Willard wiped his brow with his handkerchief.

'You really think your lady could be in danger?' Fuller asked, from the doorway.

'If those creatures are down there, yes.'

'If they exist, they could be her relatives,' Fuller pointed out.

'Several times removed.' Tom stood in front of the washstand, gazed at the envelope, then ripped it open. 'If I'm not back by lunchtime, come and get me,' he read aloud. 'That's where she's gone, all right.'

There were heavy feet in the lobby, and he went out to find Cal Simpson standing there, looking irritated. 'Just what the hell is going on?' he enquired.

'Read this.' Tom gave him Shirley's note.

Cal scanned the brief sentence and raised his head. 'Explain?'

'Listen,' Tom said. 'When I was attacked by that snake, it was because I was exploring a cave we'd found, with a passageway leading off.'

'Leading off where?'

'That's the point. I never had the chance to find out; the snake got in my way.'

'And you reckon that's where Shirley has gone? By herself? She'd have to be crazy.'

'Just enthusiastic. We have to go after her, Cal. She could be in deep trouble.'

'You reckon that cave could be the way in to these creatures' lair? Man, that's going it a bit. We don't even know they exist.'

'I know they exist,' Tom said. 'So does Shirley. So does Glossop. And you believe it, don't you, Professor Fuller?'

'I'm prepared to believe it,' Fuller said, cautiously.

'So I'm going out there,' Tom said.

'You'll never make it,' Cal objected.

'I will if I have some help. I'm asking you to help me, Cal. Whether you believe me or not, we can't just abandon Shirley out there

279

in that bush. According to that note, she intended to be back for breakfast. But she isn't.'

'Yeah,' Cal said thoughtfully. 'Okay, we'll come with you, Tommy. I just hope it ain't some wild good chase and we don't come home to find her sitting in the bar.'

'How many men can you bring?'

'How many do you need?'

'I believe there could be a whole nest of these creatures,' Tom said.

'Okay, I'll bring my policemen.'

'I'll come,' Glossop volunteered. 'They murdered my Billy.'

Cal gave him a dirty look, then turned to Fuller. 'You coming, Prof?'

'Ah ... if it's all the same to you, I won't,' Fuller said. 'I'm not all that good at crawling around jungles any more.'

'Doc? We may need you.'

'I'm due to hold another surgery,' Willard said. 'But I hope you do find the young lady, quickly. And if she's harmed in any way, then you bring her back here as fast as you can.'

'You can count on that,' Cal agreed. 'All right, gentlemen, fifteen minutes? We'll assemble at the district commissioner's office.'

Tom was pleased to see that Washington had also volunteered to accompany them. So they made up a party of eight, Cal and four policemen, Washington, Glossop and himself. He couldn't find his revolver, so he guessed Shirley had taken it, but Cal had his, and the four policemen had automatic rifles. He reckoned they were a powerful enough unit to handle anything they were liable to find. What did he expect to find? He was praying nothing, except an exhausted Shirley. But if she had gone into that cavern, alone ... Even if there was nothing there, it had been a foolhardy thing to do.

'You all bring that lady back, eh?' Rimmer told them.

Cal grinned. 'She's my witness. I'll bring her back. By the way, this is Professor Fuller. He's keeping a kind of watching brief. He knows about animals and critters.'

'Mind if I ask you some questions, Mr Rimmer?' Fuller asked. 'I'm trying to build up a picture of what these creatures are like.'

'You can ask,' Rimmer agreed. 'But I ain't never seen one. I don't even know if they are real.'

'But all these attacks...'

'Yeah,' Rimmer said. 'Come inside, Professor.' He opened the door of his office.

'What's down there?' Fuller asked, glancing along the corridor.

Rimmer grinned. 'That is the cell. It ain't need that much.'

Fuller frowned. 'But there is someone in there now.'

'Oh, sure yes, Professor. That is the one what blew up the plane. That is what the superintendent is saying.'

'Good heavens,' Fuller commented. 'Is he safe?'

'He won't be coming out until I let him out,' Cal said. 'You all have a nice chat. We'll be back ... well, some time.'

The posse was equipped with two jeeps, Washington's and one of the police vehicles. They drove up the hill, and as they did so it started to rain.

'I reckon we've had the dry season up here,' Cal commented. 'Shit!'

'Haven't you got a kagool?' Tom asked, innocently.

'I have my poncho, and that ain't going to be too much good, either.'

The rain was indeed very heavy, pounding on the canvas roofs, thudding into the trees and bushes to either side, rapidly turning the track into a skidpan – water spurted away from their wheels. Progress slowed, but eventually they reached the rest house.

'It's about half a mile along the bank,' Tom said.

'Well, it'll have to keep for half an hour,' Cal said. 'This rain should have stopped by then.'

'Look,' Tom protested. 'Shirley is out there in this. She could have fallen. She could drown.'

'So could we,' Cal pointed out.

They went inside, where the noise of the water drumming on the corrugated iron roof deadened even the roar of the Falls. The policemen lit cigarettes and produced a pack of cards; Washington joined them for their game while Cal and Glossop stared at the water thudding past the windows, and Tom walked up and down until his leg started to hurt and he sat in a corner. But at last the rain slackened.

'You're not going to wait for it to stop altogether?' Tom begged.

'I think we could make a move,' Cal agreed, dropping his poncho over his head.

They trailed out of the rest house and made their way along the path. This had all but disintegrated, and the drizzle continued to soak the ground and raise little pimples all across the surface of the river. Behind them the Falls continued to roar sullenly. Tom found the going especially hard, as his leg was now really aching. But he gritted his teeth and kept moving, even as he prayed for a sight of Shirley, emerging from the bush, bedraggled but safe.

'Pity about the rain,' Cal said. 'Otherwise there would have been tracks. How much further?'

'We're there.' Tom pointed across the river at the little bay on the far bank. 'Now we strike off at right angles. It's less than a quarter of a mile.'

Cal produced a ball of strong string and tied one end to the bole of a tree. 'Let's go.'

'I never thought of anything as simple as that,' Tom said admiringly.

'Getting lost in this forest, in the rain, is no fun,' Cal pointed out.

'Think of Shirley.'

She should be able to hear them coming, he thought, for the eight men sounded rather like a tank crashing through the bushes. But he led them confidently, remembering much of the terrain, as obviously did Glossop, and it was Glossop who first pointed at the rocks.

'Just where did you get too close to that snake?' Cal asked.

'It was inside the cave.'

'Still, where there is one bushie there is often a mate, or even a family. Keep your eyes open,' Cal told his policemen, who promptly unslung their rifles.

Tom wasn't all that happy to have them behind him, but he went forward and pointed at the aperture. 'She'll have gone down there.'

Cal peered at the opening. 'Okay. Torches.'

'I'll go first,' Tom said.

'Forget it. You're barely standing now. Wallis, Brereton, you come with me,' Cal said. 'The rest of you wait here. We'll call you if there's a possibility of getting anywhere.

Tommy, you see any sign that Shirley was here?'

'Well, actually, I don't. But it's where she would have come.'

'Right.' Cal switched on his light, which sent a powerful beam into the aperture. He took out his revolver and checked that all the chambers were loaded. 'Not that I want to shoot anything,' he remarked. 'Or anyone. Now, first things first.' One of his men handed him a loudhailer, and he presented this at the cave. 'Anyone in there?' he bawled.

The sound seemed to go in and come back out with a rush, echoing over the forest.

'That would wake the dead,' Glossop remarked.

'But not Shirley, apparently,' Cal pointed out, and tried again. 'Hey!' he shouted. 'Shirley Richards! You in there?' Once again they were surrounded by echo. 'I guess we'll have to go in,' Cal decided.

He handed back the loudspeaker, bent double and inserted himself into the opening; he was a considerably bigger man than Tom. As were his constables, who followed him, the beams of their torches scouring the walls. 'I see your passage,' Cal called over his shoulder. 'Now ... Holy Jesus Christ! Out! Get out!' he shouted at his policemen.

They re-emerged in considerable disarray, one of them dropping his rifle. Cal followed them, having picked up the weapon, but he

285

had lost his cap.

'What is it?' Tom asked, heart pounding.

'That passageway is alive with bush-masters,' Cal said. 'Three of them. Christ!' Despite the rain he pulled out his handker-chief to wipe his brow. His constables levelled their rifles at the opening, but the snakes did not emerge.

'You mean Shirley is in there, with a nest of snakes?' Tom asked, aghast.

'No, I do not mean that,' Cal said, replac-ing his handkerchief and then cap, which had been retrieved by one of his men. 'If Shirley had gone in there she would be lying on the ground dead.'

'But she could be beyond the snakes.'

'There is no way any human being could have got beyond those snakes,' Cal said.

'I got beyond the one who bit me,' Tom said. 'It came up from behind.'

'Yeah, well, I think you were goddamned lucky. Let's get out of here.'

'You can't just walk away from it,' Tom protested. 'Shirley—'

'Tom,' Cal said earnestly. 'Shirley isn't in there. There is no way she could ever have been in there. Bushmasters don't carry away the bodies of their victims. They leave them lying about.'

'But ... her note...'

'Said what? Come and get me. She didn't say where you were to get her. You yourself have just said there is no evidence that she, or anyone else, was ever here.'

'The rain has washed away the tracks. *You* said that.'

'Sure. If there were ever any tracks to begin with. Now, I reckon we have a serious problem here. Shirley has wandered off and got lost, in this bush. We are going to have one hell of a job finding her. So we'd better start now.'

'She could have been nobbled by one of the creatures,' Glossop suggested.

'What creatures?' Cal asked, disagreeably. 'If there are any creatures, they sure ain't down there.'

'We don't know that,' Tom protested.

'You suggesting these creatures have a working arrangement with those snakes?'

'They've been around here for sixty years. The creatures, I mean.'

'Those snakes have been around here one hell of a lot longer. For Christ's sake, Tom, be reasonable. There is no indication that Shirley ever came here. There is a lot of evidence that *no one* has even been in there, and lived. Save you. And if you'd been by yourself you'd be dead. If we're going to find Shirley, it needs to be someplace else.'

'Like where? Her note indicates that I know where'll she have gone. That can only be here.'

'And nowhere else? You didn't try looking

anywhere else?'

'Well ... we did try looking at the foot of the Falls.'

'Then that's where we'll look, right?'

'We abandoned the idea, because there's no way through that water.'

'That's not to say she won't have looked again. That's the way women's brains work.'

Tom looked at Glossop. 'Isn't that where you say your friend was attacked?' Cal asked, sensing that he was winning the argument.

'That's right,' Glossop said. 'But I don't know—'

'That's where we'll look next,' Cal decided.

It was impossible to argue against his entirely logical policeman's reasoning. Tom allowed himself to be carried along, even if his instincts kept telling him that Shirley could only have been referring to the cave when she had written 'come and get me'. Equally, he couldn't argue with the certainty that she could not have got past those snakes, that if she had tried she would have been lying there, dead or dying. He thanked God she hadn't been. But then where was she?

They drove back down the track to within half a mile of the village, which was where Washington estimated they were as close to the Falls as they were likely to get by jeep. Now the noise was tremendous, and the trees were soaked with drifting spray, even if

288

they were some distance away from the falling water.

'Where was your friend attacked?' Cal asked Glossop. He had apparently decided that Tom was not likely to be a coherent witness at this point.

'Not around here,' Glossop said. 'It was down by the stream.'

'What stream?'

'They got a lot of offshoot streams around here,' Washington said.

'Cheer me up,' Cal said. 'You know what, Tommy boy, this *is* a wild good chase. Shirley could be anywhere.'

'We're not abandoning her,' Tom said.

'Let's you and me have a little chat,' Cal said, beckoning him away from the rest of the party. 'Now listen carefully. You're my old school chum, and I think your Shirley is a dream boat. But it is my business to keep the peace up here, and your appearance has sure made a hole in that. You come to Georgetown and start asking questions, and, bingo, Claude Diamond is dead. You fly up here, to ask questions, and, bingo, Carl Lemmon is dead, together with three of his passengers. The State Department is asking questions of its own. You two ask some more questions, and, bingo, a young woman is attacked. You say one of your party has been murdered. We have no evidence of that. Now your lady friend has gone walkabout and missing. Tommy, anyone who goes walk-about in this bush, all on her own, is begging for trouble. I'm not talking about creatures that may or may not exist. I'm not even talking about snakes and alligators, although we know they're there. But in this bush you lose track of where you are for one second and you stand a good chance of never finding out where you are again.'

'Not here,' Tom objected. 'All you have to do is go towards the sound of the Falls.'

'Okay. I guess you can hear the sound from here. Where's the village?'

'Ah ... over there.' Tom pointed.

'You reckon? Where's the track?' Tom pointed again. 'It isn't, you know. It's over there. And the village is over *there*. Now, I reckon you know by now just how exhausting it is trying to find your way through this bush. You probably don't know how despairing it can be to walk for an hour and find yourself right back where you started from, even supposing you know where you started from.'

'So you mean just to abandon her,' Tom said angrily.

'What you need to understand is this,' Cal said. 'I reckon you know there have been a few disappearances up here over the past few years. You figure these have been caused by your friends the creatures. Common sense suggests that they were caused simply by people going walkabout. The point is, we haven't turned out the whole world to find them. These things happen. Now you are asking me to turn out the whole world to find someone who isn't even Guyanese. I'm a policeman. I have a terrible crime on my hands. I'm willing to concede that the crime may well be related to your absurd quest. But it is still the crime that is my prime concern. As I said, I have the State Department on my back wanting to find out how three of their nationals got themselves blown up in a country where terrorism isn't a daily occurrence. Now I have a suspect. It is my business to get to the bottom of this business just as quickly as possible. And that is what I am going to do.'

'You're forgetting that Shirley is also an American citizen.'

'No, I am not. Now, I will be very happy if we return to the village, where I will assemble all the villagers and you will call for volunteers to help you search the forest for her. But I, and my policemen, simply have too much to do to drop everything in a search for one woman. Much as I regret having to say that.'

'And you don't reckon I am going to get much support from the village.'

'Frankly, no. But I will throw my weight behind your appeal.'

'I love that girl,' Tom said. 'You know that?'

291

'I kind of reckon you do,' Cal said. 'And I'm sorry, man. I hope to God you find her. I'm asking you to understand my point of view.'

'Sure I do,' Tom said, and held out his hand. 'No hard feelings, right?'

Cal squeezed the offered fingers. 'I hope the hell not. Let's get with it.'

They rejoined the bedraggled group of searchers and began the drive back to the village.

'What about Shirley?' Glossop asked, sitting next to Tom.

'Cal reckons the police have done their bit. So it's up to us,' Tom told him. 'Me, at any rate. And whatever help we can raise in the village.'

Glossop considered. 'You can count on me, you know,' he said.

'You mean you're not going out with them?'

'My aim in life is to get the critter that killed Billy Milton,' Glossop said.

Tom realized that this very complex character was also a very tough character. 'Glad to have you along,' he said.

'So tell me what we do next.'

'Cal's idea is to appeal to the villagers for help. That makes sense: they know the area far better than we do.'

'Yeah,' Glossop said. 'Meanwhile, that little girl has been missing for a hell of a long time.'

Tom didn't reply; he was all too aware of what Glossop was saying. The thought of Shirley being attacked by those snakes ... But she couldn't have been attacked by the snakes, or they would have found her body. Well, then, the thought of Shirley being attacked and seized by one of the creatures ... Was that possible? Surely they would have found some evidence of a struggle. But that would only have been had she been attacked at the cave entrance. He thought he was going mad, and his leg was aching more than ever.

It took them half an hour to regain the village, where, despite the still drizzling rain, they were immediately surrounded by an excited crowd.

'Man, you is all wet,' Mrs Smith pointed out. 'Mr O'Ryan, you should change your clothes or you going catch cold on top of everything.'

'In a minute,' Tom told her.

'You ain't find her, then,' Rimmer remarked.

'No sign of her,' Cal said. 'Now, listen to me, all of you.' He stood on the top step of the commissioner's office, the better to address them. 'Miss Richards has gone missing. It is most likely that she went for a walk and got lost. Mr O'Ryan would like your help in finding her. Who will volunteer to form a search party?'

'You ain't see it raining, Superintendent?' someone asked.

'You seeing the time, Superintendent? It done past three. It going be dark in three hours.'

'All the more reason to get out there and find her now,' Cal said. 'You can't leave her alone out there in the dark.'

'She gone by sheself,' a woman pointed out. 'Let she come back by sheself. Out there got them critters, right?'

'That is mere supposition,' Cal declared.

'You thinking so? What about that Martindale? He see the critter what kill that O'Brien.'

'And he done gone out of he mind.'

'And what about that Monica? She see the critter what attack she.'

'And she done gone out of she mind.'

Cal sighed, but he was not going to give up. 'All right,' he said. 'Maybe there is something out there. But as you have just said, it only attacks individuals. It will not attack groups. We'll form search groups, of not less than four people in each. That way you'll be quite safe.'

'But, Superintendent,' someone argued, 'if the critter did get the white woman, she is long dead. What we searching for?'

'We are searching because the odds are

that her disappearance has nothing to do with any critter,' Cal shouted. 'She may still be alive, lost out there.'

'I say let she come back when she is ready,' said the first woman. The crowd nodded its agreement.

Cal turned to Tom. Who gave a wry smile. 'As you said, Cal. Thanks for trying.' He went up the steps on to the porch of the hotel, where Fuller had been looking on.

'You mustn't blame them,' he said. 'I reckon they're pretty scared.'

'I'm not blaming anyone.' Tom went to his bedroom to change his clothes. How empty it seemed without Shirley; her scent was still evident. What was he going to do? Logic told him that Cal had to be right, and she was lost somewhere in the forest, perhaps already dead. Instinct told him that she had gone to the cave. And somehow got past the nest of bushmasters? Or been bitten, and crawled away from them, to collapse in the bush and die? That was a possibility they hadn't taken into account.

He had to go back there. But as someone in the crowd had said, it would be dark in under three hours. Did he dare risk it in the dark? Perhaps that was the safest time. Snakes, like all reptiles, were cold-blooded creatures. They needed their blood to be warmed by the sun to be active. At night they were usually torpid and inoffensive.

295

Unless disturbed! In any event, he couldn't hope to cope with three bushmasters, at the very least, and however sleepy, on his own. Glossop had said he would help; he found that thought strangely reassuring. But even the two of them ... He wondered if Washington would come back with them. Washington was an odd fellow. It was his girlfriend who had been attacked, yet he had never shown any great emotion about it. He was the game warden, and therefore had to know the entire park better than anyone else, but he had never volunteered any information or suggestions as to what they should do. Maybe he was just shy. He went into the bar, where Glossop was seated, with Fuller and Cal and Willard.

'No joy, eh?' the doctor asked. 'You mean there was no cave, no passage into the earth?'

'There could be,' Cal said. 'But there sure as hell is no way any human being could get down there. Or any monster, either, in my opinion.'

Willard looked distinctly relieved; clearly he had not relished the thought of having to stitch Shirley up.

'I think there is a way,' Tom said.

'Oh, don't start that again,' Cal begged.

'Listen.' Tom told them his theory.

'It's possible,' Cal conceded. 'But if she had been attacked, and, as you say, crawled away to die, there would have been tracks, even after the rain. Broken branches and that kind of thing.'

'I still say it's worth another look.'

'I'm game,' Glossop said. 'We'll leave at first light.'

'I was thinking of leaving now.'

'And what about ma dinner?' Mrs Smith demanded; she had been listening from the doorway.

'Perhaps you could feed us first,' Tom suggested.

'You mean to go back to that cave and those snakes, at night?' Willard enquired.

Tom put forward his theory about snakes. Cal scratched his head and looked at Fuller.

'It has a sound basis in zoology,' Fuller said. 'After all, when you hunt alligators you do it at night, don't you?'

'I have never hunted alligators,' Cal pointed out. 'My business is hunting men, and the men I hunt don't sleep at night. I'll wish you joy of it.'

'You all can eat now,' Mrs Smith announced, having checked the state of her cooking.

'Do you think Washington will come back with us?' Tom asked, as he drank thick soup – he didn't care to ask what it might be made of.

'We can ask him,' Glossop said.

'And we'll need weapons. Can you let us have some, Cal?'

Cal considered. 'I can let you have a hunting rifle. But I'll want it back.'

'You'll have it back. And cartridges?'

'It'll have a clip.'

'One?'

'Just how many of these critters you expecting to find?'

'Well ... we may have to shoot a lot of snakes.'

'Who will all be asleep, you say. You can have my revolver as well. That's fully loaded. That's a total of eleven bullets, to deal with a critter and, maybe, three snakes. That's all you're going to have. I can't have you shooting up the entire park.'

'You're all heart,' Tom said.

'You want me to make you up some thermos and thing?' Mrs Smith asked.

'That's a good idea. Maybe you could lace it a little,' Glossop said.

'Lace it? I ain't got no lace, man.'

'He means add a little rum to the coffee,' Tom explained.

'Well, I could do that, sure.' She departed for the kitchen.

'You almost make me wish I was coming with you,' Cal said.

'You can always change your mind,' Tom said, as invitingly as he could.

'I'm game,' Willard said. They all looked at him, and he flushed. 'Well ... it'll be an adventure,' he said defensively. 'And, as you suggested this afternoon, if you do find Miss Richards you might need me.'

'I'd be delighted to have you along, doctor,' Tom said. 'Well, let's get—'

Booted feet pounded on the front porch. 'Man, what you trying do?' Mrs Smith demanded. 'Tramp down me hotel?'

'The superintendent,' a voice panted. 'I must see the superintendent.'

Cal put down his napkin and got up. 'What the hell? Berridge?'

'Yes, sir, Mr Simpson. Man, you must come with me. Is Mr Rimmer.'

'Something's happened to Mr Rimmer?' The other four men also got up.

'Is he send me, Mr Simpson. He say you must come quick.'

Cal grabbed his cap and ran down the steps. The others followed. As was so often the case, the rain had stopped with the dusk, and it was a fine evening. A crowd had gathered outside the commissioner's office, muttering. Cal elbowed his way through them, and Tom and Glossop, Fuller and Willard followed, hurrying up the steps to the porch, where two more constables waited. Rimmer was inside, sitting down and fanning himself. He looked in need of a drink.

'What happened?' Cal demanded, standing above the commissioner, almost menacingly.

'That Ledden,' Rimmer said. 'That Ledden...'

Cal pulled open the door leading to the corridor to the cell. Here there was another constable, who came to attention as his boss appeared. Cal stepped past him. Tom attempted to follow, but was checked by the policeman. He could see into the cell. His first impression was that Ledden had somehow escaped. But now he could see the little man, seated on his bunk, leaning against the wall, turned away from the corridor so that his face was invisible. But it became visible a moment later as Cal grasped his shoulder and Ledden fell back across the bunk, his eyes staring sightlessly at the roof of the cell.

'What the hell happened to him?' Cal demanded.

'How I am knowing that?' Rimmer enquired, having got up and joined the throng in the corridor.

'I found him, sir,' said the constable on duty. 'I came to bring him his dinner, and there he was. Just like you see him. So I called Mr Rimmer.'

'He must have had a heart attack,' Rimmer said.

'My ass,' Cal commented, and began examining the body. 'Doc, come in here. And keep those people out.'

As he hadn't specified Tom or Glossop or

Fuller, they all waited.

'He was the witness, wasn't he?' Fuller whispered.

'The only possible lead,' Tom agreed.

'You tell me how this man died, Doc,' Cal said.

Willard made a cursory inspection. 'Looks like a heart attack.'

'I'm not buying that. You examine him properly.'

Willard glanced at him, then bent lower over the body, opened the eyelids wide, then the mouth, sniffed... 'Christalmighty!'

'Yeah,' Cal said. 'I want a post-mortem performed tonight, Doc. He's going to have to be buried before it gets hot tomorrow. And I want to know the poison that killed him. And how the poison was administered.'

'Must've been a dart,' Glossop said.

'Then it would still have been in the body,' Cal pointed out. 'You get started, Doc.' He came into the office. Tom had never seen him looking so grim.

'You reckon he was murdered?' Rimmer asked.

'Yes,' Cal said. 'I reckon he was murdered. And I intend to find out who did it.'

Eleven

Pursuit

Shirley's immediate reaction to the sight of the snakes was to hurl herself backwards, with the result that she cannoned into Wishart, throwing him off balance. They hit the floor of the passageway together.

'You stop this stupid behaviour,' he panted. 'Those are our guardians. No one can get in while they're there. And no one can get out, either.'

Despite her fear and discomfort she was intrigued. 'They do what you tell them?'

'In a manner of speaking. The boys handle them. There's a chamber just off to the left where they can be put when we want to use the entrance. When we want to be safe, they're released, like now. So come along, let's go back. You're really getting to me, granddaughter.'

He heaved himself to his feet, and Shirley, rising to her knees, shouldered him behind his knees. She wasn't sure what she hoped for, if this was the only way in or out of the cavern, but she was determined to keep herself going as long as possible, because surely Cal would know how to deal with those snakes. And if she couldn't keep herself going long enough to be rescued, she was equally determined to go down fighting.

Her attack took Wishart, still out of breath from his pursuit and fall, by surprise, and he went down again. Shirley jumped over him, and ran back down the sloping passageway. By now her eyes were all but accustomed to the gloom, and she easily made out the crevasse and the pit. She knew she could jump it. She paused to catch her breath and tense her muscles, listening to Wishart shouting curses behind her, and then ran forward and hurled herself into space. She landed safely enough on the far side, staggered to and fro for a few seconds, and then went forward. She thought she could hear shouts from in front of her now, too, so it was necessary to find that side passage as rapidly as possible.

She went as far as she could, running her hand along the wall as she moved, and came to a bifurcation. She turned down the secondary passageway, into a deeper darkness, which left her blinded and meant that she had to slow to a careful advance, against the wall, feeling her way with both hands and feet in case there was another pit. The thought that there might also be another of those snakes down here made her flesh crawl, and when there was a flutter of sound above her head and something brushed her face she had to stifle a shriek.

Clearly it had been a bat. A vampire? She knew that South America was one of their natural habitats, and while she wasn't worried about being turned into a vampire herself, she also knew that they were the most virulent carriers of rabies – and that she could do without. But the bat had not bitten her, so far as she knew. She moved forward again, still going downwards, she was sure, and thought she saw a slight lessening of the gloom in the distance. This indicated that the passage might debouch into the main cavern. She checked, panting, wondering if that was her best bet. But if she remained there they would find her easily enough. To remind her of that she heard shouts from behind her, echoing through the darkness. If they were behind and above her, then she had a chance of regaining the cavern and finding another branch along which she could perhaps escape and find a hiding place. She ran forward, and a moment later entered the cavern and stared at the Amerindian girl, who had returned from the search for the phial, apparently unsuccessfully.

'Can you speak?' Shirley asked. The girl nodded. 'Is there somewhere I can hide? *We* can hide,' Shirley said, as winningly as she could. 'People will be coming to help us, soon. If we can just hide—'

'You can't hide,' the girl said. 'They going catch you, and beat you too bad.'

Shirley refused to panic. 'All of these passageways...'

'They knows them all,' the girl said. 'You ain't knowing them.'

'Do you?' The girl shook her head. The shouts were very close. Shirley took a deep breath and ran across the cavern, turning into another opening. She ran up this, panting, fell to her hands and knees, seeming to hear shouts all about her now, but shrouded in an impenetrable blackness.

She needed to think, to work things out. The snakes! They guarded the entrance, in some way controlled by the brothers. They had not been there when she had come in, or she would not have got in; Wishart had been angry about that. Now they had been loosed to stop her getting out, and to stop anyone following her from getting in.

She still wanted to believe that the snakes would not have stopped Tom and Cal if they were coming to rescue her, but the fact remained that they had not yet come; she was expecting too much of a man who had already been bitten by a bushmaster and one who did not believe in the creatures anyway. They would come, eventually, when they had exhausted all other possibilities – but when would that be?

Snakes! She tried to remember everything she could about them. Contrary to most legends, they were not creatures who lurked in darkened places and struck unseen. They were creatures of the daylight and the sunlight. Forest snakes, anyway. She looked at her watch. It was seven o'clock. She had been away from the settlement for twelve hours. Surely the whole village must be alerted by now. But if it was seven o'clock, it was dark outside. Wishart had said the snakes were controlled by his grandsons. But now was when they would be under control, both because they would be ineffective and because no one risked the forest at night. If she could get back to the exit...

She crept along the corridor. She thought she could hear shouts in the distance, but couldn't be sure above the roar of the Falls. She had no idea where she was going, was only concerned with not falling into another pit, or encountering one of her cousins. Every so often she paused for breath, conscious of a creeping exhaustion; she had not eaten since yesterday, and she had not had anything to drink, either. And she was suddenly cold, naked as she was from the waist up. But she had to keep going, until Tom or Cal came for her. They had to have read the note by now.

She had no idea how much ground she covered. The various tunnels seemed to stretch forever. She imagined she might eventually drop dead and never be found, in this labyrinthine world. It was past midnight before she suddenly smelt humanity. However far she had wandered, she had come full circle, as it were, and in front of her ... She could not believe she had been down here this long, and no one had come for her. Had they abandoned her? She couldn't believe that, either. But in front of her, she was sure, there was one of her cousins. What had they been doing all this time? Eating, certainly, and looking for her. But if he was in front of her, there had to be a reason. She crept forward, sure now that she was in familiar territory, too aware that they could see in the dark, at least to a certain extent, and came to another bifurcation. She had a sensation that she was in the main passage-way. After so long. Ahead of her was the pit, and the exit; she could see no glow of light, but that was because it was the middle of the night.

And in front of her was one of the creatures, keeping watch. That could only be because the bushmasters were no longer awake. If she could get past him ... She drew deep breaths. It would have to be a great rush, a leap and then another great rush. And then the jungle. All of those things had to be faced. Because there was no alternative.

Shirley tensed her muscles, rose to her feet and ran forward, giving as she did so a great shriek, hoping to frighten her adversary. But all he did was stand up himself, a huge, looming, dark figure, towering above her. Shirley checked, and he reached for her. She turned away and ran back down the corridor, panting and gasping, hearing him behind her. She had run several feet, and gained some distance on him, when she realized she was back in the original corridor she had taken, bending to her left.

Ahead of her was the glow of phosphorescent light from the main cavern. But she had no choice now; the creature was behind her, and if she could run faster there was no way she could turn back. She burst into the main cavern, looked right and left. They had been eating, all right; bones were scattered about. And the Amerindian girl was there, apparently asleep, but waking up, blinking, at the sudden intruder.

Shirley knew better than to waste her time asking her for help again. And her pursuer was very close, summoning help with loud triumphal shouts. Acting on instinct, Shirley ran across to the outer cave, where there was more light. She had a sense that her cousins were still somewhat in awe of the Falls themselves, if not actually afraid of them.

She stared at the solid wall of water, falling past the lip of the cave, and the pools that came back from the Falls to gather in and around the shattered wreck of the plane. Looking left and right she saw an opening in the right-hand wall. She ran for this, senses reeling from the enormous noise, splashing through the puddles, and reached the opening. It was narrow, but there was definitely space beyond. Another passage? She squeezed in and discovered that it was not a passage, merely an aperture about three feet deep. But it was dark and it was concealed, and, in any event, she had no alternative now, as she turned to look back at the cave and saw the brothers emerge, clearly directed by the Amerindian girl. Shirley didn't suppose she could blame her; she sought only to avoid beatings or mistreatment herself, and she had never seen Shirley before today.

She pressed herself against the wall, subconsciously trying to hold her breath, although there was no way either of the brothers could possibly hear her breathing above the roar of the water. They hunted around the wreckage, and then advanced to within a few feet of the Falls themselves, looking at each other and muttering in their half-gibberish.

If they thought that she had thrown herself over ... Perhaps they did, for after a few minutes more they turned and went back into the inner cave. Shirley gave a great sigh of relief. She looked at her watch: two in the morning. She had been gone nineteen hours, and had spent most of them on her feet; she was exhausted, her throat was parched and her stomach was rolling, even if she knew she would not be able to digest any of the raw meat on offer down here.

Tom and Cal would certainly be on their way by now, though. She expected them to come bursting through the caves at any moment, armed and dangerous. Instead ... she saw Wishart come through the opening, followed by the sisters and the children, chattering as usual. They, too, went to the lip and looked at the water, clearly debating. But Wishart was shaking his head, vehemently. He had worked out that she was not the sort of woman to have committed suicide.

He began pointing. The sisters and the children separated, following the wall round. Lynette was the one on Shirley's side, with two of her daughters. Shirley's instincts told her to leap out and make another run for it. Her brain told her that would be a total waste of time. She simply had to stay put and hope she might be overlooked. She flattened herself against the rock wall, and again attempted not to breathe, stupidly. Because while she could not be heard, there was no escape. She sensed Lynette's approach, and a moment later one of the little girls confronted her.

'Here'm,' she announced, very loudly.

Shirley lunged forward, attempting to force the girl out of the way, but Lynette was far the stronger woman, and where Shirley's hands slipped on bare flesh, Lynette's fingers twined themselves in Shirley's jeans and jerked her out into the cavern. Wishart gave a shout and came towards them, as did Margaret. Shirley panted and struck at them, but had her arms seized. She tried to kick, and realized that the brothers had come back into the cavern as well, and now she was lifted bodily from the ground.

'Bring her along,' Wishart said, and put his face close to hers. 'We are going to make you holler, first,' he told her.

Suddenly terribly aware of having lost her shirt, Shirley was carried through into the main cavern, the children as usual cackling beside her, pulling and prodding at her. She wriggled and fought against the men, but even one of them was far too strong for her, much less both. She panted and gasped, and now knew real fear. Wishart was angry, and the idea of fathering a son by her, which was grim enough, had been overtaken by his wish to hurt her.

'Lay her down,' he said. 'But keep hold of her. Strip the bitch.'

Shirley was laid on the floor. She tried to sit up, and was forced flat again by the clutching hands.

'Help me!' she screamed at the Amerindian girl.

'How I am going do that?' the girl asked. 'You ain't know they is ruling here?'

Shirley felt their breaths on her body as they unfastened her belt with interested comments, pulling down her jeans, commenting again at her knickers before tearing these off as well.

'Bastards!' she yelled, getting an arm free and striking at the nearest face with her nails.

It was one of the brothers, and he gave a howl of pain and reared back, clawing at his face; she had split his cheek.

'Bitch!' Wishart had joined them as she was finally naked, held on her back.

'Listen,' she panted. 'I'm your granddaughter. I came here to find you, to help you, to take you back to civilization. Please listen! You can't want to hurt me. Please!'

'You came here to destroy us,' he hissed. 'We don't want help. We don't want you. But as we have you ... Shit!'

She saw his problem. No doubt arising from all the exercise she had forced him to have in the past several hours.

'You have her,' he told Michael. 'Make her squeal.'

Michael grinned. Shirley tried to bring her legs together, but had them grasped and pulled apart by the two sisters, assisted by the children, cackling their excited pleasure at what they were about to see. Wishart himself was holding her arms above her head, as Lyle was still recovering from the wound she had inflicted. But Wishart was their weakest link. As Michael came down on her, she jerked her arms free, striking upwards once again with her nails. Wishart reared away from her, falling over, and she sat up, swinging her arms to and fro, causing Lynette to grunt as she was struck on the face and knocked over, and Michael to shout his pain and anger as Shirley managed to bring up her right knee. Then he threw himself forward again, his weight pinning her to the ground before she could roll away from him, Margaret shrieking her enthusiasm as she saw her brother about to make an entry ... And the cavern was shaken by a huge, reverberating explosion.

'You are talking as if we are all under arrest,' Glossop remarked.

'You are all under suspicion,' Cal said. 'So nobody leaves the village until I get both a true cause of death and a time of death from Dr Willard.'

'But what about Shirley?' Tom demanded. 'You mean we can't go looking for her?'

'Not tonight.'

'That is absurd,' Tom snapped. 'We were all out with you, all afternoon.'

'So, if Ledden died during the afternoon, you're clear. That is, supposing he wasn't killed by some slow-acting agent.'

'I was here all afternoon,' Fuller remarked.

Cal grinned. 'So you were, Prof. I'm sorry to have to say it, but you're as much under suspicion as anyone. Now...' he looked left and right. 'Mr Rimmer, and you, Braithwaite, and Miss Lloring, I want you to sit down and write down the names of everyone who was in this office today and this evening.'

'Man, that is one hell of a lot of people,' Rimmer complained.

'I'm sorry, but it has to be done.'

'We going to be heah all night,' Claretta said, but she sat behind her desk and took out a sheet of paper. PC Braithwaite did likewise at his desk, while Rimmer retired to his office, muttering.

'I suggest you fellows go back to the hotel,' Cal told Tom.

'What a fuck-up,' Tom grumbled, as they did as they were told.

'Eh-eh,' remarked Mrs Smith. 'I am hearing they got a dead down at the office.'

'You are hearing right,' Glossop said.

'Is that fellow what they arrested, eh? Now that is a strange thing. I did see him this very

314

morning.'

'Doing what?' Fuller enquired. 'He was in the cell, wasn't he?'

'Oh, yes, man, but I got the concession to feed who is in that cell. So I take he his breakfast. I sent his dinner down, too, just now. Now it going spoil. You know, they ain't got people in that cell too often. There ain't no money in it for the cook.'

'There's no money in it for anyone, now,' Tom said wearily, pouring himself a beer.

'Excepting maybe the doctor,' Glossop said.

Tom stared into his drink. It really was a fuck-up, as he had said. But he was growing more and more determined to end it one way or the other, the moment he got the go-ahead from Cal. Even if he had to storm the snake pit with all the firepower he could command. Meanwhile there was nothing to do but wait, as it seemed the whole village was waiting. Glossop sat at the table and played endless games of patience. Fuller was hardly less patient, but in a more relaxed manner. He didn't even want to talk about the creatures he had come up here to investigate, just sat and stared into space.

Tom couldn't keep still, walked up and down, went out on the verandah, having visions of what Shirley might be going through. She was a funny kid. Obsessed, he had thought when first they had met. He wondered if she still was. More than that, he wondered about his true feelings for her. She was a hell of a lot of woman, and a gutsy and determined one, as well. He knew he could very well slip over the edge that separates lust from love. But did she want that? They had been thrown together in rather bizarre circumstances, she had suddenly found herself out of her depth and she had turned to him for succour. All logical. Equally it was logical that when this adventure was over she would look at him and say to herself, what did I ever see in this soak?

He thought he had revealed a few guts and some determination himself, over the past week or so. But few women based their concept of love on that, except in the very short term. All academic, if by now she had been murdered and eaten. Or worse.

He was also concerned about Fuller. A man who had just appeared out of the blue. No, that wasn't true. He had been here for years and years and years. An anthropologist, Cal had said. What he didn't know about Kaieteur wasn't worth knowing. Because he had been looking all these years for a way to get behind the Falls ... and hadn't succeeded, because he, like them in the beginning, had supposed it had to be from the front of the drop rather than the top?

But Fuller hadn't appeared sufficiently

interested to take part in the search for Shirley. Because he had known there wasn't a way past the bushmasters? Or because he needed to remain in Takdai to deal with his accomplice, Ledden? Or was he just hallucinating, becoming paranoid, because of the poison in his system?

Cal arrived at eleven, looking grim. 'He was poisoned,' he said.

'You mean he *was* shot with a dart?' Fuller at last appeared interested.

'No, he wasn't, Prof. It was something he ate, or drank.'

Mrs Smith appeared from the kitchen. 'What you saying?'

'That Ledden was fed poison, most probably with his breakfast. He died about three o'clock.'

'You accusing me?'

'You served him his breakfast. And you prepared it as well, right?'

'And for that you think I poisoned him? Tell me why I should do that?' She did not look the least alarmed at the accusation, only annoyed.

'I am hoping *you* are going to tell *me* that,' Cal said.

'Man, you crazy,' Mrs Smith said, and retired to her kitchen.

'Jesus,' Glossop said. 'She's been feeding us for the past week. That pepperpot...'

'If you'd had what Ledden got you'd be dead by now,' Cal said.

'What was it?' Fuller asked.

'Doc Willard can't be sure,' Cal said. 'He'll need to take the samples back to Georgetown to analyse them. But it's definitely a virulent and quick-acting poison.'

'Wouldn't Ledden have complained about stomach pains?' Tom asked.

'He may well have done. But Rimmer shuts up shop every afternoon for his siesta, so the poor chap's hollers probably weren't heard. And, like I said, it was a quick-acting poison. He was probably dead in a matter of minutes. And when Rimmer and Miss Lloring and Braithwaite went back after their rest, the fact that Ledden was apparently sitting quietly on his bunk wouldn't have seemed odd; he's done nothing more than that since he was arrested.'

'So what happens now?' Fuller asked, looking up as Willard himself came in, looking tired. 'Doc?'

'Well, he'll have to be buried first thing in the morning,' Willard said. 'We can't keep a corpse hanging about in this heat. And, then, the sooner we can get down to town the better. I need to have those samples analysed.'

'Are you going to arrest Mrs Smith?' Tom asked Cal.

Cal grinned. 'If I did, you guys wouldn't

get fed.'

'You seriously think we're going to eat any more food she prepares?' Glossop asked.

'Like I said, if she meant to poison you, you'd know about it by now.'

'But she has to be guilty,' Fuller pointed out.

'I don't know about that,' Cal said. 'Jessie ain't stupid. She had to know we'd realize Ledden had been poisoned, and that she was the one who prepared the food. I think we need to find out just how many people had access to her kitchen yesterday, and just when she prepared Ledden's breakfast. I need to have a long chat with her. Meanwhile, Tommy, if you're dead set on going through with this snake fight, I guess I can't stop you.'

'But you won't come with us.'

'I have quite a lot on my plate here, wouldn't you say? You going, Prof?'

'Like I said, jungles aren't my scene any more. Especially at night. I'm sorry.'

'Don't forget me,' Willard said. They all looked at him. 'Well,' the doctor flushed, 'after that PM I could do with a bit of fresh air.'

'You got it,' Tom said. If only because those snakes might *not* be asleep.

'We'll still need that gun,' Tom reminded Cal, taking him aside.

'Like I said, here's my revolver, and you can have the hunting rifle. Eleven cartridges. There were only three snakes.'

'At home. Powerful torches. Glossop's and mine are a bit low key.'

'We have two; you can borrow one.'

'Transport.'

'Washington says he'll drive you up to the rest house. He ain't happy about going any further.'

'Well, then...' Tom held his arm. 'May I have a word?' Cal gave him a curious glance, then followed him down the corridor to the bedrooms. 'How long have you known the professor?' Tom asked.

'Old Fuller? Years and years?'

'Since he came here, I'll bet.'

'Well, close after.'

'And before?'

Cal was frowning. 'What are you at, man? I didn't know him before he came out here. But he's a world-famous anthropologist.'

'I think you need to check him out.'

Cal's frown was deepening. Now he suddenly grinned. 'You think he's Falby?'

'Or a clone.'

'That's ridiculous. Like I said...'

'He's a world-famous anthropologist. You ever looked him up? He's been hunting for a way to get behind the Falls for years. But he wouldn't come with us this afternoon. He needed to stay here, to slip into Mrs Smith's kitchen and poison Ledden's breakfast.'

Now Cal stared at him. 'He's not coming with you tonight, either,' he said slowly.

'Quite. He's spent the last twenty years crawling around this jungle, now he suddenly says it's not his scene, especially at night. He means to stay here and maybe get rid of those samples, so they can't be identified.'

'I think you're crazy, man,' Cal said.

'Just remember what I told you. I'm going to sort him out, the moment I get back with Shirley.'

He returned to the lounge where the men waited, looked from Glossop to Willard. 'Shall we go?'

Late as it was, the village was still humming with activity, at least partly because it wasn't raining. There were still people gathered round Rimmer's office and the cell, presumably still containing the dead man. There were others frequenting the rum shop and very readily getting drunk. Cal had his policemen on duty, guarding the office and the cell, and he himself had returned there to study the various statements, although it now seemed certain that the poison had been fed to Ledden by Mrs Smith, whether or not she had actually put it in his food.

Washington was waiting with his jeep. 'You knowing it ain't safe in that bush at night?'

he asked the three white men.

'You reckon it's safe in that forest during the day?' Glossop enquired.

Washington made a sound that might have been a raspberry, and started his engine. Glossop sat in the front. Willard sat beside Tom in the back; he had even brought along his little black bag, and was obviously prepared for anything.

'What exactly are you hoping to find?' the doctor asked. 'Your theory is that Miss Richards got past the bushmasters, some way or another, and that she followed a passageway that led to a cavern beneath the river and behind the waterfall.'

'*A* cavern?' Tom asked.

Willard shrugged. 'Could be more than one. But it is a reasonable deduction that there will be a cavern of some sort behind the Falls, eaten away by the centuries.'

'That was our idea,' Tom agreed. 'I was just wondering how you knew.'

'Cal was telling me about it on the way up. And it's your idea that this creature, or creatures, live down there.'

'That's right.'

'And that they are Shirley's relatives, descendants of the people on the plane that crashed in 1942.'

'That's her idea.'

'But you have come along to prove whether or not this could be true.'

'She's a nice girl.'

'You mean you don't believe it?'

'I didn't, really, in the beginning. But there is some kind of creature living in this bush, or beneath the Falls, or somewhere. And I did find that hair ... Did you know about that?'

'Cal told me,' Willard said.

'And then these guys...' He bit his lip, gazed behind the jeep's headlights as it slid and jerked its way over the muddy track leading up the hill.

'What guys?'

Tom sighed. But Willard seemed so entirely sympathetic to all their ideas, everything they had done ... He told him about the heavies in London, the note at the hotel.

'How do you think it got there?'

'Haven't a clue.'

'Did you have Cal check Whitling out?'

'It couldn't have been Whitling, because he knew we weren't coming back on the Grumman. Not on that day, anyway. So planting a bomb would have been a waste of time.'

'Hm. And you believe this is all linked to the murder of Diamond, the blowing up of the aircraft?' Willard asked.

'Has to be. Cal Simpson thinks so, too.'

'Must be something pretty valuable that was on that original plane. The one that crashed in forty-two.'

Tom shrugged. In for a penny, in for a

pound. 'How about the elixir of life?'

'Come again?'

'It's in a letter I have back at the hotel,' Tom said. 'But here is the gist.' He told him the story.

'That has to be nonsense,' Willard commented.

'I agree with you. But there are people who believe in it, and have apparently believed in it for sixty years.'

'And you think it is this elixir that has kept these creatures alive for these sixty years?'

'No, I don't. I told you, I don't believe in it. I believe the creatures, if they exist, have been kept going by a sort of Sawney Bean existence.'

'Sawney Bean,' Willard said thoughtfully. 'Pretty unpleasant. And if they have got hold of your Shirley ... I can see why you're in a hurry to get her back.'

'I'm glad somebody does.'

'But then who is after this elixir? And is prepared to kill to get it?'

'That is Cal's business. Mine is to find Shirley and get to the bottom of this creature business.'

Willard mused, 'But you can see that Cal also has every reason to be preoccupied.'

'Sure. But I also feel that he should play along with us first, help rescue Shirley, help get to the bottom of this creature problem, and at the same time help find out whether there *is* an elixir of life. That would draw the enemy out of the wood, right?'

'And make Cal a laughing stock if the story got out and there was nothing to find.'

Tom grinned. 'You're a devil's advocate, Doctor. I'm giving you my point of view.'

The jeep had reached the top of the hill. The Falls roared sullenly to their left, the forest loomed silently to the right. Tom presumed it wasn't quiet at all. If he hoped and prayed his theory about the bushmasters was correct, he also knew that the forest at night was far more alive than the forest during the day, that there would be cicadas clicking, lizards rustling, jaguars hunting, spiders lurking, monkeys howling ... Only the snakes and the birds and the alligators retired during the hours of darkness. But all the other noises were covered by the roar of the falling water.

Washington left his lights on while they climbed out and unloaded their gear. Then he switched them off. 'You guys want me wait?' he asked.

'We'd appreciate it,' Tom said.

'No chance of you changing your mind and coming along, at least a ways?' Glossop asked. 'Like to where you kept watch the last time we were here?'

'I'll wait for you right here, Mr Glossop,' Washington said. 'What time you got?'

'Just past one,' Tom said.

'Well, I figure it's gonna take you a couple of hours to reach that cave and sort things out. I'm supposing you can do that. Then I'm thinking that if there's a way in you're gonna need an hour or so to get down there into whatever's there and have a look around. Then a couple of hours back. And an hour to spare. I'm gonna wait here until seven o'clock, right? That'll be past dawn. You guys be back by then, because then I'm going home.'

'You're all heart,' Tom remarked.

Willard squeezed his shoulder. 'No point in antagonizing him,' he muttered. 'I think he's doing very well.'

'Yeah. Right. I'll take the revolver. Which of you wants the rifle?'

'I've done some hunting,' Glossop said.

'Apart from learning to deal with snakes. You're a treasure, Fred. Sorry we don't have anything for you, Doc.'

'I'm not into weapons,' Willard said. 'I'm here to pick up the pieces.'

'Well, at least you can carry the big torch.' Tom handed it to him. 'Okay, Washington, see you at sun-up.' He led the way into the night.

Tom used his torch to light the track. The others followed close behind. To their left the river drifted by, dark and silent. Above their heads the moon flitted in and out of the clouds, almost as bright as the sun.

'At least it's dry,' Glossop remarked.

'Don't count your chickens,' Tom advised. He knew the way pretty well by heart by now, and after just under an hour began searching the bushes to his right; there was no way any of their torches would shine across the river to pick out the little bay on the far side. But to his relief he found Cal's marker easily enough, and the coil of string.

'Got your compass?' he asked Glossop.

'Right here.' Glossop took the lead, following his compass bearing and using the torch, while Tom and Willard followed, paying out the string.

Branches slapped them across the face and thorns pulled at their clothes. Now, too, they were assailed by hordes of mosquitoes, rising out of the stagnant forest water, buzzing around them, trying to pierce their thick, button-downed sleeves and equally thick pants, attacking their faces and having to be swept away.

'I'm not even sure citronella will keep this lot off,' Willard remarked. 'Could be some cases of malaria coming up.'

But a few minutes later Glossop doused his torch, and when they got up to him they could make out the loom of the rocks. Tom made the string fast to the nearest tree and checked his revolver, holding the torch in his left hand.

'You stay close,' he told Glossop. 'But

don't waste any shots. Doc, can you cover us with that big light?'

'Will do.' Willard switched on the big torch, played it over the rocks.

'Keep it on the aperture,' Tom said. Willard advanced, shining his torch on the opening; he carried his medical bag in his left hand. 'Now the ground to either side,' Tom said. 'Just in case one of them is out on the town.' The powerful beam moved left and right, but revealed nothing, and no movement. 'So here goes,' Tom said, and went forward. For some reason he found himself bending double, as if the bushmasters might be armed with rifles and about to take pot shots at him. His skin seemed to be crawling, as he remembered that heavy body thrashing at him, the searing bite of the fangs.

Glossop came behind him, ponderously; Tom could only hope he was as good a shot as he was with a knife. The trouble was, there was no way of telling when he would have one of his mad panics. He reached the aperture, and heard no sound. Now he was bathed in the light from Willard's lamp, and if there was anything living inside it would have to know he was there. He switched on his own torch, sent it into the darkness. He could see nothing save the bare rock, and heard no movement. But the memory of that afternoon three days ago, the slithering sound that had meant the bushmaster was creeping up behind him, was threatening to take over his mind, and he was pouring sweat. He hunched his shoulders and stepped into the cave, torch moving to and fro. Reassuringly, he heard Glossop close behind him, but for the moment he was on his own. Now he was entirely inside the aperture, still moving his torch to and fro. But the cave was definitely empty.

'Okay,' he said over his shoulder. 'They must be asleep.'

'Asleep where?' Glossop asked.

'I haven't a clue. But they're not here. You guys with me?'

'You bet.' Willard had come right up to the cave, and now sidled in.

'Switch that thing off,' Tom recommended, as the huge beam turned the cave as light as day. Willard obliged. 'Follow me,' Tom said, and entered the passage. He kept his torch shining on the way ahead and they followed the single beam of light, slowly downwards.

'Man, this is something,' Glossop said, speaking loudly because the noise of the Falls was now reverberating through the passage.

Tom was continuing to beam his light to and fro and ahead, as the passage took a turn. He was listening as hard as he could, but because of the falling water he knew someone could be on guard duty only a few feet away and he wouldn't hear him. He was actually hoping the torch beam might activate someone and give them some idea of who, or what, and how many, they might be opposing. But they hadn't had to use a single bullet yet. Then the ground suddenly ended beneath his feet, and he plunged downwards into darkness. Glossop, following behind, gave a shout of alarm and fired his rifle.

Twelve

For Ever and Ever

The sound of the shot reverberated through the cavern for several minutes; Shirley felt the roof might be going to come down. It was some seconds before she realized that she had been released. The Wisharts were staring at each other in consternation. But Don Wishart had not been a member of the armed forces for nothing, however long ago it might have been.

'That was a rifle shot,' he snapped. 'Someone is inside the cavern, firing a rifle.' He looked at his grandsons. 'The snakes?'

'Lock'm up,' Michael explained. 'Dark outside.'

330

'Fool,' Wishart said. Slowly Shirley pushed herself into a sitting position. 'Oh, no you don't,' Wishart said. 'You keep hold of her,' he told the women.

'I told you they'd come for me,' Shirley said, the relief leaping about her brain now tempered, for the first time, by real fear. 'I'm your only hope. Let me intercede for you. I can explain to them.'

'That we're the creatures who're responsible for all of those disappearances and deaths over the years?' Wishart asked. 'You have to be out of your mind.'

'What to do?' Lyle asked.

'First thing is to find out how many people there are,' Wishart said. 'If there are just one or two, we can manage that, even if they do have a gun. If there are more than that, then they probably have more than one weapon. So we must make sure they don't find anything.' He looked at the two prisoners.

'You can't be serious!' Shirley shouted. 'You—'

'Gag her,' Wishart commanded. 'And her.'

The two women held Shirley's arms, while Michael tore her discarded shirt into strips and used one of these to bind her mouth. Another strip was used to tie her hands behind her back. Then he took the other strip to the Amerindian girl.

'Please,' she said. 'I ain't carrying your child?' Michael hesitated, looking at his grandfather. Shirley strained against the gag, trying to get the girl to scream. The sisters had released her, but they were all around her, and she didn't want to be manhandled again, not until Tom – it had to be Tom – was much closer.

'There'll be others,' Wishart said. Michael nodded. The sisters moved to the pregnant woman and held her arms while she, too, was gagged. Then Wishart jerked his head towards the outer cavern, and the Amerindian girl was pushed towards the aperture.

'Find out who and where those intruders are,' Wishart told Lyle. The big man nodded, and hurried to the inner passageways. Wishart grasped Shirley's arm, and forced her also towards the outer cave. 'You watch this, and remember it could happen to you,' he said.

Could! But might not! Shirley wanted to scream with relief. But the Amerindian ... 'Mmmm,' she begged. 'Mmmm.'

'Just watch,' he advised. They were in the outer cavern, beside the plane wreck. The sisters and Michael had already carried the girl to the far end, where the roaring water was descending only feet away, and the cavern itself was filled with spray. The girl was writhing against the restraining hands, but was quite helpless. The five children were clapping their hands and jumping up and down; Shirley realized they had seen this happen before. To Billy Milton's body? Now they all looked at Wishart. He extended his hand, the thumb down, and then passed it across his mouth.

'She has to scream,' he shouted into Shirley's ear. 'The gods need her to scream.'

The gag was being taken from the girl's mouth. Shirley thought she was going to burst her own gag with the power of her breathing. With an enormous effort she tore herself free of Wishart's grasp and ran forward. She had no idea what she was going to do, but in any event she tripped over a piece of wreckage before she had covered more than a few feet, throwing herself to one side to avoid smashing her face into the rock floor, and Wishart was upon her. He knelt astride her thighs and dug his fingers into her hair to bring her head up, making her watch what was happening. The sisters and Lyle were forcing the girl forward. They were laughing and shouting, even if Shirley could not hear what they were saying above the roar of the water. The girl threw back her head and screamed, and Shirley was sure she heard *that*, an unearthly sound that she knew would ring in her ears for the rest of her life. Until it was her turn to scream.

Then the pregnant girl was gone, pushed on to the edge of the cavern lip. She turned round, arms thrown up in a last, beseeching, act, then the tumbling water caught her and she went back, and disappeared.

'They all die differently,' Wishart said, with some satisfaction, pulling Shirley to her feet. 'You'll be different, too, when it's your turn.' He pushed her back into the inner cavern, joined now by the other three, and the children, all still in a state of considerable excitement. Lyle was waiting for them. He held up three fingers, then pointed downwards, jerking his hand up and down.

'Three men,' Wishart said. 'And at least one has fallen into the pit.'

'We kill'm,' Lyle said.

'No!' Shirley wanted to scream.

'Better to let them come and go,' Wishart said. 'There may be others.'

Michael pointed at the hanging meat. 'They will know,' he said.

Wishart hesitated, biting his lip. Then he came to a decision. 'You're right. They will have to die. Michael, lead them down here. Don't let them see you. Lyle, get behind them and loose the snakes.'

'Snakes no good,' Lyle said.

'In the dark. But they'll wake up in a couple of hours. Just in case these people have any back-up. Girls, take Shirley to the inner chamber and keep her there. Don't let her make a sound.' The women grasped Shirley's arms and hurried her along the passageway to the sleeping chamber, the children clustering behind them. Her last sight was of Wishart standing in the middle of the main chamber, smiling to himself.

Tom was still out of breath from his fall when the rifle exploded. The noise was so loud for a moment he thought Glossop had fallen into the pit beside him.

'For God's sake!' Willard shouted from behind.

'Sorry, Doctor, I tripped,' Glossop said. 'Tom? Tom? Where are you?'

'Down here,' Tom said, feeling himself to make sure nothing was broken. But he had landed on a springy surface, consisting of ... He felt around himself in the darkness, and decided he didn't really want to know what it might consist of. The echoes were still crashing through the cavern.

'If there's anything alive in here, that would sure have woken it up,' Willard said. 'I'm not sure the roof isn't going to come down.' He was shining his torch upwards, now he directed it into the pit. 'Let's get you up.'

'Like how?' Tom asked, testing the smooth sides.

'Give us your arms,' Willard said, suddenly taking command. 'We need to get out of here before we're trapped.'

Tom moved to the inner edge of the pit, and his foot struck something metallic. He stooped, and realized he was holding a revolver. 'Hey,' he said. 'Guess what I've found.'

'Tell us when you get up,' Willard said. Tom thrust the gun into his belt, then extended his arms. Glossop took one wrist and Willard the other. The doctor was stronger than he looked, and a moment later Tom was sprawled half across the lip, before being dragged clear altogether.

'Whew!' Glossop said. 'Now let's get the hell out of here.'

'No way,' Tom said. 'I came across my revolver down there.'

'How can you tell it's yours?'

'Shine the light.' Tom examined the gun. 'It's mine, all right.' He broke it. 'Fully loaded. It hasn't been fired.'

'And how the hell did it get down there?' Willard asked.

'Shirley dropped it when she fell in,' Tom said.

'You mean she's down there?'

'No. But I'm sure she fell in.'

'Then how did she get out?'

'Someone, or something, must have helped her. But she's in there. On the far side of that crevasse. I know it.'

Willard shone the light up and down the walls. 'I suppose we could jump it,' he said. 'Now we know it's there.'

Glossop was sending his beam further down the corridor. 'Hey!' he said. 'There's something in that passage.'

'Eh?' They all shone their torches in the indicated direction.

'I don't see anything,' Willard said.

'There was something,' Glossop insisted. 'I saw it move. Something was watching us from the darkness.' He levelled the rifle.

'Don't shoot,' Willard snapped. 'That could well start a rock fall.' Once again they peered along the length of their torch beams. 'Sure you're not hallucinating?' Willard asked.

'It was *there*!' Glossop insisted.

'Well, let's go get it, and Shirley,' Tom said. He nearly added, if she's still gettable. But he didn't want to think about that.

'You mean to go after that critter, in the dark? That's what tore out poor Billy's throat.'

'All the more reason to get him,' Tom said. 'Look, Fred, we have three torches, and now we have three guns. There's no reason for us to be afraid of any critter in the world.'

Glossop looked at Willard. 'I agree with Tom,' Willard said. 'And I think you can spare me one of those guns.' He had apparently changed his mind about carrying a weapon, or about the roof coming down, having established that Shirley had to be around.

'You got it, Doc.' Tom gave him Cal's revolver, and he put it in his hip pocket. 'Now, I'm going to be first. You chaps keep shining your torches, eh?' He retreated up the passage, took several long breaths and again tested his arms and legs to make sure nothing had been injured in the fall – he still felt fairly shaken up – then moved forward as fast as he could, launched himself into space, and landed on his hands and knees on the far side. 'Ooof!'

'You all right?' Willard called.

'Piece of cake.' Tom got up, shone his torch down the passage just to make sure there was nothing lurking, then turned back to the crevasse. 'Who's next? I'll cover you.'

'I think you need to go next, Mr Glossop,' Willard said.

'And if I fall into the pit, who's going to drag *me* out?' Glossop asked.

'My advice would be not to fall into the pit,' Willard told him.

Glossop grunted, and retreated up the passage. A moment later he was flying through space. Tom prudently retreated some distance, which was just as well because the big man did not fall on landing, but kept on coming, on his feet, charging into the darkness.

'You'd better hurry, Doc, or we won't catch him up,' Tom recommended. 'Throw me your bag.'

Willard did so, then made the jump easily enough; by that time Glossop had come back almost as fast as he had gone in. 'It's there!' he whispered.

'What?'

'The critter. I touched it.'

'Thank God you didn't shoot it,' Willard said.

'I touched it,' Glossop said again, voice rising.

'What exactly?' Tom asked.

'Fur, maybe. Hair. God, I was scared. I could feel its breath.'

'Okay,' Willard said, reclaiming his bag from Tom. 'Okay. Calm down.' He shone his torch along the passageway. 'He's not there now.' The beam swung to and fro, picked up the divergence. 'What about there?'

'He was in this one,' Glossop insisted.

'Maybe if we tried both,' Tom suggested.

'I think we should stick together,' Willard said. 'That pit may not be the only defence.'

'And the snakes,' Glossop added.

'There won't be any snakes down here,' Willard said. 'Let's go. Easy now. Mr Glossop, I think you had better be the rearguard. But stay close, and don't fire that thing unless you have to. Will you lead, Mr O'Ryan?'

Tom took a deep breath. He held the revolver in his right hand, his torch in his left, and kept the beam moving up and down as well as ahead; he had no desire to fall into another pit. Slowly they advanced down the sloping passage, until Tom saw the faint glimmer ahead. 'Light,' he said over his shoulder, and doused his torch.

Willard did the same. 'That can't be daylight.'

'Lamps?'

Willard shook his head. 'More likely phosphorescence. Now—' He was interrupted by a scream from Glossop, following which the rifle was fired, and again. As before the entire cavern seemed to shake with the reverberations.

'What the fuck...?' Willard shouted.

'It was there!' Glossop screamed. 'Right behind us. I saw it. Creeping up.'

'How can it have been behind us if ten minutes ago it was in front of us?'

'It was there, I tell you,' Glossop insisted.

'You could feel its breath again,' Willard said, contemptuously.

'There could be more than one of them,' Tom said.

Willard glanced at him, frowning. 'Okay,' he said. 'More than one. One in front and one behind. The odds are still in our favour, and at least the roof hasn't come down. Yet. Go on, Mr O'Ryan.'

Tom wrinkled his nose. 'Smells like a butcher's shop,' he said. 'And high.' He didn't like to think what he might see when they reached the light, but a moment later they were there, and he was staring at the carcasses. All animal, he estimated, and gave a sigh of relief. Willard had pushed past him, into the cavern, and was reinforcing the phosphorescent lighting with his torch beam.

'This cavern is lived in,' he announced.

Tom also used his beam, to pick up the several passageways leading off.

'We're in their lair,' Glossop shouted. 'Fuck!'

'Towards the sound.' Willard indicated the furthest opening, and they moved towards it, still sending their beams to and fro. Willard was first through, and stopped so suddenly Tom bumped into his back.

'Holy Jesus!' the doctor muttered.

Tom looked past him, first of all at the tumbling water hurtling past the open end of the cave, then at the plane wreckage just inside the aperture.

'My God! Shirley was right. Do you think...?'

'They all died? I hope so. But we'll have a look. The elixir...' Willard drew a deep breath and got his voice under control. 'The elixir could still be in there. Cover the entrance,' he told Glossop. 'And for God's sake pull yourself together.' He moved forward, put down his bag and began pulling and prodding at the wreckage. 'Sixty-two years,' he said. 'Just lying here, for sixty-two years.'

'And not a skull in sight,' Tom remarked. He was more interested in the Falls, and cursed himself for not having brought his camera; there could never be a shot to equal this. Then he remembered that he was not here to admire nature's grandeur, but to find Shirley. Who was definitely in here, with at least one of the creatures ... Her cousins?

'This has already been thoroughly search-ed,' Willard shouted, disconsolately, when Tom returned to the wreck. 'Whatever was in it, those damned animals or whatever have taken it.'

'Aaagh!' Glossop shrieked, and began firing again and again, sending bullets winging into the inner cavern. The reverber-ations hitting the water wall and bouncing back had the effect of an almost physical force.

'Fool!' Willard ran up to him and snatched the gun.

'They were there, two of them!' Glossop insisted.

'And you've emptied the magazine,' Willard said, throwing the gun down in disgust.

'I hit one,' Glossop asserted. 'I'm sure I hit one. They were so close, staring at me...'

Willard pushed him aside, picked up his bag, which he seemed afraid to let out of his sight, drew his revolver and returned to the inner cavern. He didn't lack guts, Tom thought, and followed him. He and Glossop shone their torches over the rock floor.

'Here!' Tom knelt, touched the discoloration. 'Blood, all right.'

Willard looked at Glossop, who had followed him, having picked up the rifle. 'You hit one of them. So you must have seen him. What did he look like?'

'Just like in the forest. All hair. And the eyes ... hideous.'

'Okay,' Willard said. 'And you say there were two of them?'

'At least,' Glossop said.

Willard looked at Tom.

'It's possible,' Tom conceded.

'Well, we should be able to follow this blood,' Willard said. 'There's another spot. Didn't the creature cry out when you hit him?'

'I think he probably did,' Glossop said. 'I saw his teeth. But with all this noise...'

'Come on.' Willard led them across the cavern to one of the side passages, following the drops of blood. At the entrance he stopped, sending his beam into the darkness, which seemed the greater after the comparative light thrown up by the phosphorescence.

'Now remember, if you have to, use the rifle as a club,' he told Glossop. 'And Mr O'Ryan, I'm sure you'll agree that we need to take at least one of these creatures alive.'

'To exhibit?'

Willard smiled. 'To question about the elixir.'

'And about Shirley,' Tom reminded him.

'Of course.' Willard entered the passage-way, the beam lighting his way. Tom follow-ed, and Glossop anxiously brought up the rear. Now they were moving upwards, Tom realized, even if the incline was very shallow. They must have covered about thirty yards when the Wisharts attacked them.

They had actually passed a side corridor without noticing it, so intent were they upon their forward movement. Now Glossop gave one of his terrified screams. Tom swung round, and was hit by a huge body, which seemed to be flying through the air. He was almost overcome by the rancidity of smell and sweat, and lost his balance as he was hurled against the passage wall. He dropped both torch and revolver, before he could use either, and found himself on the floor, powerful hands holding his head while even more powerful teeth snapped at his neck. Shade of poor Billy Milton, he thought.

Desperately he brought up his knees and swung his right hand, while forcing his left arm between himself and his assailant, across his neck. Teeth bit into his forearm, and he screamed with sheer agony. But the creature was grunting as Tom's knee crashed into his groin, and his grip was slackening. Tom swung his right fist again and again, landing a succession of kidney punches, which distressed the creature sufficiently for

Tom to throw him off. He sat up, gasping, blood trickling down his left wrist, wondered if he might have contracted rabies. To his right, Glossop had also thrown off his assailant, but was now running blindly back down the corridor to the main cavern, and the creature was following, a huge dark mound of moving power. To his left, Willard had coped best with his attacker, catching him a blow across the head with his torch that had sent Don Wishart staggering against the wall, and following up with a succession of punches, leaving the old man all but senseless on the ground.

Tom's assailant saw that his grandfather was in trouble, and leapt at Willard's back with a roar. Willard staggered beneath the impact and fell to his hands and knees. Tom swept his hand over the passage floor and found both his torch and his revolver. He brought them up, saw the creature reaching for Willard's unprotected neck and shot him. At such close range he couldn't miss, and the effect was devastating. The creature threw up his arms as his back seemed to dissolve in blood, and he tumbled forward.

'Michael!' Wishart shouted, trying to get to him.

But Willard had regained his breath and now checked him again, revolver thrust into his waist. 'Do you want to go with him?' he asked.

Wishart hesitated, panting, looking from Willard to Tom, eyes gleaming in the darkness. 'You have killed him,' he snarled.

'I would say that's tit for tat,' Willard said. 'Now you come with us.'

Again Wishart looked from one to the other, clearly trying to plan, but realized that for the moment he was their prisoner. He turned away, and Willard twined his hand in the long hair.

'Just keep moving nice and slow,' he said.

'What about Glossop?' Tom asked.

'You'd better go rescue him,' Willard said.

'What about you?'

'I can handle this one.'

Tom didn't doubt that for a moment, having seen the doctor at work. In fact, anything less like his normal concept of a medical man could not be imagined; he was glad they were on the same side. He went through to the outer cave, making his entry cautiously, and saw Glossop and the creature at grips again, on the far side of the plane wreckage, and within a few feet of the water.

'Hold on!' he shouted, not knowing whether or not he had been heard, and ran forward.

But Glossop was already exhausted, and terrified, and he could fight no longer. As Tom watched in horror, afraid to fire in case he hit the man who had saved his life,

Glossop was forced back to the very lip of the cave, and then hurled at the water with tremendous force. He gave a despairing scream and plunged over the edge.

Tom panted as the creature turned to face him. He levelled the revolver. 'I reckon you can understand me,' he said.

The creature was panting as well, while Tom took him in, the powerful, naked body, the long hair twined round and round his waist before dropping like a skirt past his thighs, the gleaming teeth, the muscular arms ... The creature moved towards him, round the wreckage.

'I can kill you any time I wish,' Tom said. 'Just remember that.'

Still the creature advanced, face working, shoulders hunched, very ape-like.

'Maybe you don't understand,' Tom said, and aimed past his left shoulder before squeezing the trigger. Once again the reverberations almost threw him from his feet. But the bullet had smashed into the wall behind the creature, who had turned to look at it in consternation. 'Think what that would do to your gut,' Tom suggested.

The creature turned back to him again.

'There was a woman came in here,' Tom said. 'Young. Pretty. Yellow hair. I have come for her. Where is she?' The creature grinned at him. 'If you have harmed her,' Tom said, 'I'm going to blow you into little pieces. Take me to her, and if she is unharmed I will do all I can for you.'

Another grunt, then the creature pointed at the inner cave.

'Okay,' Tom agreed. 'Lead on. Just remember I'm behind you.'

The creature moved to the aperture.

'It's okay, Doc,' Tom called. 'I have him covered.'

They entered the cavern and Tom paused in dismay. Don Wishart was just getting to his feet, his face a cloud of blood from where Willard had pistol-whipped him.

'Bastard won't tell me about the elixir,' Willard said. 'But I know he has it.'

'I don't think you can beat it out of him,' Tom protested.

'How else are we going to get it?' Willard demanded. 'What about this one? Where's Glossop?'

'He went over the Falls.'

'So this guy is a murderer at the very least,' Willard said. 'You, come over here.' Lyle moved towards him. 'Now,' Willard said, 'the bottle or whatever that was on the plane. Tell me where it is. If you don't, I am going to blow you apart.'

Lyle stared at him, eyes flickering to his grandfather and then back again. Blood continued to trickle down Don Wishart's face.

'Stuff the bloody elixir,' Tom said. 'We came here to find these creatures. We've done that. Now we have to find Shirley. Listen, old man,' he told Wishart. 'Shirley! I reckon you're her grandfather. She's my partner. I want her. And I want her unharmed. Take me to her, and I'll see what can be done to sort out this mess you've got yourself into.'

'You can do this?' Wishart asked.

'I can try. You're unique, you lot. There'll be lots of people wanting to interview you, photograph you ... You are going to be very, very famous.'

'The girl,' Wishart said. 'I will take you to the girl.'

'We'll all go,' Willard decided. 'And you can take us to the elixir as well.'

Wishart merely looked at him, then led the way to another of the exits. Lyle shambled behind him.

'At last we're getting somewhere,' Willard said. 'God, it's been a long time.'

Tom scratched his head. 'You're getting all het up about this elixir,' he remarked, 'which I don't believe exists, or has existed. It's these creatures that are important. Like I told the old man, this is going to be sensational.'

'Creatures,' Willard said contemptuously. 'You can have them, Mr O'Ryan.' Having as usual picked up his bag, he hurried behind Wishart and Lyle.

Tom followed more slowly, all manner of

questions he had not had the time before to ask himself suddenly occurring to him. He had been worried about Fuller. But ... just how had Willard known so much about what was happening, about Shirley and himself? And why was he so anxious about the elixir, which only a few hours ago he had dismissed as rubbish? Cal had never mentioned telling him about it. And he could not believe his old friend would have shown a comparative stranger Gifford's letter.

Doc Willard, with a successful practice ... which he had purchased about twenty years ago. So that he could keep looking and watching and listening, while going about his normal daily work, and all the while setting up a network of watchers and, where necessary, assassins! Godalmighty, Tom thought. He had come from America. Falby ... Willard ... In Guyana for the past twenty years. Able, and, indeed, required to come up to the Falls to attend to the people in Takdai and the other settlements, while still watching, and learning ... but never finding the vital clue, a way past the water. Perhaps he had just about given up hope of ever succeeding in his quest ... until a woman called Shirley Richards started asking questions.

They reached another chamber, utterly dark but now illuminated by Willard's light. And on the floor, on the far side of the chamber, lay the naked body of Shirley. Tom's heart gave a great lurch. He thought she was dead until she stirred, and he realized that she was gagged and that her wrists and ankles were bound together. He leapt past Willard and Wishart and Lyle and ran to her, thrusting his revolver into his belt and tearing at the strips of shirt to release her.

'Tom!' She nestled against him. 'These people—'

'They're under control,' he assured her.

'No,' she said. 'The women—'

There was a shout from Willard as the torch was struck from his hand. He fired his revolver, twice, and there was a scream of pain, but in the utter darkness it was impossible to tell who had been hit. Tom drew his own gun and rose to his feet, lifting Shirley with him. The darkness was a murmur of savage growling and high-pitched squealing. And now Willard fired again, and there was another howl.

'The women!' Shirley gasped. 'There are children, too. They can see in the dark.'

Tom realized that whatever his recent deductions he couldn't leave Willard to be torn to pieces. He regained his torch and swung the beam towards the scuffle behind him, saw Willard on the ground beneath women, children and Lyle. Wishart had seized the opportunity to escape back down the corridor.

Tom couldn't bring himself to shoot into the children, quite apart from the risk of hitting Willard. He fired over their heads, another enormous explosion that was followed by an ominous creaking from around them.

'It's coming down,' Shirley gasped.

Tom didn't have the time to worry about that. The women and children had been alarmed by the shot, and had fled after their grandfather. As had Lyle, and Willard was slowly pushing himself up, gasping for breath, looking for his bag and finding it.

'I think we must get out of here,' Tom said. 'Before the whole shooting match caves in.'

'The elixir,' Willard said. 'We have to find the elixir.'

'You mean this?' Shirley had reached into the corner in front of which she had been lying, and now showed them the phial.

'Great God in the morning!' Willard shouted, and snatched it from her. 'Sixty-two years,' he said again. 'It's lain here for sixty-two years.'

'And how many people have you and your father and grandfather killed in your attempts to get to it?' Tom asked.

'I see you've been thinking.' Willard opened his bag to insert the phial. 'Isn't it lucky I never quite got to you? I tried, but what a mistake it would have been had I made it. I was so anxious to stop you getting here first, it never occurred to me that you'd actually lead me to it.'

'You?' Shirley cried. 'Doctor?'

'His real name is Falby,' Tom said. 'Listen, you all right?'

'I've felt better. But ... Falby? You mean ... you killed Diamond? And blew up all those people? Just to stop us finding the elixir first?'

'I didn't mean Diamond to die. He was a friend of mine. I'd been through those files a hundred times. But when I heard from my woman in the newspaper office that he was coming to see you with maybe something fresh ... I told that idiot Bursil to rob him, not shoot him. The bastard lost his head. As for the people on the plane, they were nothing.' He grinned. 'I'm just glad you missed that flight, or I might never have got this.' He tapped the bag. 'I don't suppose you really knew what you were doing, but I congratulate you anyway.'

'You bastard,' Shirley said. 'You unutterable bastard.'

'I think it's time to leave,' Willard said, and fired.

Tom threw himself against Shirley and sent her sprawling. The bullet went wide, but in the fall Tom lost his torch, plunging them back into darkness. Willard fired again, then ran down the corridor behind his own light.

'Tom...' Shirley's voice quavered as from

all around them there came creaking sounds.

'Like the bastard said. We'll get him, if your cousins don't.' He held her hand to pull her up, scrabbled around in the darkness and found both torch and revolver, but the torch had shattered in the fall and was useless. 'Come on.'

He tucked the revolver into his waistband and felt his way down the corridor with his left hand, holding Shirley's hand with his right, moving towards the faint glimmer of light that was the phosphorescent cavern.

'Just what were you trying to do, anyway?' he asked. 'Going off like that? You scared the shit out of us.'

He heard her smile. 'I scared the shit out of myself as well. I just wanted to have another look at the entrance, and then fell into that goddamned pit.'

'What about the snakes? Didn't you see any?'

'No. Seems they were locked up. Those men keep them as pets.'

'And what did they do to you? Apart from not eating you?'

'I think maybe that was to come later. Much later. After I'd given birth.'

'Shit! Are you saying...'

'They didn't make it. Like I told you, I choose my men more carefully than that.'

He squeezed her fingers. Now they were very close to the exit. He checked, and they listened, but there was no positive sound above the roar of the water. He drew a deep breath, and stepped into the cavern, blinking in the sudden light.

Don Wishart sat on his stone; Margaret lay at his feet and was either dead or dying. The old man was weeping, the tears mingling with the blood on his face. Lynette knelt beside him, trying to comfort him. Lyle stood on his other side, looking humanly impotent to do anything about the catastrophe that had overtaken his family. The children stood in front of him, teeth bared.

These people are cold-blooded murderers, Tom reminded himself. Not to mention cannibals. But at that moment he knew only pity for them.

'Where is Willard?' he asked. 'The other man?'

'He shot my Margaret,' Don Wishart said. 'She tried to stop him, and he shot her.'

'Where did he go?'

Wishart gestured at the main corridor 'I told Michael to loose the snakes, when we knew you had got inside. But he's dead. You shot him,' he accused Tom.

'It was a him or us situation, old man,' Tom said. 'Now—'

The sound of three more shots echoed through the cavern. One of the stalactites fell to the floor of the cave with a resounding crash.

'There's your answer,' Shirley said.

'We'd better get up there,' Tom said. Shirley looked at her grandfather. 'Listen,' Tom said. 'Mr Wishart. You must get out of here. All of you.'

'No,' Wishart said fiercely. '*You* get out of here. All of *you*. You have destroyed my family. Leave what remains alone.'

'That's not possible,' Tom said.

'You wish to photograph us? To expose us?' Wishart asked. 'Do you think we want that?'

'You don't understand,' Tom said. 'You are guilty of a whole lot of crimes. I promised I will do what I can for you, but you will have to face trial. When we come back we will have several policemen with us. You will have to leave then. Come with us now, and it will be better for you.'

'Go,' Wishart commanded. 'Leave us.'

Shirley looked at Tom, uncertain what to do. Tom supposed he could attempt to order them out at the point of his gun, but he reckoned he didn't have more than one bullet left, and, in any event, he had no more desire to shoot anyone.

'Let them stay,' he said.

'But...' she bit her lip, and he knew what she was thinking, that perhaps they had already decided they would never stand trial.

'Could be the best thing,' he said.

She hesitated a last time, then turned and ran for the exit corridor. Tom went behind her, paused at the entrance to look back. The Wisharts stared at him.

They stumbled up the passageway together, again holding hands. They didn't speak; there was nothing to say. They reached the pit and paused to catch their breath before leaping across it, staggered against each other and went up the curving passageway, seeing light in front of them now; it still wanted an hour to dawn, but the moon remained bright.

Tom checked their progress, drew his revolver. When he reached the first light, he broke the gun; there was, as he had suspected, but a single live cartridge left. 'Wait here,' he told her, and moved cautiously forward. He rounded the last bend, and came upon the entrance. Two snakes lay dead on the ground. But the third was still alive, although it, too, had been hit. Willard was an excellent shot.

At the sound from behind it, the bushmaster reared angrily, forked tongue slipping out from the arrow-like head, then it began to move forward. But Tom had already taken careful aim, and at close range blew the head right off.

'Tom!' Shirley ran round the corner.

'We need to find Willard,' he said, and moved to the entrance. As he did so something flew through the air, struck the wall by his head and rolled down the passageway.

He spun round, recognized a grenade, grasped Shirley's hand and jerked her towards him, in the same movement hurling himself forward. The grenade exploded, fortunately just round the last corner; there was a rumbling crash and rock splinters flew around them. Shirley gave a little shriek as one slashed into her thigh. The noise of falling rock continued for several seconds, while they huddled against each other.

'Bastards,' Willard said. 'How'd you miss that?' He lay in the bushes a few feet away, and was fumbling at his satchel.

Tom leapt to his feet and kicked him in the face. Willard fell over, and Tom ripped the satchel from his grasp and threw it into the bushes, just in case the pin had come out.

'Stay down,' he warned Shirley.

But she was already crawling towards him. And there was no explosion. Tom knelt beside Willard; the doctor's face was darkening as the poison raced through his system.

'The phial,' he whispered. 'Give me the phial.'

Tom looked at Shirley, who shrugged. He went to the satchel and took out the phial.

'Quickly,' Willard said. 'Open it.'

With an immense effort Tom unscrewed the cap and handed the phial to the dying man. Willard looked at it for several seconds, then raised it to his lips and drank. His hand was trembling, and some of the liquid dribbled down his chin. But, amazingly, it was still liquid, and sufficient went into his mouth. Willard swallowed, and smiled.

'Eternal life,' he said. 'Eter...' his head drooped.

Tom checked his pulse. 'He's dead.'

Shirley picked up the phial, which had slipped from the dead man's fingers, and held it to her nose; there was no liquid left. 'Smells ... musty. Do you think it was a fake?'

'It had to be something pretty unusual to stay liquid for more than sixty years, and in this heat. Maybe it just couldn't counter a bushmaster's venom. We'll never know. At least he died happy, believing it would work.'

'We could take the phial. The boffins could probably still get something from it.'

'Do we really want to do that, Shirley?'

She glanced at him, then got up and went back to the entrance, crept inside. 'The whole thing has come down,' she said. 'They'll have to be dug out. The Wisharts, I mean.'

'Do we really want to do *that*, Shirley?'

She went outside. 'What will they do, trapped in there? Those poor kids.'

'I wouldn't describe them as poor kids; they're man-eating monsters. They can never be civilized, now. You wanted to find out what happened to your grandad, Shirley. You've done that. Do you really want him splashed all over the tabloids as a kind of cannibal king, a latter-day Sawney Bean? I think what we found is between you and me.'

She sighed. 'Didn't you come to get a story?'

'I think it's one I'd rather pass up, seeing as how it's all in the family, in a manner of speaking.'

'And Willard?'

'That's up to Cal. Here he comes now.'

Cal Simpson stood above Willard's body. He was accompanied by Fuller, Washington and two policemen. 'I should've known,' he said. 'Before.'

'How?' Tom asked.

Cal shrugged. 'Just dates and ideas.'

'But you had nothing to go on until you read Gifford's letter,' Shirley pointed out. She was wrapped in Tom's shirt.

'Yeah. So some more guys got killed. It was him put poison in Ledden's breakfast; we found out that he was the only person who entered Jessie Smith's kitchen that morning, apart from Jessie herself. That's why I came after you. To warn you and arrest him ... Tell me what happened.'

Tom took a deep breath. 'We found the passageway and got into the cave.'

'You mean there really is a cave under there?'

'Oh, yes, a honeycomb of tunnels.'

'And you found Shirley, right?'

'I fell into a hole,' Shirley said. 'I was knocked out. I don't know how long I lay there, but when I came to I couldn't get out. I thought I'd had it.'

'But you'd left that note,' Cal reminded her.

'Sure I did. But I didn't know if anyone would take any notice of it. I must've been in there for hours. And then Tom came along.' She squeezed his hand.

'With Glossop and Willard,' Fuller said.

Shirley nodded. 'They pulled me out. Then we explored the caves.'

'And found...?'

Shirley licked her lips. 'We found the wreckage of the Dakota.'

'You saying it did go through the Falls?'

'Yes,' Tom said.

'And?'

'There were skeletons,' Shirley said. 'Five skeletons. At least, we think there were five. They were all broken up.'

'You mean there were no survivors?' Fuller asked.

'It didn't look like it.'

'And what happened then?' Cal asked.

'Well, we wanted to get back out, but Willard wanted to search the wreckage. He was like a man demented.'

'He was looking for the elixir.'

'That's right. Meantime, Glossop started to be affected by the cave. Claustrophobia, I guess. Anyway, he and Willard had a fight, and next thing Willard pulled out his gun and shot him.'

'Just like that?'

'Just like that,' Tom said. 'And Glossop staggered across the cave and fell into the water. Well, Shirley and I were appalled, and we tried to take Willard's gun away from him, but he threatened to shoot us, too, and went back up the corridor leading out. His first shot had made the whole cave creak a bit, so we decided to get out as fast as we could, but he must have heard us coming, because he fired some more shots. By then we were in the outer passage, and it was clear the roof was coming down. So we ran out, and the roof did come down, just behind us.'

'But Willard didn't shoot you when you came out, after having shot at you inside.'

'He couldn't' Shirley said. 'He'd already tangled with the snakes. But he threw bombs at us.'

'Eh?'

'He had two grenades,' Tom said. 'Did you know he had grenades, Cal?'

'No, I didn't. Holy shit! But I guess they're not that difficult to get hold of in Georgetown as it is today. To think that that man was a mass murderer. But now he's dead, and Ledden, too, I guess we'll never find out about his other employees, or those guys in England.'

'Still, they have no employer now, and nothing to look for.'

'Maybe,' Cal said thoughtfully. 'So there was no elixir of life.'

'Nothing that we could find.'

'But your idea of what might have happened to the plane was pretty accurate, Shirley,' Fuller said. 'Even if you didn't find what you wanted to find.'

'Yes,' Shirley said.

Cal signalled to his policemen to place Willard's body in the waiting bag. 'All of that killing,' he remarked. 'For nothing.'

'Yes,' Tom said.

They walked behind the policemen and Washington, back to the river. Cal pointed. 'There couldn't have been a real cave-in,' he said, 'or the river would have been affected. But it's the same as always.'

'I reckon it was just the outer passageway collapsed,' Tom said.

'You know,' Cal said, 'if it's just that passageway, we could blow it open without too much trouble. Have a real look down there.'

'I wouldn't do that,' Shirley said. 'That might really bring down the roof inside. And if it diverted or lowered the river there'd be no more Falls.'

'There's a point,' Cal said.

'And there's nothing there,' Tom insisted.

'Save the plane and those skeletons. I'd say let them lie there. It's as good a grave as any.'

'One of those skeletons belonged to your grandfather, Shirley,' Cal said.

'I know. But there was no way of telling which one.'

'Weren't they wearing dogtags?'

'Ah ... I guess they were. We didn't look too closely.'

'Yeah,' Cal said thoughtfully. 'So, what's your plan now?'

They were approaching the rest house and the waiting vehicles. The noise of the Falls was very loud.

'I think we've seen as much of this waterfall as we want to,' Tom said. 'So, if you guys would give us a lift down to George-town when you go, we'll see about getting up to the Rupununi for the rest of our holiday.'

'That should be fun,' Cal said.

They made their preparations for leaving the next morning. Cal sat beside Tom on the hotel porch; Shirley was having a shower.

'You don't suppose I believe what you two told me,' Cal remarked.

'Why shouldn't you?'

'Just say it's because I'm a policeman. And then, you know, Shirley comes all this way looking for her grandfather, finds his body and just walks away from it. That's hardly logical. And what about the creatures you claim to have seen, and who you reckon attacked that girl and were responsible for all the other troubles up here over the past sixty-odd years?'

'Like you said, Cal, we must've been mistaken. People who go walkabout in this jungle disappear. Right? As for Monica, she must have had a delusion.'

'And the scratch marks on her thigh?'

'She could have scratched herself on some branch or other.'

'And Milton? Didn't you see his body?'

Tom shrugged. 'So we must have hallucinated. Maybe he'll turn up, one of these days. You reckon I should apologize to Fuller?'

'For suspecting he was Falby? What he doesn't know can't hurt him,' Cal said, as thoughtfully as ever. 'I don't suppose you'd care to tell me the truth, now, just you and me, old school chums and all that?'

'I think Shirley feels there has been too much blood spilt, as you said, all for nothing,' Tom said. 'Whoever and whatever was on that plane is history. Shirley is right in feeling that lying there behind the Falls is as good a grave as any.'

'Yeah,' Cal said. 'Well, old friend, have a good time in the Rupununi, but when you leave Guyana ... maybe it would be a good idea if you didn't come back.'

* * *

'This Rupununi,' Shirley said, as they sat in the back of a police jeep bouncing down the road to Bartica, where they would catch the steamer for Georgetown. 'Nothing ever happens up there, does it?'

'Not a lot. It's just a big prairie. We'll have nothing to do but walk, and talk, and drink ... Hey, do you realize that for the past week, apart from that medicinal whisky, I've only had a couple of beers? And I'm still here.'

'You look great. Is there liquor in this Rupununi?'

'Some, but ... I think I'd rather make love.'

'Amen,' she said. 'Did all this really happen, Tom?'

'God knows. Sometimes I think it was all just a dream.'

'All those murders ... those people in the cave...'

'Just a dream,' he repeated. 'I tell you what is real, though: you and me.'

'Oh, yes,' she said. 'For ever and ever. Just like if we had that phial, and it had worked.'